The Portal
SWITCH

Rachel Ruth

The Portal Switch

ISBN: 978-1-945190-86-5

FV-8

Intellect Publishing, LLC
www.IntellectPublishing.com

Acknowledgments

My thanks go to my husband, who supports my endeavors, and also to our two sons, for being good listeners.

To my dad and mom, toward whom I have an everlasting gratitude, for teaching me to believe in myself and reach for my dreams. Also special thanks to my friends Linda and Kathy for allowing me to weave a part of them into the story, to Kimberly for her thoughtful insight, and to Theresa and Ellie for their editing help. Also, I would like to thank my publisher John O'Melveny Woods.

In remembrance of my friend Diane, who read the beginning of this book before passing away in May of 2012, and for whom I named the main character.

The Portal SWITCH

1
Monday in Ardmore, Pennsylvania

My Monday morning started when I opened the door to a young man I'd never met, but already knew. I'd heard so much about him, but never dreamed I'd meet him in person. Yet, there he was all grown up, and looking so much like his father. The resemblance tore at my heart, as I wondered how he found me and why he was standing at my door.

"Are you Diane Duncan?" he asked.

I was speechless and in awe at the similarities in the voice. My heart was pounding as I nodded yes to his question.

"Did you know my father, Stephen Winthrop?"

I could hear the words coming out of my mouth as my mind raced with questions of my own. "I did and he was a wonderful man. You must be Evan?"

"How do you know who I am?" he asked.

"Your father had a way with words, and he managed to describe you to the tee. Not to mention you have his eyes and chin. Why don't you come in out of the cold?" I asked, as I pushed the storm door open wider with one hand, while stepping back to make room for him.

Evan came in and took off his jacket, as he looked around to see if there was anyone else around. I took his jacket and noticed it was a large, which was the same size Stephen wore. Standing next to Evan, I figured him for six feet tall, like his father, and also about the same build. I laid his coat over the arm of the antique pew bench in the front hall, motioned for him to follow me into the living room, then excused myself to go make us some coffee. It wasn't long before I heard him walking around looking at all the pictures on the walls, and all I could think was, *how did he find me?* The clinking of the spoons on the china saucers got his attention as I came back into the living room.

We sat in silence and stirred the hot steam out of the coffee for what seemed like an eternity. It was there on the couch that morning that Evan told me how his dad, Stephen, had died in a car accident a few years ago. Evan went on to explain that he was the only passenger in the car, and the last thing he remembered of that night was his dad yelling.

"He was yelling your name like you could hear him. Then he just closed his eyes and went to sleep … forever," Evan whispered. "I thought about it for years. I couldn't seem to erase that single moment out of my mind, or the sound of his voice in the darkness as he called out your name. Your name haunted my conscience for years, because I never told my mother or anyone else. I felt like your name was a secret between my dad and me, except I didn't know what the secret was, so I finally decided to find you.

"I went through all of his papers, business cards, rolodexes, anything I could put my fingers on, but I couldn't find anything. So, I decided to come to Philadelphia and go to my dad's old office. I found an older secretary, who looked like she might have been around long enough to remember my dad. I told her who I was and asked her if she remembered my dad and she did. Then I asked her if anyone named Diane might have worked with him. You were the only Diane she could remember and that's how I got here."

"So, you want to know who I am?" I asked.

"You're the woman my dad called out for before he died … and not my mom," he blurted out as he ran his hand through his chestnut-colored hair.

"I didn't hear him calling, but I knew he was gone. I always wondered how it happened. I looked up his obituary, but it didn't say how, only that his death was unexpected.

"Thank you for telling me about your father. You don't know how many times I've wanted to call and find out what happened to him, but I couldn't. Even though I knew in my heart something bad had happened, your telling me proves what I already knew in my heart nine years ago … that I'd never see him again.

"I loved your father very much. I don't say this to hurt you, but to help you understand who I am. I don't want you to walk away feeling bad about your father, because he would've never wanted that. You and your family were everything to him." I stopped to catch my breath and took a sip of coffee.

"I'm glad you're here, even though I never dreamed this day would ever come. I hope you can stay for a while. Having you here makes me feel closer to Stephen. You are so much like your father."

I couldn't believe I just said that, about loving his father, and hoping he could stay. What was I thinking? That Evan was going to want to be with me any longer than he had to?

Looking across the room Evan found some pictures of my family and asked, "Are those your children?"

"Yes, my children and grandchild," I proudly pointed out, hoping this would lighten our conversation. "They all have my late husband's dark hair and eyes."

"How long has your husband been gone?"

"Four years next month. He had cancer, and it took him within a year of being diagnosed. He was only fifty-two when he died," I said, as I took a deep breath.

"Not to change the subject, but how long are you planning to stay here in Philadelphia?" I asked.

"I honestly don't know how long I'll be here. I've got a couple of clients to see while I'm here."

"Well, the reason I'm asking is, I have an extra bedroom upstairs that you're welcome to, if you'd like."

"No. No thanks, but thank you," Evan awkwardly replied.

"Well, why don't you think about it and let me know. Even though you don't know me well and it might be uncomfortable, I feel like I know you. You are Stephen's son and always welcome here, and it's really no inconvenience to me."

"Well, thanks for the offer, but I'm not sure I would feel comfortable," Evan said as he looked out the window. "I do think I need some fresh air, and it's almost lunch time. As I walked up here this morning, I saw a place down on the corner; would you like to go down there for lunch?" he asked, and then added, "I'll pay."

"Yes, that would be nice." I needed a change of scenery, and lunch sounded good. "Let me put the cups in the kitchen and we'll go."

"Sounds like a plan."

We put on our coats, made our way out the door, and walked down the block to the corner café.

2

The sun had taken the morning chill out of the air, but not enough to want to eat outside, so we took a table inside by the front window. We both ordered a bowl of hot soup, with side servings of hot sourdough rolls. Evan had quite an appetite, or else he didn't like to talk much while eating. I let him have his own thoughts for some time before I asked him how long he had been there in Philly.

"I flew in late last night from Chicago. I went to Dad's old office earlier this morning, and then it took me a couple of hours to muster up the courage to knock on your door. I wasn't sure what to say to you or if you would talk to me. I even thought you might deny knowing my dad," replied Evan.

"I am sorry to put you through this. I want you to know your father loved your mother very much. He would've never wanted to hurt her, or to spend his life without her. He talked about you and your brother often. He kept me up on all that was going on in your lives, and how much you were growing. I even know you didn't like steamed carrots, and you hated playing baseball when you were little. He was so proud of his two boys. Did you know that you were only four years old when I met your father?"

"So, you knew my dad twelve years?"

"Yes. I got to spend twelve years with your father, and the last nine years missing him just like you. I loved him dearly. I want you to know that," I told him.

We both finished our soup in silence. Both dived into our own thoughts of Stephen, and wondered if knowing each other would help us heal and fill the void we both shared.

As Evan asked for our lunch receipt, I stood and reached for my coat that was draped over the back of my chair, when I noticed Evan wasn't standing. He motioned for me to sit for a little longer, so I sat back down.

"I'm sorry, would you like some dessert?" I asked.

"No. There is something else I need to tell you." He paused. "I halfway knew what you might look like before I flew into Philadelphia. It made finding you easier. I just wasn't sure what I was going to say if you told me you didn't know my dad. How then could I explain I recognized you? Not really knowing you, but what you looked like makes me sounds crazy. You know, I'm still not sure any of this makes sense, but seeing you this morning made me realize I'd definitely seen your face before. Maybe I'm just talking to hear myself think."

"What do you mean, 'seen my face before'? Like in a picture? I'm not sure I follow you."

"Not in a picture, but in a dream."

My heart stopped. It was too weird, and I thought maybe I had heard him wrong. *How could this possibly be? He's seen me in a dream?* I felt scattered for a few moments wondering if he was crazy or maybe I was. *Is it possible he's testing me, or did he really see me?*

"Are you okay?" Evan asked in a whisper, as he leaned in and over the table.

"Sure. I'm fine. I was just wondering if I heard you right?"

"Let me try to explain. I know this is going to sound off the wall, but for the last couple of months when I go to sleep at night, I have this dream," he said, as he drifted off.

"What kind of dream?" I asked.

"A dream that picks up where it leaves off the night before. I know that sounds crazy, doesn't it? Anyway, there's this girl in my dream and we spend time together. Well, that is, until I wake up in the morning. I saw you a couple of times in these dreams. One time you were in a market and another time you were walking behind this girl and me on a sidewalk. Please don't think I'm totally nuts; it's only my dream that's wacky."

"Why did you think this woman was me?" I questioned.

"Have you ever had a gut feeling? First, my dad yelling your name, and then these dreams with the same woman in the background made me think there had to be a connection. I just couldn't shake the thought. My dreams are weird enough as it is, so why wouldn't the woman be you? Who else could this mysterious woman be but … the woman in my dad's other life. Not only did I need to find you and find out why my dad yelled out your name, but I also had another reason. I thought if I found you, I could find this girl."

"It does sound coincidental. But why do you believe this girl is real?"

"She's got to be real. I figured out who you were through my dreams and some searching, didn't I? From what I can tell, you're very real."

I smiled, because he was very witty and resourceful like his father.

"Do I sound ridiculous?" he said, with a hint of being annoyed.

"No, but you remind me of your father."

"Will you help me find her?" Evan asked desperately.

"Why do you think I can help you find her?"

"Because you were in my dreams, and now you're here, so she has to be close."

"But I don't know what she looks like."

"No, but I do. I thought that maybe, if you don't mind, I

could hang around with you for a couple of days. You know, go with you where you normally go, and maybe she might show up somewhere. She has to be somewhere around here. It's all I've got to go on," he said as he waited for me to respond.

"You're welcome to hang out, but I have to warn you there's nothing too exciting going on in my life. Although, I do have one condition, and that is you stay at my place instead of the hotel."

3
Tuesday in Ardmore, Pennsylvania

Evan was the perfect guest. His mother and Stephen had done a wonderful job raising him; he cleaned up after himself and was very quiet. If he hadn't said good morning when coming into the living room, I would never have heard him.

Evan seemed to be okay with taking the nine a.m. train into Philadelphia with me to pick up some fresh produce from Sandy's Market. I told him I also needed to stop by the church to pick up a visitation list, because I was part of the homebound committee, and then we'd head home for a quick and easy dinner.

What I didn't tell him was that he wasn't the only one who had a secret to share. I just didn't know how it would affect him, but I knew at that point I needed to tell him. I had never told anyone my secret, but I knew sooner or later he'd be asking more questions. Who in the world would ever believe I'd ever have to tell my secret? The love Stephen and I shared was never meant to hurt the people we loved the most. The last thing I wanted to do was hurt Evan by talking about Stephen and myself.

Evan wanted to pick up a paper to read on the train, although I didn't think he'd be doing much reading because of what I had to tell him.

We found two seats toward the back of the train, away

from all the other passengers. Even though I tried to miss the rush hour, there were still quite a few people left on the train. Evan and I sipped on our cups of hot coffee, and watched all the people standing outside waiting for the next train to somewhere. I could tell that Evan was scanning the crowd for the girl in his dreams. My heart ached for him, and I wanted so badly to tell him not to worry, that we'd find her. But how could I promise that?

"Any sign of her?" I asked, hoping for a good lead into what I had to tell him.

"No. I don't see her."

"Have you tried asking her in your dreams where she lives?"

"I've tried several times, but there's always an interruption. At least you and Dad never had the problem of finding each other."

"No. We didn't have that problem, but there were problems. You know, I was always told it's not the problem itself, but it's how you handle it."

"You and Dad had problems?"

"We knew each other for many years, and things came up." I thought *maybe this was the perfect time to tell Evan how his dad and I met, but I couldn't put the words together.*

"I wish this girl and I could have met during the day, and not in my dreams. I keep asking myself if I've gone crazy. I'm not sure what I would say to her if she stepped on the train right now. 'Hi, I'm the guy who dreams about you every night.'"

"Have you thought that far, what you are going to say if you find her?"

"I thought it would just come naturally, like in my dreams. We're so comfortable with each other," Evan said, as he drifted off into a dreamlike state.

"Are you okay?"

"I was just wondering … is she going to know who I am?"

I listened quietly and didn't have the answers. I didn't want to promise him that she'd know him, even if he found her. Or, that she would be happy about him coming into her life.

"What did Dad say to you, when you met?"

"He introduced himself and then told me he had eight people in the conference room who would need coffee."

"That was real nice of him," Evan said sarcastically. "I'd never ask my support person to bring me coffee. She'd probably laugh at me."

"Things have changed a lot since I was a secretary. Back then, we girls didn't think anything about bringing coffee in for everyone."

"So, that's it? How my dad and you met?" Evan asked.

"Well. Not exactly," I replied. I guessed this was my chance to tell Evan the secret that Stephen and I kept for all those years. Waiting was making me anxious, so I decided the "ready or not" approach was the best.

"Your father and I fell in love in a dream, or what I thought was a dream."

Evan choked on his coffee but managed to keep it down. "What do you mean?" he finally coughed out. "Why didn't you tell me?"

"What do you mean — 'Why didn't I tell you?'" I said, as I wondered, *why would I?*

"First of all, I didn't know how, and until today, I never thought I'd have to. It's not the most comfortable situation, discussing the relationship I had with your father. You see, your father and I promised each other that we'd never tell anyone about us. We never felt like we'd have to, because we met every night when we fell asleep. Somehow, we were both able to SWITCH between day and night. We could never figure out how we did it; so you see our situation was different from yours because we found each other together. Does that make sense?"

"The whole thing is confusing. So, you knew my dad before you started meeting in your sleep?"

"I didn't know him well, but I'd seen him at the office."

"Did he know who you were?"

"I think I knew before your father did. I knew that I was having the dream. Every night I would go to sleep, and your father and I would meet much like any two people who have just met. We would talk for hours and laugh until we cried. Every day, I looked forward to falling asleep at night so I could see him.

"Then it got to the point we would tell each other about our day. Sometimes I already knew about his day, and it was really hard for me to keep that to myself. I thought if I told him, even in my dreams, he'd get scared and go away. Anyway, you'd think I'd have been exhausted when I woke, but I never was the least bit tired. I can remember pinching myself to see if I was awake at the office. I even started wondering if the office was part of my dream. Or maybe everything was a dream."

The train stopped. Evan and I got off and started walking toward Sandy's Market. I dug in my purse and retrieved the list of things I needed to get and slipped it into my pocket.

"So, tell me more about you and my dad," Evan said.

"Well, it was spring, and I remember feeling bold, like a flower wanting to break out and bloom. Or like a trapped animal just wanting to run. The feeling was overwhelming, like I had to let loose of myself just to survive. It was all so surreal. I'm sorry. There I go again.

"Anyway, getting back to your father, he happened to be at the office visiting for a week to meet with all the sales executives. I was assigned by the secretary pool to coordinate the paperwork for your father's meeting." I added, "And coffee."

We both laughed.

"Speaking of coffee, I need to find a wastebasket for my empty," Evan said.

"Me too. Mine has gotten cold."

We found one not far up the road by a park bench. I sat down for a moment to collect my thoughts and enjoy the morning.

"So, what happened?"

"I stayed close to him the whole time he was in the office, hoping down deep he would recognize me. Although I knew he was married, I kept telling myself I was nuts.

"Then, one day I was in the break room and he walked in to get himself a glass of water. All I could do was smile at him, and to my surprise he froze for a moment and just stared at me. I could tell by the look on his face he must have recognized me, or else I was hoping he had. I don't know if he was embarrassed or in shock, but he just shook his head and left the room.

"I'll tell you one thing — I was in shock. I didn't want to come out of the break room. I felt naked, like your father could see through me. I never felt so exposed. I had fantasized about him having the same dream, but couldn't comprehend the idea that it could really happen. Even though I wanted him to know, that moment was heart wrenching and yet exciting at the same time."

We got to Sandy's Market a few minutes early, so we had to wait with a few other customers for the doors to open. Neither one of us said anything else about what I had just told him. We both needed a break, and Evan seemed to be trying to process the possibilities of what could exist.

We had fun picking out the produce. Evan said he had never felt cantaloupe before, as he turned it from end to end. I had to giggle, because the look on his face was priceless. We both started laughing and couldn't quit. I have to admit, it was much more fun shopping with Evan than alone. We left the market with two bags of produce and started back to the train depot to catch another train.

4

The train was less crowded than the nine o'clock train. We settled into our seats as if we'd been through a workout, and maybe we had, emotionally. Evan was holding the bags of produce as if they were Christmas ornaments. I told him sometimes the train ride itself can challenge the inner equilibrium, and it wouldn't be the end of the world if a piece of produce got lost along the way. He smiled softly, like he heard me, but his eyes told me he was a thousand miles away.

"Please don't get down in the dumps, this is only our first excursion," I consoled him.

"Yeah. I know I was just zoning. Sorry."

"I tried to warn you that hanging around me would be boring."

"You're not boring, but I do think I'll close my eyes for a few, if you don't mind? But, don't think for a minute I've forgotten about your dreams or my dad," Evan said, as he smiled and leaned his head back.

"You go right ahead. We have about a twenty-minute ride," I said, as I rounded the lower part of my back into the seat to get rid of the dull ache that had settled in.

While Evan slept, I rehashed our talks earlier that day and they made me think of Stephen. I felt flushed thinking about him. The urge to be with him never ended, not even at my age. I can remember his hands and the shape of his nails. His hands were always warm, unlike mine. I remember the vein that ran across his left temple and how it would pulse when he laughed. He had a contagious laugh … it would light up an entire room. His teeth were perfect. If a man could be beautiful, then Stephen was that. Although what I remember most about Stephen were the sparkles in his eyes. They were forever dancing this mischievous cha-cha-cha. He was such a kid at heart. God, I loved everything about him, and still did.

"What are you smiling about?" Evan brought me back to reality.

"Oh. I didn't know you were awake. How was your nap?"

"Perfect. I like catnaps. How long did I sleep?"

"Ten minutes."

"Good. That leaves us ten more, right?"

"You're right."

"So, you're not off the hook yet," Evan said jokingly. "Tell me more."

"Where did I leave off?"

"You were in the break room, and my dad gave you a weird look."

"That's right. When he looked at me the way he did, I could have sworn he knew what I was thinking."

"What were you thinking?"

"I was wondering if he knew I dreamed about him, and wondered if it was written all over my face? The look on your father's face startled me, as much as the possibility of us having the same dream. I even wondered if it was a dream. You know, being with your father seemed as real as sitting here with you.

"Well, anyway, I had to find out, so I intentionally took the same elevators at the end of the day with your father. We started talking about his meeting, and then before I knew it, he was leaving the building. He told me to have a good evening, and I replied by telling him that I'd see him a little later and to have sweet dreams.

"I'll never forget the look on his face. He walked back to me, but before I could say anything, he told me to never stop dreaming, and that he wouldn't as long as he could keep dreaming of me. Then, he asked me if I wanted to dream about him. I told him I wanted to dream with him. That's when he asked me if I had time for a drink, and we found a small pub a couple blocks away.

"We had a drink and joked around about our dreams until we realized there was a little truth in every joke. The whole conversation was like a dream. Neither one of us could believe it was possible for two people to meet up each night when they fell asleep. Believe it or not, we went our separate ways, knowing that we would see each other later that night. That's how it all started," I told Evan, as I pointed to a street sign outside, to show Evan we were only a couple blocks away from our stop-off point.

5

The sun felt warm through the windows of the train, but when we got off, the coolness in the air persuaded both of us to zip up and button our jackets. We walked in silence toward the steeple, carrying the bags of produce. The gold accents on the cross blended in with the bright sun, the leaves were beginning to show their true colors, and the squirrels were scampering from tree to tree gathering acorns for the coming winter. The simplicity of life at its best unfolded in front of us, and I was hoping Evan was enjoying the sights as much as I was.

The front doors to the church were locked, so we entered through the side door and walked down the hall to the office. Mary, the secretary, handed me the visitation list, which only had two names on it. I was glad the list was light that week, because it would give me more time to help Evan.

The secretary introduced herself to Evan and he told her he was an old friend of the family. I had to bow my head to hide the sudden smile that spread across my face. I couldn't believe how nonchalant Evan was with his clichéd response. I knew she would never believe he was a hot date, so friend of the family worked well.

We left just in time to start thinking about lunch. I told Evan that today it was my treat. We settled on a bistro two blocks from the church. The menu wasn't much to write home about, but we both found a warm bowl of soup and sandwich to fill our stomachs. When we finished, we picked up our bags and started heading for the train.

"This time of day reminds me of when I was in college. I would take my books to a nearby park, spread a blanket under a big tree, and study until I fell asleep. You know, the world stops when you lie under a tree. All the branches seem to be reaching up towards the heavens. It's almost a spiritual experience. Those days were great. I guess it's not safe to fall asleep under a tree now. I apologize. I'm rambling about nothing again," I said.

"I don't mind," Evan replied.

"I've always rambled. Your father used to tell me I was good at thinking out loud. That was his way of saying, 'Diane, please be quiet.' I would tell him I didn't have a problem thinking out loud, because I didn't have any secrets. In fact, my secrets were his. That was our little inside joke, pun, pun," I added. "Anyway, getting back to the first night your father and I met, we decided to never talk about our dreams, but enjoy the time we had together."

"But you still met up every night, right?"

"Yes. We did."

"Do you remember it?"

"Yes. I remember walking by the river, holding hands and watching a couple of geese that had yet to migrate. Did you know geese pair for life?"

Evan nodded, yes.

"We continued to meet every night. Our relationship was much like any other. It evolved, as did our feelings for one another. We knew our dream had taken on a life of its own, and we knew the only way to be together was to dream. It wasn't always easy to think that, because when we woke in the morning, we got to spend the day with someone else. I guess for some people it would have been like heaven, but to us it was more like hell sometimes. We didn't want be without our spouses or hurt our children, but we didn't want to be without each other, either. So, we promised each other that our love would never affect our daytime lives. Remember how I told you we had our own problems? Well, this was one of them." I looked at Evan. "Is this too much?"

"No, I told you I wanted to hear about …" Evan trailed off.

"There's the train station. I don't know about you, but I'm ready to put my bag down and relax for a while."

"I can take the bags if they're getting heavy," Evan offered.

"Thanks."

Evan took the bag I was holding in his free arm and then juggled it with the one he was holding until they both rested in one arm. Before we knew it, we were on the train and heading home. I was glad to be getting back. Talking about Stephen had been more exhausting, perhaps, than the errands.

6

We got back to the condo around three forty-five, unloaded the produce and decided to go to our rooms for a while to put up our feet. I took my shoes off and lay down on my bed. I closed my eyes and tried to go to sleep, but I felt cold. I pulled a blanket up from the foot of the bed, thinking that would do the trick, but I still felt cold. I concentrated on closing my eyes and relaxing. I found myself thinking of Stephen, and wondering if I had a choice when it came to telling Evan more about his father and me. I'd never talked about Stephen before and the exposure made me feel a bit naked; maybe that was why I felt chilled.

There were so many nights Stephen would hold me and keep me warm. He had the kind of touch that warmed the soul. I felt safe and content in his arms … almost like I had always been there. I wished I could be there now. Is that why I felt cold, because he was not there? Having Evan there confirmed Stephen would never be there again.

I started to feel myself slip into sleep. I wanted to dream about being with Stephen, but I never dreamt during the day. I wanted to feel him again, like when we first fell in love. My heart would race when he kissed me. I would move into his arms, and our bodies would melt. Sometimes the heat was so intense that the linens would be soaked. We would move to the shower, and then back to the floor. We didn't care where we made love. Young love never does.

Stephen would always ask me how I felt when he made love to me. He would tell me what it felt like to him. We wanted to feel it all, the love in our hearts, as well as the love our bodies generously gave to one another. I loved it when Stephen would lie close to me and slept afterward. That was the best part, because we were always exhausted. We'd both fall asleep with smiles on our faces, thinking about waking up and knowing we would do it all over again if we had time. Time was our worst enemy; we never had enough time to relax totally. We knew when morning came, we'd be waking up to our spouses.

I often wondered if my husband could smell the love on me, or could smell another man. If he had, he probably brushed it off as impossible because I was lying there by him. He never said anything, but he probably did wonder why I was never in the mood to make love in the morning. I couldn't bring myself to conform that quickly. I told him I wasn't a morning person, and he seemed to understand. My husband and I were at that stage in our marriage where the newness had worn off years before. So, the explosive need for making love was gone, even though we enjoyed being together sexually.

Age might have had something to do with it, although I really didn't believe that because of Stephen and me. We never let age get in our way. Our feelings of new love never diminished over time.

I didn't know how long I'd been asleep when I heard a noise in the house. It took a minute to register that I had company. I must have really dozed off. I got up, put my shoes on and made my way downstairs. Evan was sitting on the couch, leafing through a copy of one of my monthly subscriptions. I was glad to see him making himself comfortable. I didn't want him to feel awkward around me, even though I knew it was hard for him.

7

Evan looked up as I entered the room. He put down the magazine and combed through his hair with both hands. Stephen always did the same thing, I thought, as Evan's brown hair gently fell back into place. He wore his longer than Stephen. It was longer at the crown and almost touched the top of his ears. It must have been the new style because I'd seen other young men wearing it the same way.

"Did you sleep?" he asked.

"Yes, for a few minutes. I normally don't fall asleep, but today I did. Thanks for giving me some time to catch up on my beauty rest. God knows I need all the help I can get."

"You look great, even if you are my mom's age," Evan laughed.

"Hey, that's not that old," I joked back. "Your father and I were the same age."

"Dad would be forty-nine," Evan said. "Sometimes I wonder what he would look like now if he were alive."

"Me, too."

"So, do you have any pictures of yourself back when you met my father?"

I hesitated, because I knew the only pictures I had were with my family. I didn't know how Evan would feel about seeing my family pictures. Would he think I was the cheating spouse, pretending to look happy standing next to my girls? Would he try to see through my smile?

"I'm sorry. Did I overstep my bounds?" Evan asked.

"No. Not at all. I'm just trying to figure out where they'd be. I didn't move here until after my husband's unexpected death. That time was such a blur, and I'm still finding things in the oddest places. Let me look in the sideboard, and if they're not there they might be up in my closet."

"That's okay. You don't have to go to all that trouble. I was just being Curious George."

"I don't mind sharing them if you don't mind looking at my family. There're not too many of me anyway, because I was always the camera lady. Good reason though … I hated having my picture taken."

"My mom was the same way. I never understood why."

"Let me go scout around and see if I can dig them up. There's iced tea in the refrigerator, if you'd like some."

"That sounds great. Would you like some? I make a pretty good host, even if it's not my kitchen." Evan stood up and kicked down one of his pant legs.

"I would love some. Thanks, Evan."

I went to sift through the sideboard, but didn't see the photo albums. There were only two albums because my husband and I weren't great at taking pictures. We had very few of us by ourselves. The bulk of the pictures were of our first daughter. We were like most couples, in that with each child the pictures become less and less. So, my second daughter had the least of anyone in the family.

I ventured upstairs to look in my closet, but ended up finding them under my bed. Who knew what else I would find under there, if I dug deep enough? I brushed the dust off of the albums, and cradled them close to my chest, as I started downstairs. I felt my heart pounding, and my stomach was in knots, because I wasn't sure sharing these pictures with Stephen's son was a good idea.

I paused on the landing and leaned against the wall as I kept asking myself, *what would Stephen have done if one of my daughters knocked on his door?* We promised never to let our love affect the lives of our children. So, was I breaking my promise to Stephen and, wherever he was, did he know? I mentally was fighting with my emotions, when I heard the sound of the ice clinking against the tea glasses as Evan made his way back from the kitchen.

I quickly pulled myself together and continued down the stairs to find Evan just sitting down as I came around the corner.

"I found them. I'm not sure what kind of shape they're in, and I'll try not to be too reminiscent," I said, as I thought to myself *the quicker we can get through this, the better I'll feel.*

"Let me go to the kitchen and wipe the dust off them. I'll be right back."

When I came back, Evan was sitting on the couch, patiently waiting. I sat down beside him and opened the first album. We thumbed through the first couple of pages in silence.

Finally, I managed to say, "Here I am when I was ..."

"So, that's what you looked like when you met my dad?"

"I never took a good picture, but it somewhat resembles me."

"Your hair was long."

"Yeah, I was a true brunette and I wore it longer back then." I reached up to smooth my shoulder-length hair that had a little help staying brown these days.

We continued to look through the albums. Evan didn't say much about my late husband. Although, he did ask where we lived and I told him we lived in Broomall, and that I'd moved here to Ardmore after he'd passed away and the girls had moved out. We looked and laughed at how much the styles of clothing had changed.

There was one picture he did go back to when we were all done. It was a picture a neighbor had taken of our family out on the driveway. We were all dressed up in our Easter best. The girls, Christine and Claire, were looking so proud with their little white gloves and patent leather purses hanging at their wrists. They were all cleaned up and ready to go.

"I like this picture the best," Evan said.

"Why?"

"It reminds me of my family, except my brother and I weren't wearing gloves or carrying purses. I think we were about the same age. Are your daughters the same age as my brother and me?"

"Pretty close; they're a couple years older than you and your brother."

Evan sipped on his iced tea, trying to put it all together.

"So, you and dad met when I was four years old and my brother was two?"

"Yes. I was about thirty when I met your father."

"All those years, and I never knew."

"I know." I stood up and patted him on the shoulder. "I know."

8

Evan and I had a wonderful dinner. We shared a beautiful bottle of wine with a couple of strip steaks and some steamed asparagus over wild rice. We spent most of the dinner talking about Evan. I had lost track of Evan's life after Stephen's disappearance from my life. Evan was just graduating from high school, the last I knew. Now, nine years later, he was a young man with his whole life in front of him.

"I attended the University of Indiana in Bloomington, and I have a business degree. Someday, I would like to go back and get my Master's, but for now I'm enjoying working at the ad agency. It's really incredible how much I've learned about business by working the last couple years."

"So, what exactly do you do at your company?"

"I'm what you call a junior account executive. I sell advertising in multiple medias, although it can be challenging because it's intangible — well, initially, anyway — before concepts are made visual. What I mean is, I sell concepts that are ideas of what could be created to help my customers grow their business. Our company has created some award-winning consumer advertising campaigns. Most of our clientele is in Chicago, but lately we've been branching out because it's such a competitive market. We have clients all over, even here in Philly."

"That's great, Evan. You know, there aren't too many people who are passionate about their jobs, like you seem to be. It's a real blessing to get paid for having fun, isn't it?"

"I'd have to agree."

"So, tell me, where do you live?"

"I have a small studio apartment within five minutes walking distance of the agency. I live in an upcoming area where many young career people are moving. I love the city. I always have."

"Your father liked big cities. You're a lot like him."

"I guess when it comes to cities, I am. I like to be right in the heart of it, where I can feel the pulse. It is motivating for me, because it kicks in my survival instincts."

"Well, it definitely never stops, does it?"

"Yeah."

"So, what's your younger brother doing?"

"Johnny just finished up at IU. He wants to do something in administration. I kind of hope he finds something in Chicago, so we can live close. I thought I'd never hear myself say that after the way we used to fight."

"Younger brothers are tough, aren't they? I have one myself. He lives in Atlanta, and I hardly ever get to see him. We talk on the phone, but it's not the same. So, I think you wanting to live close to your brother would be nice."

"Yeah, it'd be great."

"You know what else would be great? If these dishes would clean themselves," I said as I stood up to clear the table.

Evan followed me into the kitchen with his plate. "Hey, do you have anywhere we can go tomorrow?"

"Well, I need to get my hair done. Would you like to come? There's a coffee shop right next door."

"I would love to hang out with a bunch of women, but only if you'll let me buy you a cup of coffee."

"You are such a gentleman. This girl in your dreams doesn't know what she is missing."

"Not yet she doesn't," Evan said, as he leaned against the counter. "What time is your appointment?"

"Ten o'clock. You're welcome to go," I said, as I put the last dish in the washer. "I think I'm going to go to bed, if you don't mind. I'd like to read a little before I go to sleep."

I told Evan if he wanted to stay up and watch television that it was fine with me. I don't remember too much else, except for turning the light off, pulling up the covers and wanting to go to sleep where I could escape to my other life — the one Stephen and I had made — so I shut my eyes and made the SWITCH.

9
Wednesday in Blue Ash, Ohio

I woke up in Blue Ash, in the same house Stephen and I lived in, and had raised our daughter, Lauren. It was about nine o'clock on Wednesday morning and I was rinsing out the coffee pot, when Lauren came down the stairs with her light-blonde hair pulled up and a smile on her face. She said her morning class at school had been canceled, and that she didn't have to be on campus until eleven o'clock to catch up with a classmate.

Lauren was such an uplifting soul. Stephen and I called her our love child, because we hadn't been together six months before I realized I was pregnant. Stephen was ecstatic and head over heels for his little girl. She looked like her father, and in an uncanny way she looked like Evan. I had never realized it until that moment, but then again, how would I have known?

"Mom, is something wrong? You have a funny look on your face," Lauren said, as she broke into my thoughts.

"Nothing, baby. I'm just surprised to see you home. Seems like school just started and you're already having classes canceled."

"My prof had a death in her family."

"Oh."

"So, how did you sleep?"

"I slept decently, why? Was I snoring?"

"Mom. Stop joking around. You said the last few nights you've been restless."

"I guess your father has been on my mind."

"I thought he always was."

"Well, he is, but it's been different lately."

"Like how?"

"Just different, it's hard to explain," I said, as I pushed the button on the coffee pot. "Would you like something to eat? I'll make you a bowl of luscious cereal. We have flakes, fiber or puffs. Any of these knock you off your feet?"

"No thanks, I'm saving my girlish figure for a piggish lunch. Would you like to meet me down at the café in the Union Building? You know, across from the Library. I can meet you at noon?"

"Sure, that sounds great."

Lauren turned quickly, with her light-blonde ponytail following her. She could be tall and graceful, but at that moment she was being the typical college freshman, acting goofy and climbing the stairs two at a time. *Oh, to be young, full of life and feel invincible,* I thought. I remembered that feeling, and then I got to relive it through her again.

I only wished Stephen were there to see her. She had just turned eleven years old when he disappeared from our lives. She was devastated. Her emotions reeled between being hurt and mad at the world and everyone in it. She thought her father had abandoned us. I tried to tell her that he would have never left us, and that something terrible must have happened.

It wasn't until she started exhibiting signs of depression that I finally decided to sit down and tell her about how her father and I met and how much we loved each other. Not to mention how much her father loved her, and how he had always wanted a little girl.

I knew when I told her about how her father and I met each

night when we slept, that I had done a terrible thing. She wasn't old enough to grasp the SWITCH between day and night that her father and I had somehow stumbled on to, and now she was a part of that life. I should've known better, but I was desperate for her to understand that something terrible must have happened to her father. I didn't want Lauren being mad at her father or hating him.

At first, she laughed and thought I was joking. Then she started poking at me to see if I was real and then started hitting herself over and over again. I had to grab her by the wrist to keep her from hurting one of us, as she screamed and cried.

"So, we're just part of a dream? I'm just a figment of your imagination?!" Lauren shouted in a rage.

I tried to explain to her that she was just as real to me as I was real to myself, and that our world existed just as much as the world I went to when I fell asleep. I told her she wasn't part of a dream, because dreams don't last for eleven years.

She hesitantly asked, "You and Dad have another life, with other families? You have other kids? Do they know about me?"

I told her that she had two older sisters, but that they didn't know about her or about our family.

She had so many questions. Her mind was racing, and my heart was pounding. I had never felt as helpless in my life as I did at that moment. I explained to her that we both had other families and that we had decided not to tell them; that her father and I didn't know what good that would bring to anyone. We only knew we loved each other, and loved her. We never wanted to hurt anyone.

I told Lauren we never wanted to tell her, but under the circumstances I felt like she needed to know that maybe something terrible had happened to her father during the day, and that's why he was gone. I explained that her father and I had always agreed, that if one of us didn't show up one night it was because something terrible had happened during the day. I promised her that if her father could be with us, there would be nothing that would keep him away.

Our conversation was exhausting for both of us, but our life went on. I'm not going to tell you the next two years were a piece of cake. Lauren hated me most of the time. She blamed me for everything that happened, whether it was my fault or not, and I let her. We came full circle with our emotions and our life gradually became livable again. We gradually got used to the idea that we were alone and without Stephen.

Then, Lauren and I were best friends, and loved spending time together. She was all I had left of what Stephen and I shared.

It all seemed like it was just yesterday and yet there I was thinking about dredging it all up again. What kind of fool was I? Would the truth about her father's disappearance help Lauren put any closure on her feelings? If I told her how her father died, would she wonder how I found out? What kind of mother was I? She was already uncomfortable with the idea that I had another life, so why would I want to remind her that she shared her mother with another family?

10

I finished tidying up around the house, and put on my walking shoes for my walk to the café. Our house was within walking distance of the college, and I felt like I needed a brisk walk to stimulate my legs and keep my thoughts in order. I had come to the conclusion that I was going to have to tell Lauren about Evan, so she could have some closure on what happened to her father. I felt like I did when she was eleven … my heart aching for her and feeling like I had no control over my switching between my two worlds.

I was there before I knew it and Lauren was waiting at the entrance with a big smile on her face. *Should I tell her now?* She looked so happy, and I didn't know if that was a good time to rehash old feelings.

"Hey, Mom," Lauren said, as she waved me in her direction.

"Hi, sweetie. How was your meeting?"

"Sue and I just had to go over some ideas for a class project that is due at the end of the month. Is it okay if she comes over for dinner tonight? We've still got some things to work through for our project."

"Sure."

Sue was a friend from high school who had helped Lauren deal with the absence of her father. I wasn't sure what Lauren had told her, but whatever they talked about never ended up on the front of a tabloid. Sue had always remained a constant friend to Lauren, and I hoped they would remain friends for many years because I never kept up with any friends after high school. I was too busy thinking about getting married and having a family. I don't know why, but I guess that's what I thought I was supposed to do. My parents never offered to send me to college, probably because they couldn't afford it.

We sat down in a booth at the back of the café′ and took a quick look at the limited menu that was posted on a chalkboard up on the wall. Nothing looked great to either one of us, so we thought we would wait and ask the waitress about the specials.

"So, what did you do this morning, Mom?"

"Cleaned up a little and paid some bills which I dropped off along the way. The walk over was very relaxing. The leaves are just starting to change, and the air has a woody scent to it, as if someone's been cutting down trees. It took me back to my childhood, when my brother and I would walk home from school through the park."

"I wish I had a brother."

"We were lucky just to have you. Your father and I weren't that young, you know." I reached over and patted her hand.

The waitress finally came over to the table and gave us a rundown of the daily specials. We both decided on a tuna melt with a cup of English clam chowder.

"So, what time do you want dinner tonight, since you and Sue have homework to do?"

"How about six thirty? My last class is at two, so I'll be home by five thirty and I can help you. Would pasta be too big of a deal?"

"No. I can stop at the store this afternoon and pick up something. Pasta does sound good on a cool night."

The waitress brought over our lunch on a tray. One of the soups had spilled and she kept apologizing for the inconvenience and said she would be right back with a new cup.

"Do you know her, Lauren?"

"No. Why?"

"I don't know. She just looks familiar, and I thought maybe you went to high school with her."

"No, I don't know her. Maybe you've just seen her on campus before, or out and about."

She reappeared quickly with the cup of soup and apologized again. I told her not to worry. Then she disappeared in the direction of the kitchen. Lauren and I talked about her school project and how her other classes were going.

The whole time we were talking I kept wondering if I should tell her about her father. I knew if I did, then I would have to reveal to her how I knew and that would open the door to my other life and her father's, and I wasn't sure she could handle it. I knew it wasn't fair to bring it up that day, especially when she had Sue coming over that night.

My mind was toggling between telling her and not telling her. I wondered if she'd hate me if I hid the truth from her? Could I live with myself if I didn't tell her, knowing she'd probably want to know at some point? Why hadn't Stephen and I ever talked about what we would do in this situation?

My questions were flying a million miles a minute through my head, and I knew I needed to get a grip, or I'd go crazy. That was the first time in my life I felt cursed for having the ability to SWITCH, when I knew in my heart I should feel blessed, otherwise I wouldn't have Lauren. I didn't know how I could be so ungrateful when I'd had more than most. It would have been like heaven to most people to have two lovers and two lives, but the hellish part of it all was keeping the lives separate and knowing at some point they might collide.

I guessed that was where I was: my two lives had collided,

and I had to make the hardest decision I'd ever had to make.

"Earth to Mom."

"Just thinking about dinner while I'm having lunch," I stumbled through my excuse.

"Are you losing it? It's only a little pasta, and you know Sue. Are you okay?"

"Sure. I was trying to think of a way to spruce it up a bit."

"For a minute there, I thought you swallowed wrong, and that I was going to have to do the Heimlich."

"I'm fine. Really," I said, as I sat up straighter and smiled. "You know, you don't have to be in class to daydream."

"As long as it's just daydreaming, you're allowed. It's when you dream that I worry."

Was that the perfect time to tell her, or what? Or what, I guessed, because it felt like my throat had a knot the size of a watermelon in it. I couldn't tell her then.

"So, what are you going to do between four o'clock and five thirty?" I asked, as I looked at my watch.

"I'd like to go over and work out for about an hour after class. That way I won't feel guilty when I eat that pasta tonight."

"I promise you it'll be good, but I don't know if I can help in the carb department. You kids are so much more aware of what you eat then we ever were."

"You don't look so bad for someone who never watches her behind," Lauren said, as she blew me a kiss.

"Go on now and get out of here. I'll take care of the bill with the waitress."

Lauren left and I lingered for a bit as I drank a cup of coffee. The waitress was nice enough to take my bill up to the register and make change for me. Her name was Nicole, and she was a finance student in her second year. She asked me if I worked at the college, and I told her I was just a mother having lunch with my daughter who was a student. We exchanged smiles and said goodbye.

11

My walk home was most relaxing, but instead of the fresh air giving me a second wind, it made me tired. I blamed it on the walk, even though I knew it was the "after lunch" feeling. So, I decided to take a short nap before heading off to the grocer.

Lauren got home around five thirty as planned. She jumped right in and helped toss a salad to go with the pasta. We stood shoulder to shoulder at the counter as we prepped our dinner. After we got done, I folded a load of clothes while she got on her laptop to look some things up for a class. The quietness was nice and comfortable.

Her friend, Sue, soon arrived and the girls set the table as they laughed about some conversation they'd had earlier in the day that I wasn't privy to. Watching them made me smile. *They both have so much to look forward to in their lives. Who knows where they'll land, but I do hope they remain friends; Lauren needs that stability in her life.*

Dinner was chicken bowtie pasta and tossed salad. I was surprised how fast the girls devoured their food. They didn't waste any time with small talk, and I bet they could've eaten more if I'd fixed it.

"I could swear I was eating with boys the way you girls put down this food."

Sue laughed and said, "I had to eat fast at my house or my two brothers would eat everything."

"I'm glad to see you both eating well with your busy schedules."

"Sue's been working out, also. Sometimes we work out together in the afternoons," Lauren blurted out.

"Maybe that's where you two get your appetites. I'm glad you liked dinner because I hate leftovers, especially pasta because it never keeps well."

"We don't believe in leftovers … only in looking buff," Lauren said, as she giggled. "No. Really, Mom, the pasta was great. This can be a repeater."

The girls cleaned up after dinner, and then disappeared up to Lauren's room to work on their school project. The house got quiet very quickly, and I decided to go wash my face and slip into my favorite caftan. I wanted to relax with a good book and have a cup of hot tea. I settled into my favorite chair, tucked into the darkest corner of the den, and turned on the floor lamp so I could read.

The next thing I knew, the girls were in the kitchen getting some sodas out of the refrigerator to take back upstairs. I looked at the clock; I must have only dozed for about an hour. My tea was cold, and I had lost interest in reading my book. I wondered how I could have fallen asleep. The nap should have been enough that day, but I still felt tired. Maybe with everything going on with Evan, the past couple of days wore me out more than I thought. Or maybe it was the thought of both my worlds colliding, and that made me tired. Why did Stephen have to be taken away? I kept thinking, *if he were here, everything would be okay*.

I waited until the girls went back upstairs and then climbed the stairs myself and retired to my room. I flipped on the light switch to pull down my bedding and went into the bathroom to get a drink of water. I looked at myself in the mirror, thinking *what would Stephen think of me now with my frown lines between the eyebrows, and the wrinkles that were getting more pronounced at the corner of my eyes.* I went to get into bed and thought *I might read for a while*, but realized I'd forgotten my book downstairs. The light switch was closer than my book, so I hit the SWITCH and shut my eyes.

12
Wednesday in Ardmore, Pennsylvania

When I woke, the phone was ringing, and I felt disoriented. I was back in my other bed, and Evan was right down the hall, probably still asleep.

"Hello?" I said, as I answered the phone on my bedside table.

"Hi, Mom," my younger daughter Claire said. "Did I wake you?"

"I needed to get up anyway. I hate it when I sleep too late. How are you?"

"Oh, I'm fine."

"And how is my cute little grandson?" I asked, as I slipped my feet into my house shoes.

"Jacob is still asleep. So, I'm sitting on the couch enjoying a quiet moment and a cup of hot coffee."

A quiet moment, with a cup of coffee, that sounds nice. Then, dismissing the thought, I said, "So, what are you two going to do today?"

"We're going to make some cookies, clean up the house and go rent a movie or two for this weekend. Then, eat dinner, go to bed, and start all over again."

I laughed, because I was happy for my daughter. She was enjoying having a child and making the most of every minute they were together.

"So, when will Michael be back from his business trip?" I

asked.

"Tomorrow evening. Jacob and I are picking him up at the airport at five thirty. Then, we're going to come home and have a quiet evening. It's supposed to rain, so I hope his plane comes in on time. I have a special dinner planned for us. Anyway, how have you been?"

"Oh, I'm okay. The weather has been good, and the trees are just lovely this time of year. When I was your age, my favorite season was fall because you and your sister would play for hours outside in the leaves. I could've watched you forever. You two were so cute. You're still cute. Have you talked to your sister lately?"

"I talked to her a couple of weeks ago. Why?"

"No reason, really. I was just asking. She doesn't call as often as you. I know she's on the road a lot and busy with her job, so I don't expect her to. I do hope she's enjoying her new position."

"I think she's just overwhelmed right now. Hopefully, she will get things in order and her schedule will settle down in the next few weeks. She still says she is coming home for Thanksgiving."

"I hope so. I can't wait to see you all."

"I can't wait to see you either, neither can Jacob."

We both laughed and said our goodbyes. I reluctantly hung up the receiver, because I wanted to hug my big girls so bad, that my heart ached. Claire was my second-born child, and blessed with a warm spirit that spread like wildfire when you were around her. She had a way of making everyone she talked to feel like they were the only one in the world. I hadn't realized it before that moment, but it was uncanny that her nickname as a child was Little Angel. She sure grew up to be mine.

13

I slipped on my robe and tried to quietly make my way downstairs to start a pot of coffee without waking Evan up. I wanted a few minutes to myself with a cup of hot coffee in hand and a few minutes to think about the day. I knew Evan would be getting up soon and would want to go with me to my hair appointment. *He's such a sweet young man, I do hope his plan to find this girl works. I just wish I knew what she looked like so I could be of more help.*

The coffee brewing smelled good. I used the stop and pause feature to get a cup before the pot was finished brewing, because the smell was too intoxicating to wait, and then sat down at the kitchen table.

The birds were singing Mozart when Evan walked into the kitchen. He went straight for the coffee cup I had left out for him by the coffee pot. Without saying a word, he poured his coffee and sat down to look out the window with me as I watched the birds.

"Good morning," I said.

"Good morning. I could smell the coffee all the way upstairs."

"I hope the telephone didn't wake you this morning. My daughter Claire has a tendency to call early in the morning. She lets it ring once, and then calls back because she knows I won't normally pick up the phone early in the morning, especially if I haven't had my coffee yet."

"I heard the phone, but then I dozed off again. It was the whiff of coffee and the birds that convinced me to wake up. Philly has some loud birds," Evan said as he laughed.

"They might be loud, but very talented. Don't you recognize Mozart?"

We both laughed.

"So, where's your daughter live?"

"Claire? She lives east of here in Harrisburg. She got married young and has one little boy, Jason; he's two and a half and gets into everything."

"Does she get to come and visit often?"

"Here and there. Her husband travels a lot, so she usually tries to visit when he's gone, and then they usually come during the holidays. Hey, not to change the subject, but I thought of another place I needed to go today. There's a pet store a few blocks over from the hair salon that I need to stop in to pick up some suet packs for my little feathered friends."

"Great." Evan responded in a morning voice that hadn't cleared all the frogs out yet. "I think I'll go up and get cleaned up for the day."

"Take your time. My appointment isn't until ten. I think I'll cut up a grapefruit. Do you like grapefruit?"

"Love it."

"I'll put your half in the refrigerator, just in case I'm upstairs when you get done."

"Thanks," Evan replied as he walked away.

"Hey, Evan," I called out after him.

As he turned around with coffee in hand, I said, "I know it's not much fun hanging out with me when you'd rather be with her, but we can still make looking fun, right?"

His furrowed brows gave way as he smiled.

"I knew I could get a smile."

"Sorry. I guess I'm still thinking about my dream last

night. She is so beautiful. I've just got to find her."

"We'll give it another try today, but do me a favor … try to recollect anything in your dream that would give us a clue. You know: like a place, buildings, accents, type of people, or anything even small that could narrow it down."

"Let me think about it for a while."

Evan turned to go upstairs, and I started to cut the grapefruit when the phone rang again. This time it was for Evan, someone who said they'd call him back in the next hour on his cellphone. I headed upstairs to get cleaned up, thinking to myself that the morning hadn't been as quiet as I hoped, but then again what did I expect since Claire had called so early?

When I came downstairs, I noticed Evan's jacket lying on the bench in the front hall. I opened the hall closet door to pull mine out as I heard the water running and dishes clinking in the kitchen. It was good to hear someone else in the house for a change, and I hated to think he'd probably be leaving soon.

"Well, I guess we'd better get going if I'm going to make my hair appointment," I said, as Evan came across the living room. "No matter how old we girls get we still like to look good," I said, as I pulled my coat on. "Oh, by the way, some man called and said he'd call you on your cell in the next hour."

"Thanks."

"Hopefully, we'll find her today. How'd you do with trying to remember something?" I asked, as I checked to see if I had my keys in my purse. "Anything at all?"

"Well, there always seem to be a lot of young people around."

"I don't think you'll find that in my salon. Maybe the coffee shop will be a better place for you to look."

We left the house and started walking toward the bus stop. The salon wasn't as far away as the market and church on yesterday's excursion, so I had planned on catching the bus instead of the train. The bus was right on schedule, and we found a seat up front. We both sat in silence as we took in the morning. You would think at nine thirty in the morning the streets would be empty, but people were everywhere. Either the world had become much busier than it was twenty years ago or there were more people, because no one seemed to know anyone or say hello. They all seemed too busy to enjoy their surroundings.

The streets had become a place where people were never alone, but looked lonely. What happened to just taking a stroll, window shopping, or enjoying a pastry at the neighborhood bakery? Maybe Evan at his age didn't even notice the change or notice that people never returned a smile. I was lost in my own thoughts when Evan nudged me with his elbow.

"Is this us?"

"Sure is, and there's the salon over there. The coffee shop is on the corner. Looks like it's hopping. You'll probably have better luck there," I said, as I pointed in the direction we were going.

I could feel the rain coming. It looked dark in the east, and the oak leaves were all turned upside down. I was glad I brought my small umbrella in my purse. I thought *we might need it before we get back.* Evan walked with me to the salon, and then told me he was going down to the coffee shop and would be back in an hour. I nodded, as I quickly pulled the salon door open to escape the few raindrops that were beginning to fall.

14

An hour later, I watched Evan walk up the sidewalk toward the salon. I dug in my purse to get the umbrella out as he approached. As he opened the door, he handed me the cup of hot coffee in exchange for the umbrella. I was dying to ask him if he saw her, but I thought *I'll let him tell me.*

"Your hair looks nice."

"Thanks. I get a bit of brown added every third Wednesday to keep me feeling younger. I needed a trim, but she didn't have time today. My hairdresser, she's like seeing an old friend who can pick up where we left off every week. She knows everything about my life as it is during the day. She's a good sounding board for when I'm feeling sorry for myself and need someone to listen."

"You women are a different breed." Evan smiled as he winked at me.

I drank my coffee as we made our way back to the bus stop. The rain had let up and had left the outside smelling crisp. We opted to walk the two blocks over to the pet store. Evan found man's best friend and looked like a little boy lost in the moment. I had the clerk help me with the suet, as I watched Evan. He must have been the most adorable little boy. He eventually put the dog back in its cage, and we retraced our footsteps back to the bus stop.

The morning had turned out pretty nice, even though the

weather was calling for more rain in the afternoon.

"I didn't see her," Evan finally told me, as we sat down in our seats.

"Can you remember anything else from your dreams that could help? Names on buildings, or places you went?"

"Not offhand."

We both smiled and found a tiny space within ourselves to regroup for a couple of minutes.

"I think this afternoon I'll go and find a gym to work out at," Evan said, breaking the silence. "Maybe it'll help me clear my mind, and give me a new perspective on this scavenger hunt I'm on."

"I don't work out at a gym, so I'm not sure I can direct you."

"That's okay. I've got apps on my phone that will find the closest one to your place. Are you sure you're not tired of me hanging around?"

"Not at all. When we get back, I'll fix us a sandwich. Are you getting hungry?"

"Yeah. That sounds great."

Evan's cell phone rang once, and he talked to some guy at the office about a deadline on a project for one of his clients. By the time he hung up, we were on the front steps wiping off our feet. It felt good to take my jacket and shoes off, and slip on my moccasins.

"White bread okay?"

"Whatever you have is fine with me."

Evan made a couple of other calls from the living room while I piddled around in the kitchen and made our sandwiches. Evan came in just as I was taking our plates out of the cabinet.

"Do you want me to go out and refill your bird feeders?"

"Sure," I said, as I put the bag on the bench by the front

door.

Evan must have gone out the front door and around the side of the building, because the next thing I knew he was knocking at the back door.

"How's that?" he asked, as he pointed to the hanging feeder.

"Quick; you surprised me."

We finished our lunch and Evan excused himself. He said he had some computer work to get done for a meeting one of his coworkers was having the next day. Neither one of us could believe the next day was Thursday already. Where had the time gone?

Before I knew it, Evan was back from the gym, we had eaten dinner, and were both going to bed earlier than we had the last couple of nights. As I slipped between the sheets, I wondered if Evan was bored stiff, then shut my eyes and waited for the SWITCH.

15
Thursday in Blue Ash, Ohio

When I woke up, I was in Lauren's world and the skies were still dark. I lay in bed for a few minutes, and listened to the sounds of the house. I heard the furnace kick in, and the wind ruffle through the shingles, making it sound like a squirrel was chasing acorns. I wondered how Lauren could sleep through all the noises, but I guessed down deep I knew she'd stayed up late with her friend. I couldn't blame her for wanting to be a college girl and wanting to stretch her newfound independence.

I got up and made the bed, then took a hot steamy shower. I decided to get dressed early and drove down to the local bagel shop to buy a few hot bagels for breakfast. The blast of cold air welcomed me as I slipped out the front door. I slid into the front seat of the car and turned up all the heat controls to high. I didn't know why, because I knew the car wouldn't heat up enough in my short drive to do any good. I felt like an 80-year-old woman driving all hunched over the steering wheel.

I had to laugh at myself because as long as I could remember I'd always sat like that when I was cold. Although this posture was only appropriate for cars, not for ball games, sunrise services, or anywhere there were people around. Stephen used to ask me if it made me warmer to sit all huddled over. We'd laugh, and I'd usually end up punching him in the leg for teasing me.

The bagel shop was dead, and I was in and out in no time. The house was still dark when I pulled up, so I tried to be as quiet as possible when I went into the kitchen. The paper bag was noisier than any other sound I'd heard all morning. The coffee pot was on a timer and started brewing while I cut the bagels. The smell reminded me of making coffee for Evan and myself last morning. *Now here I was making coffee for Lauren and myself, twelve hours later.*

I'd always enjoyed mornings in the kitchen by myself. It gave me time to relax and read the paper while I thought about my new day. That was one good thing about having two days in one. It was nine o'clock before Lauren came down. She was all cleaned up and smelled like shampoo. Her wet hair was tied back in a ponytail, and she was wearing a new pair of jeans and one of her father's old sweatshirts.

"Hi, Mom. What time did you get up?"

"I've been up for a bit. I got us some bagels. Would you like one?"

"I never say no to a bagel. Sue had to leave early, so I'll do my best to eat hers, too."

"They're on the counter by the coffee pot," I said, as I nodded towards the coffee. "I didn't hear Sue leave. She must've left while I was picking up bagels."

Lauren turned around and walked over to scope out the bagels. She stood with her back to me at the counter, and crossed her feet just like Stephen always did. *How could she do that?* I thought. Had she seen him stand like that when she was small? He'd have been so proud of her.

"I've got my eleven o'clock class this morning again. Then I thought I'd run over to the bookstore on Colonial Street. I need to pick up a periodical for my night class. Do you want to go?"

"No, I think I'll stay here; but if you'd like to use the car today, you can."

"I was going to walk home from school and then go, if you don't mind?"

"No. I don't mind. I hadn't planned on going anywhere."

"Thanks, Mom," Lauren said, as she started towards the couch to have her breakfast, and I thought *that girl thinks the table is only for dinner.*

Then I thought about talking with her about her father, but once again I couldn't bring myself to ruin her day. I knew she would get upset, and I couldn't do that to her. She was at one of the happiest times in her life, and I was beginning to wonder if I would ever tell her at all.

We spent the morning doing nothing but piddling around the house and talking about little stuff. When the time came, we blew kisses and said goodbyes as Lauren ran out the door with her backpack slung across one shoulder, and her long locks hanging down between her shoulder blades.

She hadn't been gone long before I saw that she'd left one of her textbooks behind that I knew she needed. I slipped on my shoes and got in the car, not knowing where I'd park when I got on campus or where I'd find her.

The car was idling at a light when I saw the young woman who'd waited on Lauren and me the day before at the campus café'. She was wearing a pair of walking shoes, and carrying a large tote.

I watched her as she walked in the crosswalk across the intersection right in front of my car. She was a pretty girl, in a wholesome way. She didn't wear makeup, and had dark, wavy hair that she wore tied back. I knew it was the girl by the mole or birthmark on the side of her neck that I had noticed the day before. I had the urge to roll down my window and ask her if she wanted a ride, but I couldn't remember her name. I watched her until the light changed, and the traffic urged me along.

I found a parking place on the front circle in a fifteen-minute parking slot. I walked into the administration building, carrying Lauren's book. When I got to the main office, there was a line and that was when I decided that by the time I got through the line her class would be half over. I wasn't going to embarrass her by bringing her book to her in the middle of class.

So, I retreated back to my car and sat there for a few minutes, thinking to myself, *she's in college now, and you can't be bringing her books or lunch if she forgets them.* Upon my return home, I decided to put her book back on the table where she left it, and not mention to her that I'd tried to bring it to her.

16

Lauren came home from the bookstore, changed clothes and ran out the door to the gym. I knew I had to get used to not having her around as much, but at the moment I was missing her. Maybe it was because I knew when she got home from working out, she'd be getting ready for her night class. I told myself that Thursdays were going to be busy for Lauren, so I better just get used to it or adopt a hobby to fill up my time.

I made us both a hot sandwich for supper, and we had a short time at the kitchen table talking about the day.

"I'm sorry I'm eating on the run," Lauren apologized.

"Don't be sorry. I'm glad you like school."

"I love it. I'm glad I picked this college. It's close to home and my professors are nice."

"That's my girl. You are going to do great."

"I still don't know what I'm going to major in."

"Why should you? You just started. Why don't you concentrate on your core classes for the first couple of years and then maybe you'll have narrowed it down?"

"You're probably right."

"I know I am," I said. "Hey, are you thinking about joining a sorority?"

"I don't know yet. Maybe."

"I want you to experience it all, only because I didn't. I want you to make friends that hopefully you'll have for the rest of your life. It'll be nice to reminisce someday with your girlfriends about your college days. Some people call these the glory days, you know."

"I like college so far, Mom, but it's only been a couple of months. I'm still learning my way around campus. It's not that I don't want to belong to a sorority or club, I just haven't gotten that far yet."

"Hey, you better get going, or you'll be late. Make sure you lock the door when you get in and out of the car. You can never be too careful."

"Mom." Lauren drew out her response in a derogatory manner.

"I'm serious. You can never be too careful. Now get out of here."

Lauren jumped up, pulled her sweatshirt over her head and grabbed her book bag, as she asked, "I should be home around nine thirty. Will you still be up?"

"Long enough to know you got home okay," I replied.

"Well, if not, I'll knock on your door to let you know."

"You're such a sweetheart."

"Love you, Mom," Lauren said nonchalantly, as she ran out the door.

I cleaned up the few dishes we had dirtied up. Then I made sure all the lights were turned on outside, so Lauren would be able to see when coming in. I left one light on in the kitchen, headed upstairs to change into my nightgown, and washed my face.

I didn't want to leave Lauren, but I was tired and ready to talk with Evan. My curiosity was getting the best of me, and I was wondering if Evan had remembered anything from when he fell asleep. Being with Evan was making me feel closer to Stephen, maybe because we could talk about him. I liked the feeling of being closer to Stephen, but guilty for sharing these moments with Evan instead of Lauren, who still avoided talking about her father.

I fell asleep trying to figure out why I felt guilty wanting to make the SWITCH, and leaving Lauren all alone.

17
Thursday in Ardmore, Pennsylvania

When I woke up, it wasn't Lauren knocking at my door, but Evan.

"Diane, are you okay?"

"I'm okay," I replied in a startled voice I didn't recognize as my own.

I jumped out of bed and quickly pulled on a pair of khakis and an old rugby top I inherited from one of my daughters. I noticed it was nine in the morning, and wondered how I could have slept that long. I washed my face, brushed my teeth, and straightened up my hair the best I could. I felt like I was getting ready for something really important, and I wondered what Evan had to tell me.

I smelled eggs and bacon, and knew Evan had made himself some breakfast. I was a little embarrassed that I wasn't a better hostess. I found my boat shoes by the closet door and slipped them on. When I got down to the kitchen, Evan was sitting at the table reading the newspaper

"Hey, you got up early," I said, as I went for my first cup of coffee.

"Yeah, I've been up for a couple of hours. I was beginning to get worried about you, and I didn't know whether to wake you up or not."

"No. I'm glad you did. The extra beauty sleep really doesn't work anymore for me. Although I'm not sure I ever get good sleep, because it seems like I'm always awake."

We both laughed.

"Yeah. I've been wondering about that. How does that work, anyhow?" Evan asked.

"I'm not sure. All I know, is I wake up in Ohio, in another house, and in another life. It took me years to realize that Blue Ash is a different city during the day."

"What do you mean?" Evan inquired.

"Well, the streets, stores, businesses and people are all different. One time, I tried to look up Christine and Claire online from Ohio, and there was no record of them. So, when I made the SWITCH back to Ardmore, I've looked up people I know in Blue Ash and they weren't anywhere to be found. Then, another time, after my husband had passed away, I took a road trip to Blue Ash, to see it during the day, and I didn't recognize a single person. The streets were different, the buildings were different, and my house wasn't there.

"All I could come up with was Blue Ash must be some kind of portal. I know that doesn't explain how Lauren can be there 24/7 and never see how everything changes, unless it's some kind of black hole. You know, kind of like the Bermuda Triangle where people disappear, except in this situation they're there half the time. In other words, their nights are a void, and for those like me that can SWITCH, it is a portal. Who knows? Maybe Blue Ash isn't the only portal out there."

"I'm not going to try and understand that. I thought I was doing well with the dreaming thing every night, but this SWITCH you do sounds much more complicated than just drifting off to sleep and meeting up with someone."

18

Evan and I both drank the whole pot of coffee as we talked and read the paper, and by the time we got up from the table it was eleven-fifteen, and almost time for lunch, but neither one of us was hungry. I had waited two hours for him to tell me something about his night with this girl, but I guessed he was in no hurry.

So, finally I broke down and asked, "Did you find anything in your dream last night that could help us find your lady friend?"

"Maybe. I noticed a place called Del's on a store front, although the signage looked very outdated."

"Were you walking or driving?"

"We were walking."

"Evan, can you remember if you were in the city?"

"Yes. We were in the city and so was this place called Del's."

I thought to myself, *this is like pulling teeth*. "How about this girl? Did she give you anything to go on?"

"Like what?" Evan asked, as he folded up part of the newspaper that was lying on the table in front of him.

"Well, have you ever met anyone she knows?"

"No. Not really. We've never visited any of her friends."

"What kind of purse does she carry?"

"What?"

"Purses tell a lot about a girl."

"Really?"

"No," I said, as I laughed. "But we don't seem to have anything else, so I'm asking out of desperation."

"Well … I don't think she carries a purse or if she does it's inside her backpack."

"Backpack? Is she a student?"

"Yes. She goes to a university, but I think she's only taking a few courses."

"Why didn't you tell me that to begin with?"

Evan looked down at the table as if he'd been scolded. "I didn't think it was important, because I'm never with her at the university, and it's not where we met."

"Where did you meet her?"

"I bumped into her at a music store. We both like the same kind of music. I just figured that she would be where you are sometimes, since I've seen you around us."

I shook my head as I ran my fingers through my dirty hair, and my thoughts went to taking a shower. I told Evan that I needed to clean up and rethink our options. I excused myself and aimlessly went upstairs to think about why I couldn't think of a darn thing. The only thing I could come up with was a music store up by the university that I went into one time. It wasn't a regular music shop, but it definitely showed more promise than any other clue Evan had provided.

All of a sudden, I felt like we had wasted two days and a lot of energy in all the wrong places. *University? I'm totally out of the loop. The only university I know is the one Lauren attends, but that doesn't do me any good here.* I simply couldn't remember ever going near a university here in Philly.

I took my shower, and put on some clean clothes, then went back downstairs to see if Evan had come up with anything new. He was on the phone with his office explaining to someone that he was going to take a few more days of vacation. When he saw me, he smiled and handed me a sheet of paper with some directions to a campus bookstore he had found at a nearby university. He motioned to me that he would be off the phone in a minute.

I went into the basement to get a load of laundry going, and when I returned Evan was standing in the kitchen looking hopeful.

"I thought I could try that bookstore and see if I recognize any memorabilia. Do you want to go?" he asked.

"Sure, but before we leave do you have any dark clothes to put in the laundry? I just started a load."

"I do. Thanks. Let me run upstairs and grab them."

I got my windbreaker out of the hall closet, and went to find my purse in my bedroom. When I went down, Evan was coming up from the basement. As he walked through the living room, I heard a knock at the front door. I motioned for Evan to stay in the living room. I went to the door and looked out the peephole, only to find the mailman with a package. I thanked him, and returned to the living room where Evan was sitting.

"It's not that I don't want anyone to know you're here. It's just that I don't know how to explain you to some of my neighbors who have lived close to me for the last several years. I like my neighbors, but through my own doing, they probably know too much about my family and children. I'm not in the mood to get into a conversation with them now. I can bet they know you're here, especially the lady next door, and I can guarantee she's chomping at the bit to find out who you are. You'd give her something to talk about for the next month."

I laughed, but Evan didn't look like he thought it was funny.

"Are you sure my staying here is a good idea? I don't want to make you feel uncomfortable around your neighbors."

"Oh, I don't care what they say, I just don't want to deal with them at the moment. I heard you say that you plan on staying a few more days. I hope that means you're staying here because you're always welcome," I told him, trying to smooth over the comments I just made about my nosy neighbors.

"I am going to extend my time off, in an effort to find her, but I don't want to be an inconvenience. I need to give you some money for letting me stay."

"You have been a pleasure, so don't even think of giving me any money," I said. "And, if I might add, I'm kind of enjoying the scavenger hunt. Let me take this package to the kitchen table and then we'll go, okay?"

"Yeah. I'll get my coat on."

19

We caught a cab at the corner and took it to the university. The fall leaves fell generously at our feet, and we walked around the campus. We finally had to ask one of the students where the bookstore was, and were amazed at how close we were. I'd never been in a university bookstore, and I was quite impressed on how they kept the class books organized by subject and course number — not to mention all the paraphernalia. The prices were no surprise to me, since I'd just paid for Lauren's a couple of months prior.

Evan meandered around with a blank look on his face, like nothing was jogging his memory. I felt sorry for him, because I knew he was losing his momentum and hope of finding his girl. We walked past the administration building, where we'd been dropped off by the cab, and wound our way through the campus until we came to a busy road.

"Nada?"

"No," Evan replied.

"I remember going to a music store over here one time. I think it might be within walking distance. Do you want to try looking there?"

Evan perked up. "Sure."

I couldn't tell if he was perking up because he liked music, or if it brought back some glimmer of hope.

"Let me get my bearings. It's on the main college strip, if I remember right. Let's cross here and go up a couple of blocks."

"So, how long has it been since you were here?" Evan asked.

"Oh. It's been a couple of years," I said, pointing to the left-hand side of the street. "Over there, Evan, I think that's it."

"Okay," Evan answered as he followed me across the street and into the store.

Stepping aside, I watched Evan disappear into the rock aisle, scan all the people in the store, and then jot down a couple of titles I guessed he wanted, before motioning to me that he was ready to leave. Unable to read Evan's facial expressions as we walked out of the store, I was at a loss for words and happy when he pointed out a German pub he wanted to stop into.

"I sure could use a beer. How about you?" Evan asked.

"Sounds good to me," I told him

The waiter took us to a booth, where we found a list of import beers a mile long. Evan helped me pick a beautiful amber beer that wasn't too yeasty, and dark ale for him. Not wasting any time, he guzzled down the first beer, and had started on his second before saying, "The music store made me remember something."

"What?" I asked, as I swallowed wrong and coughed.

"She's got a mole on the side of her neck. Right here," as he pointed to the left side of his neck. "Or else it's a birthmark," he said, taking another drink.

"How big is the mole on her neck?"

"I don't know, maybe the size of a pencil eraser," he said, as he rubbed his neck.

"I know I've never asked you, but what color hair does she have?"

"Dark brown."

"Is it long or short?

"Longer, I guess. Not real long, though, and kind of curly sometimes," Evan added.

My mind was racing, because the birthmark on her neck threw me for a loop. I knew I had seen a girl with a birthmark on her neck, but where? It absolutely drove me crazy when I couldn't remember things. I was constantly forgetting people's names and then remembering them in the middle of the night. *Maybe if I let it go, I'll remember. I won't say anything to Evan, until I know for sure.*

"You know, you've never told me her name," I said, as I made a conscious effort not to let him know I was shocked by his last comment.

"I think its Nicole, or Nicki. I know that sounds silly, but when I wake up, I can still see her face; although beyond that I don't remember many details, except I want to see her again."

"Don't beat yourself up, Evan. You can't control what you dream about or how much you'll remember. I'm glad you remembered the mole or birthmark, though. It'll give me something to look for while I'm trying to help you," I said, as I further committed myself to the program.

We had probably overstayed our welcome, because we'd had a couple of beers first before ordering our dinner, and then had a hard time finishing the heavy German food, probably because we'd filled up on beers.

When we finally left, it was dark, and we had to walk a couple of blocks to catch a cab. We were barely inside the front door when we both said goodnight, and went to our rooms.

I got ready for bed, and then remembered the package that had come earlier. So, I went back downstairs to open it. I could tell by the writing on the box that it was from my daughter, Christine. She was always showering me with gifts from her travels.

That one was from San Diego, and it was a box of chocolates from the San Diego Zoo. The chocolates were in shapes of animals, and next to the box was a picture of her hugging a polar bear statue. There was a handwritten note, taped to the top of the picture.

Hi, Mom. I am planning on being in Philly next weekend and thought I would come by to give you a big kiss. I'll give you a call. Love you, Christine.

I was so excited, I opened up the chocolates and ate the bear and giraffe, but it dawned on me that Evan could still be here. That could be a problem since my two girls here didn't know about Stephen and me. *How would I explain Evan?* I wondered. I decided not to fret about it until she called, and then I'd deal with it. I just hoped she'd give me the courtesy of calling ahead. I loved my daughter and all, but she was not the most dependable when it came to schedules, probably because she was always on the go.

I went back upstairs and got into bed feeling like I was hiding something. I had never felt like this when Stephen was around. Children have this way of making a parent question everything. I was not sure I'd ever been the best mother on earth, but then again there aren't any trial runs for motherhood. My three girls were all wonderful in their own way, and that made my heart hurt, especially for Lauren, who knew of her other siblings but would never have the chance to meet them.

With that thought, I was ready to make the SWITCH, so I turned off the light and shut my eyes.

20
Friday in Blue Ash, Ohio

I woke up feeling tired, but remembered where I had seen the birthmark and on whose neck. It was that waitress who'd waited on Lauren and me at the café on the college campus. *I knew I would remember, but now that I did what was I supposed to do? It can't possibly be the same girl Evan was talking about in his dream, because she is in mine.* My head started to hurt just thinking about it, so I got up and made a pot of strong coffee.

After my third cup, I finally stopped pondering the questions I had about this girl and started to focus on the weather channel. It looked like we were going to get some rain. I thought to myself how fall rain wasn't the same as spring rain. It had a damp, cold feel to it, and it didn't make everything smell fresh like it did in the spring.

I traipsed upstairs to find one of Stephen's old fisherman sweaters to throw on with a pair of jeans. As I was brushing my hair, Lauren walked in and flung herself across my unmade bed.

"Hey, Mom."

"Hi, sweetie."

"What are you doing?"

"Brushing my hair and now thinking about when you were little and how you used to come running into our bedroom and jump into bed with us. You were so little. I can still see your little feet. You were just a prissy little thing. Your toenails were always painted some pearly pink color because it was your favorite and your hair hung in long curls and was usually halfway out of your elastic band. Your father would tuck your hair behind your ears, and you would giggle because it tickled. Your father's hands looked so big next to your little face," I said, as I laid down my brush and pulled my hair back into a ponytail.

"I'm not sure your father would have let you come flying into our bed now; you might have crushed us," I said, giving her a wink.

Lauren got up and followed me out of bedroom, and back down the stairs.

"You've already made coffee? How long have you been up?" she asked her mother.

"I've been up for a while. I can't sleep as late as you do. I decided if I cleaned up and got dressed early, then maybe I'd get something done today."

"Like what?" Lauren asked in a playful way.

"Like I don't know, but I need to get something done. Do you have a list for me?"

"Well, let me see. It's nine-twenty and I've got my first class at eleven. Hmm, maybe a ride to school, since it looks like it's going to rain. I wouldn't want to ask to borrow your car, especially if you need to get something important done today."

"You can use the car, if that's what you're asking. I don't care."

"Really? I'll be back when my two classes are over. Around four, okay?"

"Sure," I said, as I thought, *that should give me enough time to figure out how I'm going to find this girl on campus. Hopefully, she'll be working at the café, and I won't have to play detective with the other employees.* I had to talk with this girl for Evan's sake. I just needed to make sure I went during one of Lauren's classes, because I didn't want to take any chances on her seeing me. Sneaking around made me feel like a horrible mother, but it was the only way to protect Lauren from what we never talked about: my second life and all the other people in it.

Lauren got ready, while I straightened up around the house and watered all the plants. She found me on the back patio, trimming a few peony bushes in preparation for the winter months.

"Mom, do you know where the keys are? They're not in their usual."

"Give me a second and I'll look for you," I replied, as I laid down the clippers.

I went for the coat pockets first, but eventually found the keys on my bedside table. Lauren hit the road as soon as the keys landed in her hand. I looked out the window and it wasn't raining yet, although the skies were getting pretty dark. I decided to change my shoes, stick enough money in my back pocket to cover lunch and walk over to the campus. I knew with it being Friday, I had to do it today or else I'd be wondering about this girl all weekend.

It was eleven-fifteen when I got to the café and it was quiet enough to be the library. I made my way to a booth in the back corner as a waitress came over, and I ordered some coffee. I had picked up a newspaper at a corner store on my way over, so I would have something to read and hide behind if I had to.

I didn't see the girl anywhere, as I breezed through the paper and drank my coffee. The lunch crowd was beginning to filter in so I decided to order a bowl of soup and take a chance that maybe that girl would come in. I hadn't even opened my pack of crackers when I noticed her rushing in, and quickly disappearing behind the kitchen doors. She came out with her t-shirt changed and her hair tied back and glanced in my direction, but was apparently assigned to the tables on the other side of the restaurant.

I asked my waitress if I could move to a window table on the other side of the restaurant so I could read better. She had no problem with my request and helped me with my bowl of soup.

I sat down and glanced out the window to check on the weather and make sure Lauren wasn't around. There was distant thunder and a hint of rain that was hitting the canopy of leaves on the old oak trees that majestically towered above the buildings. I was glad to be inside and not walking home, with the way the skies looked.

I pressed my back against the hardwood of the booth and glanced around to see where the girl was, in anticipation of what I would say to her when she came to my booth. I knew that I had to say something, but I didn't know how or what. It wasn't long before we made eye contact, and I thought *she probably thinks I need something.*

Coming over to my table, she said, "Hi, I'm Nicole and I'll be taking care of you. Is there anything I can get for you?"

"No. I don't think so," I said, as I looked at her neck and saw what I thought was a mole. Thinking to myself as she walked away, *this is just a coincidence. She can't be the same girl in Evan's dreams, even though she has the same name and mark on her neck. Could this possibly be her?*

21

Fortunately, Lauren didn't show up during the lunch hour, and I knew she had a one o'clock class, so I hung around for a bit. Most of the lunch crowd had thinned out, and I ordered a piece of apple pie that I really didn't want but felt like I needed to order if I was going to stay.

"Is everything okay here?" Nicole asked, as she stopped back by after wiping down a couple of tables.

"Sure. You know, it seems like I've met you before. Are you from here?" I blurted out before I knew what I was going to say next.

"No, I grew up in Bowling Green, Kentucky."

"Hmm, I don't why you look so familiar. Do you work anywhere else?" I asked.

"No. I got this job last year. I probably should have found another job this last summer closer to where I live, but I didn't."

"Oh, you don't live here in Blue Ash?"

"No. I live in the city. Not right downtown, but on the outskirts."

"That must be quite a commute?" I kept probing for answers.

"I take the bus. It's only a twenty-minute commute. It's not that bad and it gives me time to get some of my reading done."

"You still at home?"

"I live with my brother. He's a couple years older than me. He was a student here until last semester, and then he decided to take some time off. I just moved in with him last spring. I don't know why he didn't choose to live closer to campus, but it's okay."

"So, what year are you?"

"I'm a sophomore. Are you a professor?"

"No," I chuckled. "I walk over sometimes to go to the library, because it's closer than the public library. Furthermore, the campus is exhilarating and makes me feel young again," I told her, as I lied through my teeth.

I wanted to tell her I had a daughter there, but I decided not to go there since Lauren didn't know I was there.

"Well, it was nice talking to you. I've got to get back to work."

"Oh, I'm sorry. Let me finish my coffee and I'll get out of here."

"No rush," Nicole said, as she turned and smiled over her shoulder. "I'm here until two."

I finished up my coffee, and left Nicole a generous tip for occupying the table for so long. Then I paid my bill with the cashier, and left the café. It wasn't quite one thirty, so I knew I had plenty of time to relax and enjoy my walk home.

The ground was still dry, so the weather report must have been wrong. The dark skies and little rain that fell had passed over, and there was a slight fall breeze that felt wonderful against my face. I tried to clear my head and think about what Lauren and I could do with the rest of our day together. She had said she wanted us to go shopping. Maybe we could get out of the house for dinner and spend some time together, providing she didn't have too much homework.

I got home, slipped off my fisherman's sweater and put on a t-shirt. Then I laid down on the couch to ward off a headache

I knew was coming. I didn't know if it was from the stress of talking with Nicole, or the change in the weather.

I closed my eyes but all I could see was Nicole's face. She seemed like a hard worker and a good girl. *Her parents must have done a good job raising her,* I thought. I told my absorbent self to stop thinking about what I didn't know. The only thing I did know was that if that was the girl in Evan's dream, things were going to get a lot more complicated.

Lauren came home a few minutes before four, plopped her backpack in the chair and took a seat on the floor next to the couch.

"Hey, Mom." Lauren announced her arrival.

"Hey. How was your Friday?"

"Okay. This one professor I have is such a trivial son of …"

"Hey, I don't want to hear you talk that way, it cheapens a girl to talk like that," I said, as I repositioned the pillow under my head without opening my eyes, knowing Lauren was still sitting there. "What did this professor do that's got you so upset?"

"He wants us to clip a newspaper article out of tonight's paper and type a two-page paper by the next time we come to class."

"Well, clip the article tonight and then work on it off and on this weekend. It's not that big of a project. You've had much bigger projects."

"I know. It's just the idea of it. I feel like I'm in high school again. I guess I'm just questioning the purpose of the assignment."

"It's an assignment, and it's a grade. Sometimes you don't question, you just do what you're asked to do. Someday you might have an employer that will ask you to do a menial task or things you don't like to do, but that's all part of life. There are times I don't feel like cleaning or cooking, but I do. Why? Because life is not all roses–it's hard work sometimes. Raising you hasn't been a piece of cake," I said in a joking tone.

"Mom."

"You said there was some shopping you would like to do? I know it's Friday night, but I thought if you didn't have plans, we could go out on the town tonight. I know I'm not very exciting, but I'll even spring for dinner, if you like."

"Well, let me see, hot date or Mom? Let me weigh this out. Hard decision, but you win," Lauren said, as she yanked at the corner of the pillow under my head. "When do you want to go?"

"Give me a half hour, and I'll meet you at the car."

"It's a date," Lauren said, as she unfolded her long body from sitting on the floor.

22

We got in the car just before the sky opened up to the rain they'd predicted all day. Lauren wanted to go to the mall to find a new pair of jeans and look at some sweaters. Unlike her mother, she didn't have to try on ten pairs of jeans before one fit well. The jeans were the easy part, but shopping for sweaters was the challenge. Lauren had a time deciding if she wanted the sweater to be fitted or loose, blue or green, or striped or solid. I think she'd figured out how to wear her old mom down, because I ended up buying her two sweaters.

We found a place to eat in the mall, where we could sit down and order off the menu. I'd always had a pet peeve about fast food places and buffets. Stephen would always laugh at me over my idiosyncrasies. I can hear him say, "Diane, you still can't see what goes on in the kitchen of nice restaurants either or know how clean the people are who are fixing your food."

"Mom. Earth to Mom," Lauren said.

"I'm here," I said, startled.

"Yeah. Right. You're staring right past the top of your menu. Which, by the way, offers French onion soup, one of your favorites."

"That does sound good. I'm not sure I need anything heavy right before I go to bed. I need to lose a couple of pounds before the holidays so I can fit into my clothes."

"Ever since I've been little, you've been losing a couple of pounds."

"Well, I'm either neurotic or like every other woman in America. Hopefully, you'll never have these worries."

Lauren ended up ordering a Caesar salad with grilled chicken, and I had my old faithful bowl of French onion soup. We must've worked up an appetite shopping, because it only took us twenty minutes to eat.

It was still raining when we went out to the car. I unlocked the doors, and Lauren jumped into the passenger side, throwing her bags into the back seat all in one motion. I wasn't too far behind, shutting the door behind me. I hadn't realized how hard it was raining until I noticed how wet the inside of my car door had gotten. I brushed my hair out of my eyes and looked over at Lauren, and we both laughed at getting wet. I loved those mother-daughter moments. I turned on the ignition, adjusted the heater, and locked the doors.

"What do you want to do now?" I asked Lauren.

"I thought we were going home."

"Is that what you want to do? It's your night out."

"What time is it?" Lauren asked, as she pushed the sleeve of her sweat shirt up so she could see the face of her watch under the streetlights that were illuminating through the rain on the windshield.

Her hair swung down and hid her profile as she looked at her watch. Actually, it was one of Stephen's old watches she'd asked for a couple of years ago, and gotten a new band for with her allowance. She wore it every day, which said to me that she wanted to remember her dad. She'd gotten much better talking about her father over the years, but only on her own terms. There were times she'd still cry or get mad if I mentioned something about her father, and I hadn't quite figured out what triggered those emotions.

I did understand her willingness to believe her life was real, and that was where I went when I fell asleep in the dream. How could I expect her to understand it, when I wasn't sure I did? To be honest, sometimes I'd questioned it myself. After all the years I'd made the SWITCH, how did I know which life was the dream?

"It's seven-fifteen, whoa … we're doing good," Lauren said, breaking into my world of worries.

"Okay, you wild young woman. What do you suggest we do?"

"We could take in a movie. Do you want to drive by and see what is playing?" Lauren asked, as she looked over. "You don't look too excited about my choice."

"I said it was your night."

"I changed my mind. I'm allowed to do that since I'm a girl, you know."

"Well?" I said, waiting for this great revelation.

"I want to go to the coffee house a couple of blocks from the campus. Everyone has been talking about it. How does that sound? We could go and check it out," Lauren said in a playful voice.

"Chai Latte, here we come."

"Cool."

The car had warmed up, and the rain had dwindled down to a sprinkle. I turned on the windshield wipers to the slowest setting and adjusted the rearview mirror from when I straightened up my hair from the earlier downpour. Lauren pulled down her visor at the same time and put on some lip-gloss and combed her hair.

"Did you forget something?" I asked, as I looked at the dash lights.

"What?"

"Your seatbelt. I hope when you take the car you wear it.

It only takes one time for something to happen."

"Mom. I do wear it, so don't worry."

Then I wondered to myself if Stephen was wearing his seat belt the night he died.

23

We had to parallel park on a busy street almost two blocks away from the coffee house and walk. Fortunately, the rain had stopped and the street lamps made it somewhat easier to see that we were walking on an old sidewalk that had seen better days. Over the years it had buckled and cracked from tree roots that had grown underneath and pushed up against the concrete.

At one time, that quaint neighborhood with its small Cape Cod type homes had probably been one of the more popular areas in Blue Ash to live. Although, now that the branch college had expanded so much, a lot of those little homes were probably rented to the students if not sold to young professionals. The yards were well groomed, and it seemed to be a safe area to walk at night.

"There it is, up there across the street. See it?" Lauren pointed out.

"You mean the one with the big picture of a coffee mug hanging over the door?"

"Yeah." Lauren nudged me with her shoulder. "Maybe they'll have some live music to listen to while we have our coffee."

"By the looks of it, there's a crowd. I hope we can find a seat."

"Me, too. You want to cross now? It looks clear."

"Sure," I said, as we crossed the street. "Well, at least the sidewalk on this side of the street is better. I can take my eyes off where I'm walking and look up," I said, as I reached in my coat pocket.

"I thought I had a twenty-dollar bill in my coat pocket, but I guess not. Don't worry, though, I still have enough to get us a couple cups of coffee apiece."

"I've got some money, Mom. It's left over from what you gave me last week."

We entered the coffee house and I had to stand for a couple of seconds at the door to scan the place to see if there was room for two more people. From the outside of the building the place looked small, but on the inside, it took on a life of its own.

There was a small room up front that had a few pub-style tables with swag lights hanging over them. The second room was larger, and it smelled like incense, coffee, and bad hygiene, all mixed together. There was a combination of tables from five different decades and an area with a great assortment of large pillows and some scattered stools. The stools looked like the ones I had seen in antique shops, or that used to belong at my grandparents' house.

Just about the time we spied out two stools, a table opened up. We quickly made our way across the room and seated ourselves. There was a large chalkboard that hung above the bar area, that listed all the different flavors of the week. I ordered decaf African java mix and Lauren settled on a cup of green tea with lemon.

"Look, there's a guy with a guitar," Lauren said in an excited voice.

"I hope he plays classical, that would be great."

"Mom, this is a coffee house," Lauren said, like I was ancient. "Maybe if you're lucky he'll play some hippie music."

"Well, that would have been my second choice. Do you

think we should get another drink before he starts playing? Otherwise, it could get pretty busy in here."

"I knew there was a good reason I hang out with you," Lauren joked. "Even if you are my mom and like weird music, you're still pretty smart."

"I don't know about smart, but I do have common sense. Let me go up and get us another drink real quick. We'll have a cup for each hand, while we listen to the music."

"I like this place. Now I know why everyone's been talking it up."

"Lauren, will you drink another tea if I get you one?"

"That would be great, Mom, but sit for a couple of minutes," Lauren answered in a somewhat dreamy voice.

The guitarist started playing, and the room got very quiet. Lauren swayed and melted into the college headiness of the moment. I wouldn't have traded the moment for anything. I just wished Stephen could have been there to enjoy his daughter as much as I was.

We talked about clothes, classes, working out, and some guy she'd had her eye on. He was in one of her classes, and he was from Tennessee. That was the most she'd ever talked to me about a boy.

She had her own agenda on what she felt comfortable talking about and I didn't push it, because she had been through a lot in her short life. I was flattered that she felt like she could confide in me. Her eyes danced while she was talking, and she glowed with the look of infatuation that made me feel young all over again.

"So, tell me, does he have a car?" I asked, as I sat down with our second round of drinks. "Will he be coming over to the house soon?" I joked with Lauren.

"I don't know, maybe."

I didn't want to push it, so I changed the subject. "So,

how's your tea?"

"Good. I like it. Thank you." Lauren looked down. "Hey, Mom, can I ask you something?"

"Sure."

"How do we live like we do? I mean, you don't work, but we live comfortably."

"Well, your father worked as a marketing consultant … you know, and he was very conservative with his money, and made good investments. Your father was also well-prepared to take care of us in case something ever happened … and I'm glad he did. Why do you ask?"

"Because I never have, and I guess I never thought about it before now. Well … I thought about it, but not until … uh, I thought about getting a job."

"Getting a job? When did you decide you needed to get a job?"

"I don't know. I've been thinking about it since school started," Lauren said, before finishing off her first cup of tea, and then pushing it aside to make room for the new one.

"Well, we're not destitute, so you don't have to work if you don't want to. There's no reason to get in too big of a hurry. You're still a freshman and have barely got your feet wet. You might even want to join a sorority," I said, as I stirred my cup of coffee.

"Mom, I really would like to work a few hours a week. I thought a place on campus would be good, since I'm already there."

"Well, if you've got your mind made up, that's probably a good decision. Have you thought about the bookstore or somewhere in the administration building?"

"Well … I sort of already got a job lined up at the café for about ten hours a week. You know, in the Union Building where you and I ate. I know it's not glamorous, but I'll make more with the tips I'll get and I think it might be kind of fun."

My first instinct was to get upset, but then I looked at Lauren and realized how proud I was of her for taking the initiative on her own. I was also sad, because my little girl wasn't little anymore.

"That's a great idea. You might as well have a fun job during college," I replied, as I thought to myself that she'd be working with that Nicole girl. I told myself not to get worked up over what could be nothing, as I took the last sip of my African java, and smiled at Lauren.

Lauren and I both hit the hay around ten. As I lay in bed, I could hear the rain tapping on the gutter outside my window. The sound of the rain was therapeutic, and I quickly dozed off for only a couple of minutes before waking. My first thought was the caffeine, but I knew the real reason was … Lauren working with Nicole. I didn't know why that bothered me. I tossed and turned for an hour, before I finally decided to turn my light on and read.

I found one of my old subscriptions that I never read when I subscribed to it and after twenty minutes knew why. I was ready to make the SWITCH, but not ready to leave Lauren after we had such a wonderful evening together.

24
Friday in Ardmore, Pennsylvania

I woke up not quite ready to face my day, so I wrote a note for Evan to let me sleep in because I'd had a restless night. I taped it to the outside of my door, so he would be sure to find it.

When I woke up the second time, it was thundering. I had to look twice at the clock, because I couldn't believe it was after ten. I bolted out of bed, threw on some old khaki pants, then made my way downstairs to see what Evan was doing. When I got to the living room, I found a note from Evan that said he'd be back late afternoon.

I walked around the house, out of one room and into the next, feeling lonely. Evan had been staying with me less than a week, and I was already used to him being around. I should've been happy to have some time to myself to relax, but between worrying over the possibility of Evan not being able to find the girl he loved and Lauren juggling work and school, I didn't feel very happy or relaxed.

I knew one thing though: fretting over the possibility that Evan's girl lived in Blue Ash and was working with my daughter, Lauren, wasn't going to do me any good. My head started to hurt from thinking that Evan could be able to SWITCH lives when he dreamed, just like his father and I. After all, Evan had seen me in his dreams, but until I met that Nicole girl it never dawned on me that his dream could send him to Blue Ash, Ohio. How could I tell him I thought we'd been looking in all the wrong places and that I might have found her?

I decided I needed to get out of the house to clear my head, so I grabbed my umbrella to protect myself from the swell of clouds that were closing in on the treetops.

I walked several blocks to a plant store I'd wanted to visit, and spent most of my afternoon in awe at how beautiful and serene the greenhouses could be. Some of the plants were so large they'd need a moving truck to deliver them. I ended up with one wimpy-looking philodendron that looked like it needed a good home.

When I left the plant store, the clouds were slightly less obtrusive, and my umbrella was a nuisance to carry. I thought to myself that life was that way. We as people only needed cars when they worked and umbrellas when it was raining, and God forbid that an umbrella break when we needed it.

The grandfather clock in the front living room struck three o'clock as I was coming in the back door, but there was no sign of Evan. I kicked off my shoes and leaned my umbrella up against the frame of the door, and then made a home for the plant on the kitchen counter.

I scanned the kitchen for anything that needed to be done, but it was clean. The apple didn't fall far from the tree. Evan was a gentleman when it came to cleaning up after himself, just like his father had been.

I think that was why I was attracted to Stephen, because he was my partner in everything. There were never any expectations, because he didn't assume it was my job to do one thing or his to do another. We wanted to do everything together. I helped him with yard work, and he helped me cook.

Some of my greatest memories were when we bought our first house. Stephen would get in the kitchen and cut up vegetables, and then eat half of them before they got cooked. He also liked to play pinch the cook, but then again, so did I. We laughed at ourselves all the time, and we often agreed that we were just alike and that is why life found a way for us to be together.

I wasn't sure how I got off on that train of thought, or how I ended up sitting in one of the kitchen chairs, but decided to move into the living room and put my feet up. The next thing I knew, one of the pillows fell off the couch and woke me up. I sat up and looked at the clock, thinking that it seemed much later than four thirty. Evan was still gone, and I hoped that meant he'd finally found the girl, and that she wasn't Nicole after all. If not, I didn't know where else to take him to look. Especially since my gut told me I'd already found her.

25

I was in the kitchen cutting up salad when Evan came in the front door. I wiped off my hands on a dishcloth and straightened up my clothes from lying on the couch earlier.

"Hey, Evan, I'm back here in the kitchen!" I yelled.

I heard footsteps coming through the living room and then they stopped. I put down the bag of carrots and walked over to the doorway. Evan was standing in the dining room, looking at some paper he had pulled out of an envelope.

"Would you like something to drink? I've just started cutting up a salad."

"Sure, water would be great," Evan said, as he looked up. "Hey, I should've called today. I apologize."

"Oh, you don't have to apologize. I'm not your mother; plus, you're a grown man."

"It's just that you've gone out of your way to let me stay here and help me find her …" Evan trailed off.

"Evan, are you all right?"

"Yeah, I spent the day walking around and trying to figure out what I am going to do next. I'm having problems with meeting some production deadlines for one of my largest accounts back at work and I feel like I'm wasting vacation days looking for a needle in a haystack.

"So … I hope you don't think I'm ungrateful for all you've done, but I bought an airline ticket to go back to Chicago tomorrow. I'm not giving up. I just need to go back home and sort some things out, instead of staying around here and spinning my wheels. Plus, I don't want to end up stressing you out or become an inconvenience."

"You're anything but an inconvenience. I've enjoyed having you around. Will you come back?"

"Hopefully, in the next week or so. I just need a week to get some work done, and find out more about the girl I'm in love with. Maybe a few more nights with her will give me some more clues. To be quite honest, I thought that when I found you, I'd find her, too."

"Well, I just wish I could've been more help," I said, thinking of Nicole. "The only thing I know to tell you is to keep looking, and when you're ready to come back your room upstairs will be ready."

"Thank you. You've been so kind."

"I mean it," I said, as I pointed at him. "When you come back, you'll stay here, won't you?"

"I'd love to, if that's okay. Like I said, I'll be back soon."

"You'll have clean linens. What time is your flight tomorrow?"

"Ten-thirty," Evan said, as he folded up the ticket and put it back in the envelope.

"Then how does a glass of wine sound with dinner, since you don't have to catch the plane at the crack of dawn?"

"I would love one, but if you don't mind, I think I will excuse myself and go get cleaned up after all the walking I did today."

"You have plenty of time," I told Evan. "We're not going to eat for another hour, at least."

Evan went upstairs and I went back in the kitchen to finish up the salad. I understood why he was frustrated, but I truly didn't know where else we could look. Well, I did know one more place, but I couldn't tell him about that yet. I couldn't even tell him I had a hunch. I needed time to talk with Nicole, and even then, I didn't know if she'd be honest with me.

Now that I knew Evan would be away for a few days, I could plan what my next move would be. Should I go to the café on Monday? I would need to find out when Lauren's first day was and what her hours were, so I didn't open another can of worms. I would also need to figure out how I was going to approach the subject with Nicole.

Just then, a light bulb went off in my head. *I need a picture of Evan before he leaves.* I decided that I would tell Evan half of the truth. I'd tell him I needed a picture of him just in case I found her while he was gone. That way, I could show her his picture to see if she knew him. I didn't think he'd have a problem with that, as desperate as he was to find her.

26

When Evan came down for dinner, I was pouring wine into our glasses. My presentation of food had always been better than my cooking. I could remember an old friend telling me one time that presentation of a meal is the most important thing when dining, and good cooking is an added bonus. I'd never had anyone turn my cooking down, but I was definitely no gourmet chef.

"I could smell dinner all the way upstairs. Whatever it is, it smells great," Evan announced as he came in the kitchen.

"Good," I said. "I fixed Chicken Cordon Bleu. I hope you like it. Hey, go taste that wine and tell me what you think. I've never tried that brand before; I hope it's not too sweet."

I took the baby potatoes out to cool and checked on the bread. When I turned around, Evan was back in the kitchen holding a gift.

"I thought you went to taste the wine?"

"I did taste it, and it's a good one. I didn't want to leave without giving you something to let you know how much I appreciate you letting me stay here. I know my type A personality doesn't allow those around me to relax much, so I hope I didn't wear you out. I'll lay this right here on the counter, okay?"

"That's fine, but you really didn't have to get me anything. Your being here has helped me put some closure to your father's disappearance in my life, and gave me the opportunity to get to know you. Your father would have been so proud of you. You know that?" I asked Evan, as I spooned the vegetables neatly on each side of the meat.

"Thanks. Let me help you with that platter. It looks heavy," Evan said, as he moved in my direction. "I've enjoyed getting to know you. It was hard at first, but now I can see how my dad …"

Evan stopped short as he turned and walked toward the dining room with the platter.

I could tell he felt weird about what he had just said, because of his mother and all. I thought it would be best to breeze over his comment, so I forced myself to make small talk as I followed him into the dining room with the rest of the food.

"Do you like bread pudding?" I asked, as we sat down.

"Sure," Evan replied, after hesitating a moment.

But I could tell by the tone of his voice and the way he'd hesitated that he probably didn't care much for bread pudding, but was just being polite. I decided to let him off the hook by telling him his father hated bread pudding and so did my other late husband. So, I told him not to worry, that I was joking and hadn't fixed it for that night's dinner anyway.

"That's good," he quickly answered, and then further explained. "Bread pudding's okay, but it's not one of my favorites."

I laughed.

"Well, how about tapioca?" I asked.

"When we were kids, we said it looked like fish eggs, and I still haven't got past that," Evan told me.

"Not high on my list either," I confessed, as I picked up my wine glass. "*Bon Appetit.*"

We both dug in like there was no tomorrow, and after a couple of minutes of eating in silence, I made the comment that

I was hungry enough to eat a horse.

Evan smiled as he finished his bite and said, "Let me see, first bread pudding, then tapioca, and now a horse? Lady, if you eat horses you can count me out."

I nearly choked. "I've been good while you've been here and haven't cooked any 'possum."

"Thank goodness."

"Not to change the subject, but I wish I had a picture of you."

"I'm not leaving forever."

"I know, but if I find this girl and you're not around, a picture would be helpful."

"My business card has a picture of me on it," Evan responded, as he got up and walked toward the kitchen. "Will that work?"

"Yes. I think so."

"Good. I'll go up and get you one in a few minutes, but first I want you to open the gift I bought you."

I nodded yes, as I thought it had been a long time since I opened a gift that was wrapped so pretty.

"Did you wrap this yourself?" I asked, as he handed it to me.

"Are you joking? I don't think I've ever wrapped a gift in my life. Dad and Mom always took care of those kinds of things."

I wiped my hands on my napkin and then opened the small box. Inside was a beautiful broach pin that was shaped like a leaf. "Oh, Evan, it's gorgeous. I love it."

"I liked the colors of the stones. I don't know, it just reminded me of you. Like the first day we rode the train and you told me about lying under the trees and looking up through the leaves and branches. Remember? Anyway, the pin had your name all over it."

"Well, I truly love it, and I'll cherish it forever. Thank you."

As I was admiring the colors of the stones on the pin, Evan excused himself and went upstairs to get me one of his business cards. When he came back down, he gave it to me and I told him how handsome he looked in the picture before tucking it inside my shirt pocket.

Then we turned on the television to watch the weather, so Evan could see what the conditions were going to be on Saturday morning, since his flight was at ten-thirty. He was happy the radar was clear. He told me he planned on leaving around seven-thirty, and that would give him time to catch a cab to the airport. I agreed with his plan to leave early, because the traffic could be unpredictable and the lines at the airport long. It wasn't but a few minutes after the weather was over, that we both retired to our rooms.

Lying in bed, I thought *about Stephen, and how he'd once told me he fell asleep holding his cell phone, and made the SWITCH with it in his hand. He'd said he couldn't use the phone because it couldn't pick up a signal, so it didn't work. He thought it was probably because the phone wasn't recognized and didn't have any reception.*

I wanted to try and take Evan's business card with me when I made the SWITCH that night. I wanted to see for myself if it would work. I'd taken his card out of my shirt pocket when I was getting ready for bed and laid it on my bedside table. I knew I had to hold onto it when I fell asleep. I knew it wouldn't transport with me if I put it in a pocket, because I always woke up in different clothes. I always woke up in different pajamas.

Evan didn't know that I was attempting to take his business card with me that night. Nor did he know that my plan was to show his picture to Nicole. Thinking to myself, *I know there are some things better left unsaid, and this is one of them. I don't want to complicate his life anymore than I want to complicate mine.*

Trying hard to ease my worries, I closed my eyes and thought about seeing Lauren. Holding on to Evan's business card in my right hand, I fell asleep and made the SWITCH.

27
Saturday in Blue Ash, Ohio

I woke up in Blue Ash, Ohio, with Evan's card still in my hand. It had worked and I was in total awe. Getting out of bed, I cracked one of my bedroom windows to let some fresh air in. It smelled clean from rain we got overnight. Everything was still wet, but the sun was peeking through the grey blanket of clouds trying to say good morning to what was going to be a good day.

I walked back across the room and sat down at my vanity to brush my hair through a couple of times when the phone rang. It was only eight-fifteen, and knowing it couldn't be Lauren, because she was probably still asleep, I didn't answer it. The early mornings were my selfish time to do whatever I wanted, and I didn't want to talk on the phone.

I was just about ready to get into the bath when the phone rang again. It was still early, so I ignored it. Finally, when it rang the third time, I heard Lauren's door open and then her telling someone she'd be there by nine-thirty. It was Saturday morning, and she didn't have a class, so I thought maybe she was meeting a friend. I went ahead and took my bath and was toweling off when Lauren knocked on my door.

"Mom?"

"Yeah, honey. I'm here," I said, as I slipped into my robe and walked out of the bathroom.

"My new manager called, and they had two people call in,

so I guess I'm starting my new job today. Is that okay? The café′ is only open from ten to four on Saturdays."

"What time do you have to be there?" I asked, even though I already knew.

"In twenty minutes. Can you take me?"

"Sure," I said, as I put moisturizer on my face. "When do you get off?"

"Probably four," Lauren replied as she shrugged.

"Well, let me get my clothes on and we'll leave, okay? I need the car to run some errands today, otherwise I'd let you have it."

"Thanks, Mom," Lauren said, as she turned on one heel and disappeared out the door.

Now I knew I was going to have to tell Lauren about eating lunch at the café last week and talking with Nicole, without telling her what she didn't need to know until I could be sure that Nicole was Evan's girl. I sure didn't want Nicole to remember waiting on Lauren and me, and then mention to her that she saw me there last week.

When I came out in the garage, shutting the kitchen door behind me, I saw Lauren sitting on the passenger side with a nervous look on her face. When I opened my car door, the heat reached out and pulled me in. Sitting down, I reached up to turn down the radio, because I knew I needed to tell her. I didn't have a choice.

"Thanks for heating up the car," I said, as I turned the ignition.

"No problem, that's the least I can do."

"Well, I'm excited for you. Are you nervous?"

"A little."

"You'll do fine. Just remember, everyone there was new at some point. Hey, if you have a chance, get me a piece of their chocolate pie when you leave. If they don't have that, then pecan would be good," I told her, as I riffled in my wallet for a bill.

"You remember the menu? We've only been there that one time."

"You're right, we have only been in there once, but I was out walking a couple of days later and got hungry. So, I stopped in there and ate by myself," I said, as I waited for the questions to fly.

"Where was I?"

"You were in class, if I remember right. Yeah, it was Thursday."

"Why didn't you tell me?" Lauren fired away. "We were together all last night, and you didn't mention it. Not even when I told you I had a job there."

"I didn't think it was a big deal. Like I said, I was walking and got hungry. I had remembered the café was close and I stopped in. I guess I didn't think it was noteworthy."

Lauren shook her head and looked out the passenger side window. I reached out to turn the heater down for something to do as I looked over at her.

"Why are you acting like this?" I asked, as I adjusted the rearview window.

"Never mind. I just think it's weird."

"Well, it might be, but so is your dear old mom. Hey, I had the same waitress that we had there. Anyway, I think her name was Nicole. She told me what year she was, but I can't remember."

"Pull up to the back of the building. I am supposed to go in the back door."

"Okay, sweetie. I hope you have a good day," I said, as I took a breath of relief.

"I'll let you know what time I get off, but if it's nice out I might walk home."

Lauren got out of the car and disappeared behind the door of the restaurant. I sat in the car for a second, wondering if her last comment was out of retaliation or if she wanted to walk. After all, she did walk home quite a bit, because it was only a couple of blocks.

I backed up the car and headed for the grocer. I had a few items to pick up for dinner to get us through the week. By the time I pulled into the driveway, brought the groceries in and put them away, it was almost time for lunch. I made myself a sandwich and went out on the back patio to feel the warmth of the autumn sun shining through the trees. I was finishing my last bite when the phone rang, so I ran to pick it up, hoping it was Lauren, and that she was in a better frame of mind.

28

"Hey, Mom. It's me," Lauren said on the other end of the receiver. "I get off at three."

"Okay. Well, do you want me to pick you up?"

"No, I think I'll walk home. I'll see you in a little."

I couldn't tell if she was still upset with me or not, but I knew one thing: I didn't plan on making a big deal about going to the café and getting myself some lunch. The only plan I had was to hopefully go again next week with Lauren for lunch, and then conveniently stay for coffee after she went to class. *Maybe that should be my plan from now on until I can figure out if Nicole is the girl Evan's been searching for.* I hung up the phone and grabbed the newspaper before heading back outside on the porch.

After I finished my lunch, one of the chaise lounges was screaming at me to put up my feet. I took my plate into the kitchen, grabbed the afghan off the back of the couch, the newspaper from the table, and headed for the chaise. After getting settled, I covered up my legs and put the newspaper on my lap. Fortunately, my glasses were hanging around my neck, so I was ready to relax and read about all the wonderful things happening in the world. I hadn't gone through the first section, when I fell asleep. The next thing I knew, I awoke to a horn honking somewhere down the way.

I laid there for a while thinking about when Stephen and I used to bring the air mattresses out here and sleep when Lauren was a baby. We'd put her in the playpen right inside the screen door going into the kitchen where we could still see her, and camp out there all night. We would pretend we were on vacation for one night. I would pack us a midnight snack, which was usually cheese and wine, and Stephen would bring a flashlight and whatever book he was reading at the time to share with me.

I honestly believed I could get lost in the past and lose touch with reality, that is, if I knew what reality was. I forced myself to look at my watch and was surprised it was five past three. Lauren should be coming home soon, and I hoped in a better temperament.

I walked back into the house, laying the folded-up newspaper on the kitchen table on my way into the living room to put the afghan on the couch, when I heard Lauren come into the garage through the 'man' door and then open the kitchen door.

"Hey, Mom, when are you going get all of the stuff in the garage moved, so we can start parking the car in there?" she asked, as she walked in the living room

"Yeah, I know I need to do that soon. How was your day?" I asked.

"Good. I did some paperwork, got the café tour, learned how to work the register, and for a couple of hours I got to wait on people. I could only remember the special, but for anything else I had a cheat sheet. It was fun, and the other people that work there are all nice."

"Well, good," I said, thankful that she had dropped the attitude.

Turning back towards the kitchen, Lauren took off to go upstairs and I walked out into the garage to take a look at our collection of stuff. We hadn't pulled the car in for I didn't know how long, which made me wonder what prompted

Lauren to notice it then. The thought of cleaning all that stuff up made me tired. I sat down on one of the boxes and mentally planned how I should organize it, and then call Salvation Army for a pickup while I looked the other way. *That would probably be the easiest*, I thought, as I got up and walked back into the kitchen for a drink of water.

In the meantime, Lauren had gone down and made herself comfortable on the couch. I listened to the television show she was watching while I prepped dinner, until the teapot started to whistle. Then I made myself a cup of hot tea, and went in to sit with Lauren.

Lauren grabbed the afghan, and as she covered herself up, she said, "Hey, I met that girl at work today. You know, the one that waited on us. Her name is Nicole."

"I think that's the same girl that waited on me the other day also."

"Anyway, she trained me on the waitress part."

I took a sip of tea and waited for Lauren to tell me more about her day, but she didn't. Finally, after staring at the television for ten minutes, I asked, "So, do you know when you have to work again?"

"No, but the manager said he'd start me out with a few hours this week. I'm supposed to stop in there on Monday."

"If you'd like, I can meet you there before your one o'clock class on Tuesday and we can have lunch again. I'll buy?" I asked awkwardly.

"You're going to become a regular if you don't watch out."

"Now that you're working there, you're probably right. I'll take every chance I can to see you. You're a busy young lady, and your schedule is only going to get busier."

"Are you feeling sorry for yourself?"

"No, not at all. If you weren't busy, I'd be worried, but I want you to have some fun time too. Your college days won't last forever, so make the most of them. It should be all about you."

"I love you, Mom," Lauren said.

"I love you, too."

"Tuesday it is," Lauren announced.

"Wouldn't miss it for the world," I said as I got up to run upstairs.

29

On my way back down, I passed Lauren going up to her room. I picked up the newspaper that I'd placed on the table earlier and put it on the counter, so I could set the table for dinner. We were going to have stir-fry, and I had picked up some chopsticks that neither one of us could use very well, but I thought they would be fun. So, I put them by each of our plates, along with a decorative teacup for some oolong tea, and the matching teapot in the center of the table. I'd poured oil into the electric wok that was beginning to hiss and crackle, while filling up the teapot on the stove, when Lauren reappeared in her sweats.

"Can I help?"

"Would love it. Can you turn down the heat on the wok?"

"Sure."

"Would you like to take care of the stir-fry or the rice?" I asked.

"I'll do the rice," Lauren said, as she walked across the kitchen to pull out a pan from down below the oven. "The table looks nice. Chopsticks? Where'd you get those?"

"They had them in the oriental section at the grocer. I thought they'd be fun."

Lauren ran the tap water until it turned hot and filled the saucepan. "You crack me up, sometimes."

"Why?"

"Do you think I should put forks on the table, just in case

we give up?"

"Probably wouldn't be a bad idea. I'm not sure I could eat the rice with them, anyway."

The novelty of the chopsticks wore off quickly, and we gave in to using our forks halfway through the meal.

After dinner, Lauren went to her room to work on a report for one of her classes, and I cleaned up the kitchen as I watched the sun disappear over the horizon. The days were getting shorter and it was nearly dark outside by the time I got everything put away. I tucked the newspaper under one arm as I locked the doors and turned off the lights, and then headed up for the night.

Lauren's door was partially open and the light from her room spilled out into the hall as I reached the top of the stairs, allowing me to see where I was walking. I poked my head in to thank her for helping with dinner and let her know I'd turned off all the lights downstairs.

It felt good to get in my pajamas and get into bed. I turned on the television, which sat high on a chest of drawers in the far corner, and clicked through the channels to get to the local weather, but then realized it was too early.

So, I pulled out the drawer of my bedside table to find my reading glasses to read the newspaper, but they weren't there. I mentally scrolled through my day, hour by hour, until I recollected waking up that afternoon on the chaise and having them on. I hadn't remembered for the life of me putting them anywhere else, so I figured I had two options. I could go back downstairs and look for them or forget about reading the newspaper.

Too tired to go back downstairs, I chose the second option, and folded up the newspaper for the second time that day and tossed it on the floor beside me. Then I turned off the light and laid in the darkness, thinking about all the stuff in the garage I needed to go through, and that was enough to make me want to SWITCH.

30
Saturday in Ardmore, Pennsylvania

When I woke, it was Saturday. I found a note by the coffee pot from Evan saying he left early for the airport and to enjoy my coffee he had made. The house was quiet, and I thought to myself how uncanny it was how fast I'd gotten used to having him around. I found myself humming to fill the void as I drank my coffee and scoured out the kitchen sink. Feeling lonely, I asked myself what I'd be doing that day if Evan had never come into my life?

I decided to get out of the house and stop feeling sorry for myself. As I walked out the front door with my coat in hand, I ran into my chatty neighbor. It didn't matter that I wasn't in the mood to talk, because she was already approaching as I put on my coat.

"Hi, Diane."

"Hey, Jackie. How are you?" I heard myself say without really meaning it.

"Above ground, so I guess I'm doing well. You've had some company for the past few days. Did I see him leave this morning?"

She didn't beat around the bush, and I could hear my momma saying, "People like that are like fruit flies. They're not harmful, just pesky." I heard her question over and over in my mind, until it blew through Momma's memory.

"Yes. He had to leave. He was only here a few days, and

needed a place to stay."

"Well, he sure was a nice young man. He always had time to say hello. Where is he from?" she continued to ask.

"Chicago. He's a nephew of a friend." I frankly answered as I glanced toward the sidewalk, wondering why I felt like I had to explain. "Looks like the weather's going to be nice today."

"Sure does."

"Well, it was good to see you," I said, as I came out of that conversation unscathed and headed down the sidewalk.

The sunshine felt good on my back and was an uplifting boost for my outlook on the rest of the day.

When I got back home, I started cleaning out closets to keep myself busy. It was late afternoon before I stopped, and by that time I had three bags to donate to the clothing bank at our church. Knowing it was Saturday, and that the church receptionist, Mary, wouldn't be working, I called and left a message on the answering machine that I had donation bags to be picked up. Then I laid down on the couch for a quick nap, before mustering up enough energy to go upstairs and clean up.

I stepped out of the shower feeling less grungy and more accomplished. It wasn't until I heard my stomach growling that I knew the kitchen was calling my name, and it was all I could do to heat up a cup of bean soup and grab a handful of crackers before I retired.

Sunday and Monday were uneventful, and before I knew it, it was Monday night, which is what I'd been waiting for. Not that I was wishing my life away or anything, but I did need to go play detective with Nicole (that is if she was working on Tuesday), and have lunch with my lovely Lauren.

I rested in bed and listened to the wind outside, thinking of *all the beautiful trees with their colorful fall leaves I had seen on my walk Saturday. It wouldn't be long before all the leaves fell, and winter came. I wondered if it was my age or my great fondness of trees that made me feel sorry for the leaves. They live such a short time, but provide us with the pleasures of the new green foliage we eagerly wait for each spring; shade when we want a reprieve from the hot summer sun; and a colorful palette of nature's awesome beauty; and then, finally, after they fall, the few that survive the final raking nourish the lawns. My thoughts went to our lawn in Ohio, and then to Lauren and Nicole,* and with that thought I made the SWITCH. When I woke, it was Tuesday in Blue Ash.

31
Tuesday in Blue Ash, Ohio

I stood at my bedroom window and looked at the ominous clouds that had settled in before the sunrise, and the way the tree branches were gracefully swaying, as if they knew how to dance. I felt the need to sway with them, as if they were calling my name, and I would've if I hadn't needed to check in on Lauren.

So, I put on my robe and went down the hall to her room. As usual, Lauren's door was closed, so I slowly turned the doorknob, and pushed the door open a crack so I could see her sleeping. Then I backed away, and tiptoed downstairs, so she could sleep a few more minutes.

Down in the kitchen, the coffee pot made gurgling noises, which were by far the loudest noise in the house as I sat at the table patiently waiting for the day to start.

I was surprised to see Lauren on the stairs, because I knew her alarm wasn't scheduled to go off for another fifteen minutes. I couldn't see her face, as she appeared to be watching her step from behind two blonde curtains of hair that hung almost halfway down her arms.

"Good morning. Hope I didn't wake you by cracking your door this morning."

"No, I needed to get up anyway. I've got to read one more chapter for my business class before I leave. Hey, do we have any yogurt?"

"I think there might be a couple on the top shelf in the refrigerator."

Lauren ventured to the refrigerator, which also needed to be cleaned out. I wondered to myself, *how dirty do things need to get before they actually become "dirty"?* Fortunately, the refrigerator wouldn't be as formidable as the garage.

"Right there, honey. See them? They're behind the container of cottage cheese."

Lauren rearranged the shelf, took her yogurt, pivoted and headed for the silverware drawer as the refrigerator door shut behind her. She sat down at the table, propped her feet up on a chair and opened her yogurt.

"Would you like some coffee?"

"Maybe when I go upstairs to read. I've got to get a move on, though, because I need to be on campus by nine."

"Are you going to have time for lunch today?"

"Sure."

"Good. Do you want to meet at noon?"

"That'll work out perfect, because I've got my afternoon class at one o'clock."

Lauren finished her yogurt, poured herself some coffee and took off upstairs. I envied her energy. Standing up, I stretched, then retied my robe and went to rinse out my coffee cup. The refrigerator had to be dealt with, so I got busy and emptied out the shelves.

The kitchen counters were lined with jars, leftovers, and plastic-wrapped items that needed to be eaten two weeks ago. I normally cleaned out the leftovers regularly, but with all that had been going on with Evan, and Lauren starting school, I had become lackadaisical. There was no doubt about that, by the amount of leftovers that I threw away. I was almost done putting everything else back, when Lauren came downstairs dressed, and looked out the kitchen window.

"Can you drop me off? It looks like it is going to rain any time."

"Sure, let me finish up here. It'll only take a couple more seconds. You don't mind if I go in my robe?"

"You're not getting out anywhere, are you?" Lauren said jokingly.

"If I don't have to pump gas, I'll be doing good."

We both headed for the door, as I grabbed the keys off the hook.

32

The short trip to campus and back was a blur. Lauren and I had confirmed lunch at noon, then she was off and I was back in the kitchen looking at the refrigerator. Cleaning the refrigerator was a breeze, but I knew the garage was going to be a chore.

I poured myself another cup of coffee, and then walked out into the garage to face my next project. After walking around a bit, I decided to get to work by making two piles, one for donation and one for the garbage. The next couple of hours went quickly, and before I knew it, I was cleaned up and leaving to go meet Lauren for lunch.

I got to the café first, and had a minute to look around for Nicole, but I didn't see her. I spotted a table in the far corner when Lauren walked in, and we made our way over to sit down. Before we had finished eating, the manager came over and Lauren introduced us. He asked Lauren if she could work from three to five. Lauren agreed to work and we ate our lunch. I wasn't quite finished yet, and told Lauren I was going to stick around and finish up. She gave me a hug and ran off to class.

At one o'clock, Nicole walked in and went straight for the kitchen, as if she were running late. Luckily, today I was at a table in her area.

"Hey, you're back," Nicole said, as she approached the table.

"Yeah, except today I came over to have lunch with my

daughter instead of going to the library," I said, as I finally came clean.

"Oh, really? She's a student here?"

"Lauren's a freshman. You'll probably meet her soon. She just started working here last Saturday."

Nicole stood there for a few seconds and then said, "I think I helped her on Saturday. Is she tall, with long blonde hair?"

"Yes," I answered proudly.

"Your daughter will like it here," Nicole said, as she cleared the dishes from the table. "I got to get back to my tables."

"I understand,"

"I'll be back in a little bit, okay?" Nicole said, and smiled as she walked away.

I nodded and wondered how I would ever get to the subject of Evan with her, and wondered what she would say.

I finished my lunch and Nicole came over to take my dishes; but before she had a chance to leave, I said, "I can't get over how familiar you look. I thought that last time I saw you, too, but I just can't seem to place where I know you. Maybe you were in one of my dreams or something."

Nicole seemed to pause, but didn't respond.

"Do you think that is possible?"

Nicole shrugged. "I don't know. I'm not good at remembering what I dream."

"Really? I remember the majority of mine. I just can't think of where else I would have met you."

"Can I get you a cup of coffee?" Nicole asked, trying to change the subject.

"Sure, if I can get a to-go cup," I said, as I watched her eyes shift in the other direction.

Nicole stopped at two other tables on her way back to the kitchen, and then came back with a Styrofoam cup full of coffee.

"Maybe I have a twin," Nicole said jokingly, as she handed me the cup.

"Only if she has a birthmark like yours."

Nicole reached up to her neck with her free hand.

"Oh, I hate this thing."

"It's your beauty mark, you shouldn't hate it," I told her as I reached over to get a creamer. "Let me ask you something: Do you recognize me from anywhere?"

"Only from here, but then again my brother says I wear blinders."

"What does he mean by that?"

"I guess he thinks I'm not very observant."

"Well, some people are more observant than others," I consoled Nicole.

Nicole hesitated. "It was nice talking with you."

"I'll get out of your hair, and let someone have this table," I said, as I poured the cream into the coffee and then ran my thumb around the lid to make sure it wouldn't leak. "My daughter is working later today."

"What time?"

"Three."

"I'll be here until four," Nicole told me.

"Great, she could probably use some of your expertise."

Nicole laughed. "I hope I don't become too good at this; it's not what I want to do for the rest of my life."

"Well, try and make the most of your time while you're in college, and have fun with it," I said, as I reached over and gave her a motherly pat on the arm.

33

I was restless over the conversation I had with Nicole, because I didn't know much more about her than I started with that day. As I sat in the car, I kept going over our conversation, which was exhausting me. I didn't know if our casual conversations would ever lead to finding out if she were Evan's girl. My gut feeling told me she probably was, but she told me she didn't remember her dreams. *What if her brother was right and she's not an observant person?* I knew I couldn't keep showing up at the café and asking questions, especially now that Lauren was working with Nicole.

Not knowing how to move forward made me feel like chewing a piece of gum really hard. I dug down in my purse to see if I had any, as I thought about Evan. *At least he's gone for a few days, which gives me more time to figure out what I am going to do.*

The rain that had looked inevitable that morning finally made its appearance. The beads of water danced across the dry surface of the windshield, and reminded me of a time when Stephen and I got locked out of our car in the rain.

We had been to the grocer, and had the cart full of groceries that were packed into paper bags. I could still see Stephen desperately trying the clothes hanger routine and cursing at tearing up the sponge trim around the window. After numerous attempts that got us nowhere, we started to laugh. It probably started out as a nervous laugh, but when we looked at how drenched we were, we got to laughing so hard that other people in the parking lot were staring at us.

We ended up walking home in the rain, pushing a grocery cart. Then, if that wasn't enough, the bottom of the paper bags gave way to all the groceries when we tried to pick them up. We were cold and exhausted by that time, and all we wanted to do was get dry and go to bed. What amazed me afterwards was Stephen never said anything about getting locked out of the car, when we both knew it was my fault.

The rain pelting the windshield brought me back to the present. I put the car in reverse and started home. The thoughts of Stephen hovered over me, and it changed my mood. Instead of energizing me, like it usually did, the memories drained me. I had lost my get-up-and-go attitude, and felt tired. All I wanted to do was climb into bed and sleep. So, I did get into bed, even though I normally didn't like to take naps when I was feeling down, because I wake up grumpy.

I never went anywhere during naptime, not like at night when I went to my other life. Maybe some people could do that, but I'd never been able to make the SWITCH. That might be because, subconsciously, I didn't want to make the SWITCH. That was a good thing, though, because I didn't want to leave Lauren any more than I had to. She was the one most affected by the SWITCH, because she felt left alone in life when I fell asleep at night.

She'd even tried to wake me up during the night to see if I was still there, and physically I was. She told me I talked to her. When she was little, I guess I would get up during the night with her when she was sick or couldn't sleep, because she would thank me the next day. I never remembered getting up, and it made me feel like a terrible mom.

Boy, oh boy, for a day starting off so good, my conversation with Nicole and my thoughts of Stephen had sure brought me down. I closed my eyes and tried to clear my mind of Nicole, or how I was going to figure out if she were truly Evan's dream girl.

I slept hard. I couldn't believe it was six at night. I got out of bed and splashed my face with cold water, and then went downstairs to fix some dinner.

"Hi, Mom." Lauren announced her presence as she sat on the edge of the kitchen counter eating a handful of pretzels.

"I'm sorry, honey. I fell asleep and time got away from me. How long have you been home?"

"I don't know, maybe a half hour or so. I got a ride home from one of my friends."

"You should've called, I'd have come and got you."

"Are you sick?"

"No, I don't know what came over me. I didn't eat that big of a lunch. Maybe it was the rain this afternoon that made me crawl into bed. How was work?"

Lauren took a drink of her iced tea as she slid off the kitchen counter and walked over by the stove, and replied, "It was good. I worked with that Nicole girl and some other new girl. Nicole was a big help when I got mixed up on an order. She jumped right in and helped me in the kitchen, and you know what else? She said she's got that business book that they're out of at the bookstore, and that I could have it."

"Oh, that's great."

"I offered to pay her, but she said no. Anyway, she said she has some other stuff from taking that class last year that I could have also. She had the same prof."

"Well, good."

"We're both working tomorrow afternoon again, and she's going to bring it all in," Lauren said, as she finished her tea and set the glass in the sink. "I'm going upstairs to wash up, I feel kind of gross."

My mood hadn't changed much. I was on edge and feeling pressured. There were so many unanswered questions. Was Nicole really Evan's dream girl? If she was, did that mean Evan crossed over to the world Lauren and I knew? Would that be a good thing or not? And then the question crossed my mind, could Lauren cross over like Evan did? That thought scared me more than anything.

Lauren came back down after cleaning up and told me she wasn't that hungry, as I was making sandwiches to put on the Panini maker. We ended up sharing a sandwich, watching some television and then going to bed.

34
Tuesday in Ardmore, Pennsylvania

When I made the SWITCH it was still Tuesday, and I had awakened to sunshine instead of rain. A pair of cardinals had just arrived at the feeder, which was a sure sign that fall was there to stay. I decided to skip going to Sandy's Market that day because I felt drained and had a scratchy throat. I poured myself a cup of coffee, and went back upstairs to read the paper I had brought in. I had every intention of reading it, as I climbed back into bed and turned on the television to watch the weather, when the phone rang.

"Hi, Diane," Evan said.

"Good morning, Evan. Is everything all right?"

"Oh, yeah. I was just calling to tell you it'd probably be Saturday night when I come back. Is that okay?"

"Sure, it's quite all right."

"Good." Evan paused, "Anything new happen, while I've been gone?"

"No, not yet, but I'm confident we'll find her. Don't you worry."

"You sound confident, today."

"It's a new day."

Evan laughed. "It is good to hear your voice. I'll see you Saturday night, but I'll be late."

"I'll leave the key under the front door mat; just let yourself in."

"'Bye now," Evan said, and then he was gone.

I sat there with the receiver in one hand and my cup of coffee in the other for a few minutes after Evan hung up. He was such a vibrant soul, just like his father. I replaced the receiver and turned to the television, but the news was over. Then I did something I hadn't done in years: I finished my coffee and sank back down under the covers and went back to sleep.

When I woke it was ten-thirty, and I felt groggy from sleeping all morning. It was noon before I was cleaned up and ready to face the day. I decided to take the train and go to an art exhibit on Cuba in the 1940s that I'd seen advertised for the last month. The pictures looked more interesting than the topic, plus I had nothing better to do and I certainly didn't want another cleaning project.

The train was empty in the early afternoon and the emptiness made me miss Lauren terribly, for some reason. *Sometimes,* I thought, *living two lives seemed more hellish than the blessings bestowed.* I'd spent countless hours worrying that something could happen while I was living my other life or wondering if I'd missed anything. The train jolted, and so did my thoughts. When it stopped, I got off and looked for a street sign to get my bearings.

The museum was only three blocks up the road, and apparently it was a popular exhibit. From a distance, I could see people sitting on the steps outside the entrance. As I approached, I got the impression that I was going to have to wait, but I was wrong because the lines were moving at a steady pace. The exhibit was good, and I was parched by the time I got through it, so I bought some lemonade for my walk back to the train.

I barely got in the front door at home when I heard the phone ringing. I laid my purse down on the bench and ran to catch the phone next to the couch.

"Hello," I said, half out of breath.

"Hey, Mom, it's me, Christine."

"What a nice surprise! How are you?"

"I'm fine. How are you? You sound out of breath."

"I am," I announced. "I was just coming in the door when I heard the phone ringing. Where are you?"

"Well, I'm home at the moment, but I wanted to call and let you know my travel plans have changed."

"Really?"

"My meeting got bumped up a week. So, if it's okay with you, I'll be coming in on Saturday."

"Sure, that will be fine. I'm not going anywhere. I'm always here."

"It'll probably be between six and seven when I get there," she concluded.

"I'll have some dinner ready."

"That'd be great." Christine paused. "And, Mom, I would like to bring a friend."

"Okay, that's fine, I'll make sure I have two rooms ready," I said, as I wondered how this was going to work with Evan coming in on the same night. Unlike Lauren, she didn't know about my other life. *How will I explain this one?* I wondered.

We said our goodbyes and I hung up. I don't remember how I got to the kitchen table, but there I was back in the whirlwind of my two worlds, that were closer to colliding than I had thought.

I finally made it to bed that night with the help of a couple of sleeping pills. Sleep was the only thing I could think of that could calm my nerves. I needed to make the SWITCH.

Being close to Lauren would calm my nerves.

35
Wednesday in Blue Ash, Ohio

It was a good thing I liked mornings because I got to do them twice. Wednesdays were even better, for the sole reason they weren't Mondays and I felt like I was halfway through the week. Not that I was wishing my life away. Stephen always liked Mondays, because he said it was like having a clean slate at work. I could never bring myself to think that way, only because my father always complained about Mondays. He was never as positive as Stephen.

Lauren and I ate breakfast together and then she ran out the door. I sat at the table for a few minutes longer before deciding to go back out in the garage for day two of my cleaning project. I decided to tackle the boxes against the front wall first, because they were all still labeled from when we moved in years ago.

The first box I came to was filled with bed sheets and towels that smelled old and damp. I quickly folded the top down and took it over by the 'man' door to add to the donation pile. The boxes went fast because they should have been gone a long time ago.

Then I started with the infamous junk pile of sports equipment that was either broken, outgrown, or not in style anymore; like the wooden tennis racket we gave to Lauren for her seventh birthday that needed to be restrung, or the pair of skates she was wearing when she broke her arm. Then there were some old golf shoes that belonged to Stephen, and I wondered what happened to his clubs, because I didn't see them anywhere.

If there had been a recess bell, I heard it. I brushed myself off, and ventured back into the house. The morning had flown by and the microwave clock reminded me it was time for lunch. I fixed myself a sandwich and found a comfortable spot on the couch to lounge. There wasn't much on television that I cared to watch, so I picked up a magazine to read, when the phone on the end table rang.

"Hey, Mom."

"Hi, Lauren. Don't you have class at one o'clock?"

"Yeah, I've got to be there in a few minutes. I just called to see if it's okay if a friend comes home with me later this afternoon?" Lauren asked.

"Sure. Do I need to be cleaned up? I don't want to embarrass you, especially if it's this guy friend you told me about."

"Mom," Lauren said in a derogatory tone. "It's Nicole, from the café, if you must know."

"Just curious," I replied.

"I'm just going to wait until she gets off work and then we'll walk home. She's got those books for me and they're too heavy for one person to carry. Anyway, she said there are some things she can show me to help me with the papers and exams."

"Well, that's awfully nice of her. Are you sure you don't want me to pick you girls up?"

"I don't think so."

"Okay, see you later."

"'Bye, Mom," Lauren said, as she hung up.

I sat there with the receiver in my hand, thinking about how this was all going to play out. Maybe this was a godsend.

Nicole could trust me if she was Lauren's friend. My only obstacle was not upsetting Lauren's world along the way. I put the receiver back in its cradle next to my empty plate and reached for the remote control to see if there was something mindless on TV to watch. I needed something to focus on that would take away the sudden pang of anxiety that had settled in the bottom of my stomach and made me nauseous.

I reminded myself that my life was far from normal; otherwise, I wouldn't be stressed over a college kid who had no idea that we both might know Evan. A familiar tune on a commercial broke my train of thought and for a short moment carried me away. Then some soap opera came on, so I turned the television off.

By the time Lauren got home, I had taken a shower and made a batch of brownies that were still hot. Nicole and Lauren ate two apiece before disappearing upstairs. I wasn't about to follow, even though I wanted to, so I pulled out the telephone book and called the Salvation Army to schedule a pickup. They agreed, as long as what I was donating wasn't broken and met their requirements

When the girls came down, I was back out in the garage going through a plastic container of some proposals Stephen had spent hours pouring his heart into for his clients; and now there they were, piled in a box. I debated over throwing them away, but I couldn't, even though I had no desire to read them.

"Wow. Looks like a typhoon hit. What are you doing?"

"Oh, just going through some things," I replied, as I started stacking the folders and loose papers back in the container. "Thought I'd try to clean the garage out before the snow flies."

"Do you want me to call in some pizza?"

"Whatever you girls want is fine with me."

36

The pizza arrived in twenty minutes, and the three of us ate like there was no tomorrow. After dinner, I told the girls I needed to run out to get some more trash bags for the garage project and offered to treat the girls to ice cream and take Nicole home.

It was dark and I didn't want Nicole catching the bus to get home to late in the day. Plus, I wanted to see where she lived, so I could mentally log some landmarks for Evan. They agreed to go, so we all jumped in the car and headed for the plaza that was right around the corner.

I gave Lauren ten dollars so they could go and get some ice cream while I ran into the grocer for some trash bags. When I came out, they were sitting on the hood of the car giggling about something.

"You girls ready to go?" I asked.

They both headed around the driver's side and climbed in the back seat.

"Nicole, you're going to have to help with directions, okay?'

"Sure," she said, as she smiled at me in the rearview mirror.

She was a great navigator. It only took us twenty minutes to get to her building, but of course that wasn't during rush hour. The building was an old brownstone, but bigger. There was a dim light shining in the entryway and a staircase that looked old and steep. I wondered if the intercom buttons on the left-hand side of the door worked, as I listened to Nicole dig in her book bag.

"Thanks for bringing me home. I really do appreciate it," she said, as I heard her keys jingle.

"You're welcome. It's not that far, and besides, I was going out anyway."

I wanted to tell her it wasn't safe to ride the bus after dark, but I wasn't her mother and she might take offense to me making that comment. I waited for her to get inside the front door and disappear up the stairs. She was out of view by the time Lauren got into the front seat on the passenger side.

"Nicole takes the bus every day?" I asked, more as a statement than looking for an answer, as I put the car in drive.

"You never know how good you have it until you see how others get by."

I looked around in hopes of seeing a restaurant or a name on buildings that Evan might recognize, but there weren't any.

"Thanks for offering to take her home."

"It wasn't a bad drive this time of day. She seems like a nice girl."

"She's really nice. I think we're going to try and do something this weekend after work on Saturday. We both get off at three o'clock."

"Does that mean you'll be asking for the car?"

"Probably."

We rode in silence the rest of the way home. I'd learned to cherish those moments instead of worrying that something was wrong. Lauren and I were comfortable with the mother-daughter bond we shared. Being by ourselves had strengthened our relationship. We had grown to understand that we were best friends and could depend on each other. The silence was sometimes a quiet awakening to being content.

The streetlamps were standing majestically, like Roman soldiers guarding over the city. Their sole purpose was to make sure we could see to get home. Then they inevitably would disappear into the busy background and gradually fade with morning traffic.

My rambling train of thought quickly came to an end as we pulled into the driveway. The quietness ended with Lauren asking to borrow the car. She wanted to go to the coffee house to hear some music, and meet a friend. My knee-jerk reaction was to say no, because all of a sudden she was growing up too fast. But instead, I heard myself say okay, and didn't ask whom she was meeting because I already knew it was this boy she'd mentioned.

She got dressed and came into my bedroom to say good-bye. I was dressed for bed and lounging in a chair over in the corner of the room. The only time I ever sat in the chair was when I needed to feel hugged by Stephen. It was his favorite chair, and in the evening he would retire to this chair before going to bed. For some reason, that night I needed to feel him. Maybe it was because our little girl was going out.

"I won't be late. Okay?" Lauren asked.

"Eleven o'clock?"

"Okay."

"You know I won't sleep well until you're home."

"I'll be okay, Mom," Lauren consoled me.

"Lock your car doors," I said, with a pasted smile.

I could hear her running down the stairs. She was leaving, excited, and I was staying behind, worried. I kept telling myself I'd been through this with two other daughters, but for some reason it didn't make it any easier. Maybe it was because my being older made Lauren seem so much younger than my other two daughters. I closed my eyes and tried to remember the first time I ran out to meet Stephen, and how the anticipation overrode everything else in the world. I smiled at the look of excitement on Lauren's face when she left.

I went up to my bedroom and turned on the television, got under a blanket, and tried to wait for her to get home, but my eyes kept closing. When she did get home, she came into my bedroom and halfway pulled me back into her world with several hard tugs on my shoulder, and let me know she'd gotten home and was going to bed.

37
Wednesday in Ardmore, Pennsylvania

I made the SWITCH, and woke up feeling refreshed in the quiet of my condo. I could hear the grandfather clock at the bottom of the stairs ticking and my heart beating, but that was it. I laid there for a while thinking about Christine, and that mysterious friend she was bringing with her. She'd never had much time for a man in her life, or talked about having a family, because of her career. I'd always known it would take someone special to make her think twice about slowing down.

My two big girls couldn't be any different than night and day. Claire was two years younger and didn't have a competitive bone in her body. She had been content playing with her dolls and baking, while Christine was dreaming about setting the world on fire. It was uncanny how it had all played out, and how happy they both seemed to be in their lives.

I sat up on the edge of the bed and put my house shoes on, then grabbed my robe off the chair by the door and ventured downstairs to make coffee. I picked up my purse off the bench in the foyer, and took it to the kitchen with me, so I could pay some bills while I drank my coffee.

Two cups later, I decided to get my day started and run the errands I didn't feel like doing the day before. Sandy's Market would be my first stop for groceries, and then a quick stop by church to pick up my weekly call list. I told myself as I walked up the stairs not to forget to call the salon to see if my hairdresser could take me the next day.

I quickly got dressed and headed toward the train station. I was already dreading my stop by the church, because I didn't want to play twenty questions with Mary, the office secretary. I knew she was harmless and had nothing better to do than pry into other people's business, but she could be too much at times. I told myself to keep it short, get the list, and find out when someone planned to stop by and pick up the donation bags I had left a message about last Saturday.

The train doors opened, and I stepped into an empty car. I sat on the side where the sun was shining so I could warm up a bit. *Last time I was going to Sandy's Market, Evan was with me,* I thought to myself. It didn't seem possible that so much had happened in a week's time. I hadn't mourned this past week like I thought I would've when I found out how Stephen died. Maybe that was because I had Evan with me. I didn't know.

My thoughts took me to *Stephen when he found out I was pregnant, and how excited he was to know it was a girl. He brought me flowers and breakfast in bed one morning, right after we got the news. Lying on the bed next to me while I ate, we talked about all the things we wanted to do with her. He had this smile plastered on his face like a kid who was going to an amusement park.*

The train jolted a bit and jostled my thoughts. I scanned my outside surroundings to see where we were and then thought about all the questions Evan had for me a week ago on the train. I wasn't sure we finished, but I thought enough was said.

The train came to a stop and I got off. I picked up my pace and got to Sandy's right after they opened. Looking at the produce was like looking at a colorful bouquet. It was hard to keep from buying one of everything, but my little rolling cart would only hold so much. I could spend all day buying food if I knew someone else would fix it. Yep, all those years of fixing three squares a day for two families somehow took the enjoyment out of cooking.

After leaving the market, I headed to the church, lugging my cart behind me. It was cooler than what I remembered it being last week at that time. The sun was hidden behind some clouds and the intermittent grayness of fall snuck into the day, like a fog settles over the water in the wee hours of the morning.

I enjoyed my walk by all the brownstones, and when I got to church the door was locked. I looked in the side window, hoping to catch Mary, but she wasn't at her desk. My watch confirmed what I already knew, that it was lunchtime, so I decided to find a small café.

I stopped at the first one I saw; it was a cute little Italian sub shop, slightly tucked back in between two apartment buildings. A young man in his twenties with a heavy Italian accent took my order and made my sandwich. I chose to eat inside at a table by the window, so I could be entertained by the assortment of people passing by. Most of them were dressed in work attire, except for the few creative types who meandered along at a different pace.

38

Then I saw Mary, but it was too late because she was waving at me. I quickly finished my sandwich and grabbed my purse, but by that time she had gone in and was already talking.

"What are you doing on this side of town, Diane?" Mary asked.

"Well, I was coming to the church to pick up my call list from you, but by the time I got there it was lunchtime and you were gone. So, I decided to stop and get a bite myself."

"I don't live but two blocks, so I go home for lunch every day."

"Are you on your way back to the church?"

"Yes, I have to get back by twelve-thirty."

"If you don't mind, I'll walk back with you and get my call list for the week," I said.

"Fine with me," Mary replied.

"Hey, did you get my message about a donation pickup?"

"You were on my list to call today. They said they could come out tomorrow. If you're not going to be at home, just leave your bags by the back door," Mary said, as she unlocked the door.

We stepped into the church and went into the main office. Mary handed me an updated list of people on my call list. I kept waiting for her to ask about Evan, but she didn't. Instead, she wanted to know about what I had in my cart and why I had so much food. I thought she was digging for information, because she didn't ask about what I was donating. I made a graceful exit with my cart, and started back to the train, thinking the whole encounter was pretty harmless.

The train wasn't any more crowded that afternoon than it was that morning. There was only myself and one other lady in our section. The sun had broken out from behind the clouds and was shining through just like it had last week when Evan had been sitting next to me. It seemed like it had been longer than a week since I'd seen him. Thinking of him made me yearn to see him. If I still had his picture, I could've looked at it, but I didn't because I'd left it in Blue Ash.

The mental picture of him brought tears to my eyes because of the strong resemblance to his father, Stephen. The other lady on the train asked me if I was okay and I told her I was reminiscing over a picture I'd seen and I had gotten lost in the moment. It was similar to getting caught laughing at funny cards in the card aisle, and then noticing that you're not the only one there.

Thinking of Evan's picture made me want to dig through the albums at home in Blue Ash and look for pictures of Stephen. I hadn't wanted to do that for a long time, because it made my heart ache knowing I would never hear his voice again and feel his touch.

All my thoughts were jolted when the train slowed, and came to a standstill at my stop. I hung my purse over one shoulder, and pulled my cart full of groceries behind me as I got off the train and walked home.

I'd bought more than I thought I had at Sandy's, and the refrigerator was packed by the time I got done unloading everything. I was too tired to fix much for supper, so I ended up with an egg sandwich.

After eating, I got a stack of cookbooks and headed for the

living room to plan the menu for Christine and her guest on Saturday night. Planning dinner was the easy part, but explaining Evan coming in later was a different story, and I hadn't exactly decided how that was going to go. Believe it or not, my brain didn't start racing; it just stopped because I didn't have a planned explanation.

I thought of *Evan's picture and the sweet smile on his face, and wondered what young girl wouldn't want to be with Evan?*

Then my thoughts *went back to what I would tell Christine Saturday night. Maybe I'd tell her Evan was a friend of someone at church who needed a place to stay, and then I wouldn't get the hundred-questions routine. I think both of my daughters would be okay with that, plus I knew for a fact that Christine would tell Claire about Evan.*

To say the least, the cookbooks never got looked at, and instead I decided to lie down on the couch. Closing my eyes, I fell asleep and made the SWITCH.

39
Thursday in Blue Ash, Ohio

The last thing I remembered was Lauren coming in to kiss me good night when I woke up. I could smell the coffee as I went downstairs, and saw Lauren ready for school and having a bowl of cereal.

"Hey, Mom," she said, with a good morning smile on her face.

"Hi, honey, you're up early."

"Yeah, I want to stop by the library to look up a reference for a paper I'm working on. I've got to leave in twenty minutes or so."

"I didn't know it was that late, but then again I don't know how I got from the chair to the bed either. My brain's a little cloudy."

"You were in the chair when I came home last night."

"Thanks for making the coffee," I said, as I poured myself a cup and walked toward the table. "So, how was the music last night?" I asked.

"It was two girls on acoustic guitars. They were okay."

"Did you get to see your friend?"

"Yes. We had a good time."

With that short comment, I knew better than to expect more. Lauren probably didn't want to get overly excited about her friend, or else felt weird talking to me about him. She finished up her breakfast, gave me a quick peck on the cheek, and was out the door.

I sat down at the table to drink my coffee and think about my garage project when the doorbell rang. I wasn't expecting anyone, and couldn't imagine who would be at the front door this early. I was surprised to see Nicole when I opened the door, and for a moment wondered if she had passed Lauren, but then remembered the bus stop was in the opposite direction. Out of curiosity, and not to be rude, I invited her in the house.

"Nicole, come on in. Can I take your coat?"

"No, thanks. I'm looking for one of my books I need for class. I must've left it here last night," Nicole replied.

I walked back toward the kitchen as she followed me. "Where do you think you left it?"

"Maybe up in Lauren's room, since we were studying up there."

"Well, let's go take a look," I said, as I motioned upstairs.

We looked all over the room, but we didn't see it, and that within itself was a task because Lauren's housekeeping wasn't the best. I bent down and hesitantly looked under her bed, and I found a plate of leftover food from the day before. We both laughed, but mine was out of embarrassment.

"Maybe it's in my car," I offered.

So, we headed back down to the kitchen. I offered Nicole something to drink, and she took me up on some juice. She ended up taking off her coat after all and hung it on the back of one of the kitchen chairs as she sat down. I poured her a glass, and then went back upstairs to retrieve my car keys from my purse.

Once I got outside, I took a deep breath because I knew that might be the chance I'd been waiting for to ask Nicole about Evan. I took a look in the back seat where she had been sitting the night before, and the book was right there. I picked it up as I gathered my thoughts.

"Well, your book was in the back seat," I said, as I intentionally laid the book on the kitchen counter across the room. I watched her out of my peripheral vision as I poured myself another cup of coffee. She wasn't getting up, so I sat down with her at the table.

"So, are you working today?"

"Yeah, I'm doing my usual twelve o'clock shift."

"You don't have much free time, do you? I mean, between your school and work, you're busy."

"Yeah. Sometimes I think it'd be easier if I lived closer, but I like rooming with my brother."

"Where are your parents, Nicole?"

"They live in Bowling Green, Kentucky. My dad's deceased and my mom's just a mom. Anyway, my brother and I had to find our own way to come to school here in Philly. Last year, my brother dropped out of school and he's been working in some bottling plant," she said, as she took a drink of her juice.

"Every once in a while, we'll get a care package from Mom, but that's about it. I love my mom, and I don't want her to worry, so I do the best I can."

I reached over and patted her on the hand. "Nicole, you're doing wonderful and if you ever need anything at all, I want you to know you can come here."

She nodded.

"Do you have a boyfriend?"

"No. Not really," she said, sounding a bit shocked that I'd asked.

"You're a pretty girl. Don't miss out on too much. You'll want to have some good memories of your college days. What do you do for fun?"

"I like music."

"That's a start. Maybe you'll meet a boy in a music store."

She smiled at me like she was uncertain of what I was going to say next, but she wasn't the only one — so was I.

"Hey, I have a picture of a boy in my purse who's looking for the love of his life. Although I don't know if he works at a music store or not, he seems nice," I said, as I reached behind me to grab my purse off the kitchen counter. "Let me get his picture and show it to you."

Nicole was sitting on the front of her chair by this time and had finished her juice. I knew it was only a matter of moments before she told me she had to go, so I flipped out the tiny picture of Evan and laid it on the table in front of her.

"What do you think? He's kind of cute, isn't he?"

"What's his name?" Nicole asked, as she picked up the picture.

"His name is Evan."

"How do you know him?"

"I knew you were going to ask me that. Actually, I knew his father."

"Does he live here?"

"No, but he's close."

Nicole smiled at the thought and asked, "Does Lauren know him?'

"No, and that's a touchy subject. Please promise me you won't tell her about this picture. Anyway, she already has a boy on campus she likes."

"She doesn't know you know this Evan?"

"She knows of him, but she's never seen his picture."

"Why is he a big secret?"

"Maybe someday I'll tell you. He's a nice young man. Would you like me to introduce you sometime?"

"I don't know. Let me think about it," she said, sounding uncomfortable as she laid Evan's picture down and stood up.

"I've got to go if I'm going to make it to my class."

"Okay. I'm glad we found your book," I said, as I retreated to the reason she came by.

"Me too. Thanks for the juice," Nicole said, as she put on her coat.

"You're welcome," I said, as I stood up with Evan's picture still in my hand.

Nicole looked at it as she turned toward the foyer and left out the front door.

40

The rest of the day I spent going over our conversation in my head as I went through boxes in the garage. The look on Nicole's face when she saw Evan's picture was emotionless, but her eyes told it all. She couldn't seem to take her eyes off of him. I wanted to ask her, *are you sure you don't know him?* But I knew I had to take baby steps for Evan's sake.

The boxes were filled with stuff I hadn't missed all those years, so I neatly stacked them as close as I could to the garage door. There was only one box left that I hesitated to open because I knew it was full of family pictures and cards that I knew would bring back too many memories.

I ended up carrying the box up to my bedroom and putting it behind Stephen's favorite chair. Then I stacked a couple of blankets and other linens on top of it for safekeeping, until I was in the right frame of mind to go through them.

I washed up, changed clothes, and went down to the kitchen to start something for dinner. God knew what, but at least with just the two of us it didn't have to be meat and potatoes every night. Thank goodness, Lauren was easy to cook for and not a picky eater.

"Hi, Mom. I made pretty good time, huh?" Lauren asked, as she entered the house through the kitchen door.

I turned around and smiled, as I wiped off my hands on the dishcloth.

"It only took me fifteen minutes to get home from work."

"You made good time," I replied, but was somewhat uneasy because I wasn't sure if Lauren had worked with Nicole that day; and if they had worked together, if Nicole had mentioned our conversation or Evan's picture.

"How's a big fat cheeseburger sound for dinner?" I asked, as I tried to read Lauren to see if anything was askew.

Lauren laughed. "As long as it has more cheese than fat, I'll eat it," she said, as she whirled around the staircase banister and went upstairs.

I turned on some jazz music and hummed along as I finished making our hamburger patties. The table was set and the buzzer on the oven had just gone off when Lauren reappeared.

"So, what's on tap for the evening?" I asked.

"I'm home and I don't have much homework, so I thought I'd chill out and catch some TV."

"Good luck. Wednesday night TV isn't great for anything but sitcoms or those silly reality shows that aren't worth two cents," I told Lauren.

We ate dinner without a word about Nicole, and I was relieved. Instead, we talked about Lauren's classes, my cleaning the garage, and what we were going to do for the holidays.

In the past, we'd stayed home for Thanksgiving and flown to Florida for Christmas break, but we thought we'd find somewhere new to go. We tossed around a couple of ideas, but neither one of us truly cared where we went as long as it was warm.

After dinner, Lauren sprawled out on the floor in front of the TV, and I took the couch. It felt good to prop my feet up, close my eyes and listen to Lauren laugh over some program she was watching.

We don't laugh enough, I thought to myself. When Stephen was here the house was filled with laughter because he was quite the prankster. He loved to tickle Lauren when she was little. There were many nights I would hear her laughing as he tucked her in. Then things would get really quiet. I would ask him what they were laughing about, but he would tell me he didn't know what I was talking about. Then he'd wink at me and, if I didn't look away, he would start tickling me. He loved a good hearty laugh. He said laughing was a great stress reliever.

I wondered sometimes if Lauren remembered those moments with her father, because she never talked about her memories. I'd never been sure it was healthy that she didn't bring up her father, but she'd had a lot to deal with in her life and I'd never wanted to push her, even though I had so many good memories I'd have liked to relive with her again.

I was almost asleep when Lauren told me she was going to bed.

"Oh … I'm sorry, honey, I didn't mean to doze off."

"It's okay, you didn't miss much."

"I heard you laughing, and that's all I remember."

"Just a silly show," Lauren said, as she helped me up.

"Thanks. You go on up. I'll get the lights."

"Okay. Good night, Mom."

"Good night, honey. Sleep tight," I told her, as she headed up, and I started turning off the lights so I could quickly climb into bed and make the SWITCH.

41
Thursday in Ardmore, Pennsylvania

I woke up full of energy and decided to burn off some of it with a morning walk. The sun was barely peeking over the horizon when I stepped out the front door, which was so unlike me to be up, dressed and moving that time of the day.

The morning traffic was just starting to stack up with the over-achievers who were starting their trek to work. There were a few professional types scattered here and there on foot, juggling their briefcases and cups of hot coffee, which reminded me of Evan. They all reminded me of being younger and working, and how I'd spent years living for the weekends; until one day, when it dawned on me that I'd want all those days back. Oh, if I could've told me at thirty what I knew now, maybe I would've not wished all those days gone.

It was around eight-thirty when I got home, and the morning paper was waiting for me on the front stoop. I had either gotten hot from walking or the furnace was working overtime, because when I opened the front door the air clung to me like a wet sticky blanket. The heat thwarted my desire to drink my usual cup of hot coffee.

As I walked through the living room, I noticed the stack of cookbooks by the couch that I'd left the night before. They reminded me that I only had two days to figure out what I was going to do about Evan and Christine meeting one another.

The menu had taken a second seat to the situation at hand.

I didn't bother to sit or pick up the books; instead, I went into the kitchen and decided to feed the birds. After that, I just sat at the table in a daze, not because I was tired but because I was mentally drained.

I must have sat there for thirty minutes before I realized it was Thursday and I had rescheduled my hair appointment for that day at ten. I raced upstairs and got in the shower before the water got hot, because I needed every minute I could get. Clothes and all, it took me twelve minutes to look presentable.

On my way downstairs, I remembered the church was stopping by for my donation bags, so I put them on the back porch, grabbed my purse and the newspaper, and then headed for the bus. I was hoping the *Dear Abby* column would have something fun that day, to take my mind off my own dilemma.

My hairdresser was her normal bubbly self. We had this weird relationship, maybe because she thought of me as a mother figure. She spent most of her time telling me about her problems, instead of listening to me because I was the client. She'd been getting a divorce for the last six months and didn't know how she was going to work and manage raising her two children. My heart went out to her, because she didn't have any family close by, but something told me she was a cat with nine lives and would land on her feet.

That day, I didn't mind listening to her while she trimmed my hair, any more than she minded that I breezed through some magazines and found a couple of recipes for Saturday night.

When I left, I was feeling good about my hair and the recipes I had torn out of the magazines. The best part was, I had all the ingredients I needed and didn't have to stop anywhere else. On the bus ride toward home, I decided to call Evan and talk to him about coming in on Sunday night instead of Saturday. I didn't think he would have a problem with it, knowing the circumstances. I felt good about my decision, and it took the weight of worrying off my shoulders. Plus, I didn't think it was worth making either Evan or Christine feel uncomfortable.

My stomach was growling by the time I got home. I made myself a salad, and then laid down on the couch for a catnap that turned into a full-fledged nap. I hadn't slept that hard since I could remember. Maybe it was the release of stress over my decision to call Evan, which I knew I still had to do.

So, I got up and found his phone number and picked up the phone. I hated to call him at work but didn't want to take a chance on missing him. The phone only rang twice when I heard myself say, "Hello, is Evan Winthrop in?"

"No. He's not in right now. May I take a message?"

"No, thank you. Is there a better time for me to call back?" I asked.

"Well, he's out for the rest of the week, but he will be calling in for messages."

"Will you please tell him to call Diane? He has my number."

"Sure."

"Thank you," I said, as I hung up the phone.

The stress was back. What if he didn't call in or get my message? Why hadn't I gotten his cell phone number before he left? I couldn't call him at home in fear that his brother, Johnny, would be visiting and wonder who I was. I was right back in the same boat. Thank goodness I'd had a good nap, because I didn't think I'd sleep too well until I could get a hold of Evan.

I spent the rest of the evening sitting on the back steps with the door left cracked so I could hear the phone if Evan called. He never did, so I finally went to bed and fought with the covers until I fell asleep.

42
Friday in Blue Ash, OH

I had made the SWITCH before Lauren stirred. It was still dark outside when I turned on the lights under the cabinets in the kitchen so I could make some coffee. I thought of Stephen, when he'd ask me how I could see without the overhead lights on. He knew I hated overhead lighting, because it made me feel like I was in a department store.

I had to remind myself that it was Friday, as I stirred the cream in my coffee. The week had gone by faster than I thought it would, and I wasn't sure I got anything accomplished for Evan in regard to finding out if Nicole was his girl, but I did get the garage organized. I'd gone through everything except for the one box I carried to my bedroom, and I wanted to wait until I was by myself to do that.

Before I knew it, I'd drunk two cups of coffee and I was pushing the button on the coffee maker to keep the rest warm for Lauren. She finally came dragging down, with half her hair hanging out of yesterday's braid, and went straight for the coffee pot, as I knew she would. Lauren was not the diehard coffee drinker I was. She drank it in the morning to help wake up, unlike myself, who could drink it throughout the day. Hot coffee, iced coffee, black or white, I liked it all.

"How'd you sleep, honey?"

"Hard."

"It was probably good that you stayed home last night.

You need the rest every once in a while."

"Yeah. It felt good to hang out, and do nothing."

"Well, I'm glad you did. I've missed having you around since school started."

"I've missed you, too."

"So, what does your day look like today?" I asked.

"Busy. I've got three classes and work. Plus, I'd like to go down to the coffee house tonight, if it's okay with you? There's supposed to be a band playing. They've had their posters hanging all over campus for a while now."

"I know you went over there by yourself last time, but I'm not sure it looks good for a girl to be going alone all the time. I'd feel more comfortable if you went with someone," I explained.

"Maybe I can get Nicole to go with me."

"That's okay with me, but I don't like the idea of you driving her all the way home late at night."

"Mom, I said maybe. I'll figure it out," Lauren said, with a hint of irritation in her voice.

It was at that moment that I wished I'd gone out to get the morning paper, because I hated starting off the day feeling at odds with my daughter.

"I've got to go out this morning and run some errands. Do you want me to pick you up some chicken-fried rice for lunch? I could drop it off to you before you go to work," I asked, trying to change the subject.

"I'll be okay, but thanks for offering."

Lauren stood up and stretched. Then she took her cup and set it in the sink.

"Guess I better get going," she said, as she stared out the kitchen window.

"You've got some clean clothes I folded on top of the dryer, if you're looking for your jeans."

"Thanks, Mom."

I got up and walked toward the foyer to get the newspaper off the front steps that I should have gotten earlier, as I heard Lauren going upstairs. My thoughts drifted to Nicole, and *I wondered when I was going to see her again. I wished she lived closer so I could feel better about Lauren wanting to do things with her.*

Lauren was in and out of the shower by the time I had gone through the first section of the paper. The house already seemed empty, and she hadn't even left yet. I had fibbed when I told her I had errands, so I could get over to the café, but that didn't work. I needed something to take my mind off everything, and the cooler weather made me feel like curling up with a good book; but I had too many ants in my pants to do that.

I'd put the coffee cups in the dishwasher when Lauren came trotting downstairs. She kissed me on the cheek, and then took me up on my offer for lunch after all. I was surprised and pleased with the change, plus chicken-fried rice sounded great, and we agreed to meet outside the café at noon.

Lauren was waiting when I pulled up. We found a bench under a cluster of trees, and ate from the small pint containers that our chicken-fried rice was packed into, while we watched students move about the campus. The tea I had bought wasn't all that great, and we both agreed that we could do without it. We got thirsty before our lunch was over, so we ended up going into the café to get something cold to drink. Lauren had to start her shift anyway, so it was good timing.

Nicole came in soon after we did, waved and went straight through the employee door. I'm not the smartest, but I am intuitive, and I decided not to push my luck; so I finished my drink and told Lauren I had to go and I'd see her later at home.

43

When I got home, I went straight upstairs, hoping to curl up on my bed and read a good book, but ended up falling asleep. The next thing I knew, it was two hours later, and I was waking up and no longer in the mood to read. I didn't know what I wanted to do, so I just laid there and wondered what Lauren would do if she found out about my little talk I had with Nicole.

I wondered when she would be old enough to talk about her father and me, and if she would ever be able to acknowledge my other life. I wished there was something I could say or do to make her feel secure about my being with her and that my other life was in no way a threat to the life we had together. Even though we never talked about it, I knew it messed with her sometimes at bedtime.

She had told me before that she couldn't wait until she got married just so she didn't have to be alone at night. She knew I was somewhere else when I went to sleep and that bothered her. I suspected that when she had her own family she would feel much more secure, and I wanted that for her.

In my mind, I could see her face when she was sleeping. She still looked like she did when she was little. I used to go into her bedroom to tuck her in, and she'd wrap her little arms around my neck and hug me real hard. I'd whisper in her ear that I loved her and then kiss her on the neck below her ear. Her skin was still soft like a baby. She would giggle like it tickled, and that was the only way I could get her to let go of my neck. That was our ritual every night. She was so innocent and full of dreams. She even talked of marrying her father, who at that time was the only man in her life. Stephen thought that was the sweetest thing he had ever heard. His smile at that moment was etched in my memory forever.

I got up and dragged the box out from behind the chair in the corner of my bedroom until it was next to the bed. The intention was to put it on the bed, but instead I sank to the floor and leaned up against the bed beside the box. I tried opening the box at least three times before I finally unfolded the flaps.

The first thing I saw was a picture of Lauren in the second grade. Stephen had taken a picture of her standing by her poster, with a grin plastered to her face, after winning an art contest.

The second picture I saw was a picture of Stephen smiling at me. He was standing in front of a hotel on one of our vacations. I found myself laughing instead of crying, because he used to do the funniest things. Anytime we left a hotel, he wanted to take a picture so we could remember where we'd been. I was the designated photographer because I hated having my picture taken, and Stephen was a ham in front of the camera, so it worked out well.

I got up to stretch my legs and to get a handful of tissues from the bathroom, because I knew I would need them if I kept on looking through the pictures. There was a knot in my throat as I sat back down on the floor. Stephen was staring at me from the past and I stared back. I watched my hand run over the pictures, but they felt cold, unlike how I remembered Stephen. My heart sank as I looked at all the moments I could never have back.

Tears ran down my face and neck, but I didn't reach for the tissues because my hands were full of pictures that I'd pressed tightly against my chest. I could feel myself rocking back and forth and my heart throbbing. I could taste my pain and felt the tightness in my neck as I strained to catch my breath. That was the first time I had looked at those pictures since Stephen had disappeared, and I thought I would handle it better. Nine years of not knowing what happened to him had kept me from truly grieving, because I was more focused on how Lauren was feeling. I needed that cry, and I needed to feel the pain of losing him.

I quickly swung around to look at the clock when I heard the kitchen door open. *It must be Lauren,* I thought, so I quickly put the pictures back in the box, pulled the box across the room next to Stephen's chair, and then went into the bathroom and washed my face with cold water.

As I came out of the bathroom, Lauren and Nicole were standing at my door.

"Hey, I didn't hear you come in," I said, in a somewhat cheerful voice.

"Mom, are you okay?"

"Sure. Why?"

"It looks like you've been crying."

"No. I'm fine. What are you girls up to?"

"We're just hanging out, that's all. Is it okay if we get something to snack on?"

"Sure."

They sounded like a herd of elephants going back down the stairs.

It was hard to shift gears and put on a happy face when my heart was still hurting, so I decided to stay in my room and write in my journal. The girls had gotten their snack and come back upstairs to Lauren's room. I could hear their muffled voices and music playing, then Lauren as she walked down the hall to take a shower. The next thing I knew, Nicole was knocking on my door.

"Mrs. Winthrop?" she quietly asked.

"Yes, Nicole?" I answered her, as I motioned for her to come in."

Nicole stepped into my bedroom. Then she looked down by the bed and, before I could see what she was looking at, she'd walked over and bent down. When she stood back up, she was holding a picture of Stephen that, apparently, I had missed.

She studied the picture for a moment and then asked me, "Is this that boy's dad? You know, the picture you showed me."

I was sitting on the edge of the bed as she handed me the picture. I turned it around and looked at Stephen. He was sitting on the front steps, looking more handsome than ever. I glanced away from his picture, so I could answer Nicole.

"Yes. This was Evan's father."

"Well, they look alike," Nicole said.

"Was he Lauren's father also?"

"You're a smart girl, and to answer your question, yes he was. Evan is Lauren's stepbrother. Although she's never met him, and it's not a good thing to talk about, so I never do."

"I understand."

"Lauren's father died nine years ago, and she still has a hard time with it."

"Yeah. I know that feeling." Nicole paused before coming back to the conversation. "So, Lauren has never met Evan?"

"No. Maybe someday."

"She'd probably like him, if he's a lot like her father."

"That's a kind thing to say, and I'm sure she would," I told Nicole.

"I mean I might like him too … if I were to … ever meet him," Nicole stuttered, as she looked down at the floor.

"You mean you would like to meet Evan?"

"Sure, but does that mean I can't tell Lauren who he is?"

"Well, that might be best for now. Hey, I think I'll see him this weekend sometime. Let me see what I can arrange, okay?"

"Okay," Nicole said, as she left my room as quietly as she entered.

I was on cloud nine the rest of the evening. I wasn't sure what was accomplished, but Nicole wanting to meet Evan was progress. I couldn't wait to tell him. I was so preoccupied with my thoughts that the girls could've told me they were going to Florida and I probably would've told them to have fun.

Instead, my reality check was Lauren asking if it was okay if Nicole slept over after they got back from the coffee house. They were going to meet Lauren's other friend, Sue, for a while. I was happy to have Nicole stay, and it saved me from riding with Lauren to take her home later. I just prayed to goodness that she was the right girl, for Evan's sake.

The house got quiet after they left, and I didn't mind because it had been a mentally exhausting day. Looking through the box had zapped me emotionally and my eyes felt strained from crying. I considered myself hugged as I got into bed, and I had no desire to pick up a book or leave the light on. For some reason, I was at ease with Lauren and Nicole making it in on their own that night, so I could make my SWITCH and go tell Evan about Nicole.

I dozed in and out until Lauren and Nicole came home around eleven-thirty. I could hear them talking downstairs in the kitchen and then whispering on the way up the stairs. Lauren peeked into my room, and then pulled the door shut and went down the hall into her room. I could still hear them talking for a minute as they got ready for bed, and then I made my SWITCH.

44
Friday in Ardmore, Pennsylvania

One more day, and I still didn't know what I was going to do the next night about Christine and Evan meeting each other. Evan hadn't called back, and I had no way of reaching him. All I could do was hope he would call sometime before he showed up.

My humble abode needed cleaning and I didn't feel like getting out of my pajamas. I cleaned most of the day, took a long bath, and went to bed. My last thought before I fell asleep was, *the phone never rang today.*

45
Saturday in Blue Ash, Ohio

I had made the SWITCH and could hear the girls talking from what sounded like the kitchen, so I put on my robe and went downstairs. It was only seven o'clock, and I was surprised to see them up so early.

"Hey, Mom. I hope we didn't wake you," Lauren said, as she sat down in one of the kitchen chairs.

"I needed to get up anyway. You girls are up early."

"Yeah. Nicole is going over to the campus early to get some research work done at the library."

"So, tell me, how was the band last night?"

Lauren chimed in again, "Oh, well, not as good as they were talked up to be. How would you describe them, Nicole?"

"In between jazz and folk, but the jazz side was weak and the sax was totally out of place," she answered, as she shrugged.

"Well, it was still fun though?"

"Yeah. We had fun. The place was packed. It took us twenty minutes to get a cup of tea. We got lucky though and found a couple of stray stools," Lauren said, in between gulps of coffee.

Nicole stood up and put her book bag over one shoulder. She started towards the sink with her empty coffee cup, but I intercepted halfway to save her the walk.

"Thanks, Mrs. Winthrop. I appreciate you letting me

stay."

"Anytime. You know you're welcome here."

Lauren got up and walked around the table, pointing at Nicole's empty chair.

"Hey, Nicole, don't forget your jacket."

"Oh, yeah, thanks," she said, as she scooped up her fleece coat. "See you at work later," she told Lauren, as she headed towards the front door.

Lauren stood in one spot by the table for a moment or two, before going toward the coffee pot for a refill.

"Would you like a second cup, Mom? I think there's enough left," Lauren said, as she picked up the pot and showed me what was left.

"Sure. Do you have a busy day?"

"Not too bad. I'm pulling the afternoon shift at work," Lauren explained as she poured me coffee. "What about you?"

"Not much. The Salvation Army is supposed to stop by and pick up some of the stuff in the garage, and other than a box or so to go through, I plan on sticking around."

"Do you want to make pizza tonight and watch a movie on Netflix?"

"Sure, but don't you want to do something with your friends instead of spending Saturday night with your dear old mom?" I heard myself say, but couldn't believe it was coming out of my mouth, because Stephen and I had always vowed we'd never be old parents.

"No, it's been a long week. I just want to throw on my sweats and stay home. I actually think I'm going to go back to bed for a bit," Lauren said, as she took her coffee and started upstairs.

I set out to gather the morning paper off the front steps, but I didn't have to go that far because Nicole had laid it inside the front door on her way out. I picked it up and went back to the kitchen to retrieve my cup of coffee.

The Salvation Army came as scheduled, and before I knew it the morning was gone. I hadn't done a darn thing but get cleaned up and stare at the television.

After we had lunch, Lauren went to work and I went up to take a nap, but couldn't sleep. I tried to read but my thoughts were scattered, and I knew why. Between worrying over my situation with Evan and Christine, and the box behind Stephen's chair calling my name, I was a basket case. I wasn't sure if I could emotionally handle going through the box, but knew if I didn't go through it, I wouldn't be able to move on. The problem was, I didn't want to move on. I hadn't moved on for nine years, so why would I want to then?

An hour passed before I got off my bed and walked toward the box. I pulled it out and sat down in Stephen's chair, and then unfolded the cardboard flaps of the box and began to relive my past. I laid the pictures aside that I had gone through the day before and then slowly went through the next layer of pictures until I found the letter. I held it to my face in hopes I could still smell Stephen, but I couldn't. It was the first love letter he had written me. He didn't like to write letters, so I didn't get many.

I remembered it was my birthday, and I'd found it under my pillow with a little prompting from Stephen. He had put it under there while I was sleeping and was beside himself waiting for me to wake up. I remembered how he'd reached over to adjust the shoulder strap on my gown, as he tried to hide his mischievous smile when I opened my eyes. He told me happy birthday, and then told me to check under my pillow as he jumped up and left the room. The letter was folded, and in an envelope with my name on the front.

I remembered thinking, *it doesn't look like a birthday card*, and it wasn't. It was much more. My eyes welled up with tears as I read it over and over again.

> ***My Love,***
> ***Happy Birthday, and many more returns, hopefully with me. I would trade a whole lifetime to be with you again. You are the light in the darkness, and have made all my dreams come true. I am so happy we found this life together. I love you with all my heart. Stephen***
> ***P.S. Every minute with you has been worth all the restless nights. Ha! Ha!***

Stephen wasn't much for writing, but what he did write meant the world to me. He was one of the most tenderhearted people I'd ever met. As I relived the moment, I felt tears roll over my lips, and I wiped them off with my sleeve. Then, in my mind's eye, I saw Stephen coming back through the bedroom door carrying a breakfast tray, just like he had that morning. He had fixed me oatmeal with fresh-cut strawberries, and a freshly brewed cup of coffee with a red rose placed at the top of the tray.

As I tried to eat, Stephen took the rose and gently brushed it against the side of my neck, and whispered against my ear, "Does she love me or love me not?" I leaned over and put the tray on the floor beside the bed, and then turned to Stephen and whispered, "She loves you."

Then I let him pull my gown up over my head and take me into his arms. He brushed his warm hands down my lower back, causing an involuntary tuck of my pelvis. I could feel him pressing up against my inner thigh, and thinking about it then still gave me inner contractions. The love our bodies shared and the desire to make each other happy was explosive, and the utter quietness that followed as we blended was a feeling of total completeness. It was those memories that were worth reliving and kept me feeling young and loved; and to me, Stephen would always be young.

46

I got this surreal feeling as I reached into the box and thumbed through more pictures. I couldn't believe Stephen had been gone nine years. Thank goodness I had Lauren, but the thought of her growing up and leaving scared me. Who knew, maybe then the loss of Stephen would finally sink in, when I was alone.

It seemed like yesterday that he was there, and each picture brought back his smell, his touch, and his laugh. The memories and moments we shared were timeless, like wristwatches that wind with movement. The memories pulsated within my soul with each heartbeat.

I didn't hear Lauren come in, and I was startled like a kid who had been caught doing something sneaky. She had me in such a tizzy that I dropped the picture of Stephen, and it landed on the floor between us.

"Hey, Mom. What are you doing?" Lauren asked, as she stared at her father's picture.

"I'm going through the last box in the garage," I said, as I reached out to retrieve Stephen's picture.

"Pictures? I've never seen these," Lauren commented, as she slowly sat down on the floor. "How come you never showed these to me?"

"Well, I knew they were around here somewhere, but I didn't know where. Plus, I honestly didn't know if you wanted to see pictures of your father yet."

"Why wouldn't I?"

"I just don't like to see you get upset."

"Tell me about this one," Lauren said, as she reached in the box.

"Oh, well, those are some tulips your dad took a picture of for me. I think I saw them on the side of the road on one of our vacations, and your father stopped and took a picture of them. Those flowers are just as yellow as I remember them. Aren't they beautiful?"

"Yeah, they were pretty," she agreed, as she pulled out another one. "How about this one?" Lauren asked.

"You don't remember that, do you? I think you were about four, and we were at a friend's house for a barbecue, and that was your first rib. You had more sauce on you than the rib did. Look right there," I pointed out. "See, you even had it in your hair."

We both laughed. Lauren kept pulling pictures out of the box, one after another, and asking questions. One by one we looked at the pictures. We laughed and cried, and sat in silence at times, until we finally realized our stomachs were talking more than we were.

"Hey, how about that pizza you wanted to have tonight?"

"Can we order in instead of making it?" Lauren asked with hope in her voice.

"Now, that sounds like a good idea. What kind do you want?"

"Half cheese for me."

"I'll go down and call in a cheese pizza, okay?"

I went downstairs to call in our order, which included cheese pizza, a side order of jalapenos and a two-liter diet soda. Then I grabbed a bag of chips to keep the wolf away, flipped on the front porch light for the delivery guy, and headed back upstairs. Lauren had sprawled out, lying belly down and propped up by her elbows, looking at another picture.

"Oh, do tell," she said with a put-on Southern drawl, and flipped around a picture that made us both start laughing. "Is this a picture of your big toe, next to Dad's big toe?"

"Yep, your father and I were kind of crazy sometimes. He had just painted my toenail with this putrid pink polish, and I in return buffed his until it was real shiny. I think it was one of our first anniversaries, and we had been celebrating with a couple bottles of champagne. Your father wanted a unique picture to remember our night. So, he bypassed the corks and the ribbons from our presents, and talked me into taking a picture of our toes. Don't ask me why. I always told him I was going to have it blown up and framed or send it in to some greeting card company. Yeah, we got kind of silly sometimes. I had forgotten about that one. I'm glad you found it."

Lauren and I had more fun looking at pictures. We never got around to opening the bag of chips, or watching a movie, but we did eat pizza on my bedroom floor amongst all the pictures. It was one of the most magical nights Lauren and I had ever spent together. I'd always dreamed of this time when I could enjoy Lauren as a young woman.

As much as I enjoyed reminiscing with her about when she was little and her father and I, we both grew tired and needed to go to bed. The pizza had gotten cold as the night grew late, and Lauren offered to take the leftover pizza and soda down to the kitchen and lock up for the night.

"I love you, Mom," she said, as she stopped by my bedroom when she came back upstairs.

"I love you, too. I'll see you in the morning."

I laid in the darkness of my bedroom, and relived each expression on Lauren's face as she had looked at the pictures of her father. She had only asked to keep one, which was a picture of her and Stephen at the playground when she was about six. They were both swinging and holding hands at the same time. The moment was priceless, and their smiles looked just alike. I would have picked the same one if I were Lauren. Maybe the next day I'd try and find her a frame for it.

I could fall asleep feeling good about how well Lauren had dealt with going through the pictures, compared to when she was younger. I knew one thing for sure: my SWITCH would be seamless that night.

47
Saturday in Ardmore, Ohio

When I woke up, I didn't feel content like I had when I'd fallen asleep. My anxiety felt like an electrical current racing through my body, and my mind had hit the brick wall because I didn't know how I was going to explain Evan to Christine. There it was Saturday, and I still hadn't come up with who he was or how I knew him, and time was running out.

I propped myself up on my elbows to look at the alarm clock, and was pleased to see it was only six o'clock. So, I rolled over with my back to the window, putting the pillow over my head to hide my eyes from the first hint of light that was seeping through the fringe at the bottom of the curtains, and fell back to sleep.

It was eight-forty when I woke again, and I knew I had to get the day started. I felt like a kid going to the first day of school. I was excited, but scared of what comes with a new experience. I went downstairs to start the coffee and feed my feathered friends while I thought about what I should do first. Before I knew it, I was outside with my cup of coffee watching the birds and meandering around. My neighbor, Jackie, was just coming back from walking her dog as I picked up the paper off the front step

"Hi, Diane."

"Good morning, Jackie. How are you?" I asked.

"Great. Looks like the day is going to be lovely. Have you been out?"

"Only for a few minutes to see the birds while having my first cup of coffee. Would you like to sit on the back porch and have a cup?" I asked, having an out-of-body experience. *What was I thinking?*

"I'd love to, but I've got to go to the grocer. Do you need anything while I'm out?"

"No, I think I'm fine," I said, as I tucked the paper under my arm. "But, thank you, you're always so good to ask."

"Well, I'll talk to you a little later then," Jackie said, as she stooped down to pick up her dog.

"Sounds good. Hope you enjoy your day."

As I walked back around to get in the back door, I heard the phone ringing. It was all I could do to run, but when I got inside the kitchen door it was quiet. I stood there for what seemed like a long time, feeling scattered and distracted by not knowing how to get hold of Evan. Then the phone rang again and I was able to answer it that time.

"Hello," I said, as I leaned against the kitchen counter.

"Hi, Mom. You sound out of breath. Are you okay?" asked Christine.

"Oh, I'm fine. Did you try to call a minute ago?"

"No. Why?"

"I was outside and heard the phone ring, and ran in but didn't catch it in time," I explained to Christine.

"No, it wasn't me, but that does explain why you sound like you're out of breath. Anyway, I just wanted to call and let you know we'll be there around six."

"Great, I'll have dinner ready. Oh, by the way, does this person you're bringing have a name?"

"His name is Tom, and I think you'll really like him, Mom."

"I'm sure I will. Hey, I was going to fix the bedrooms upstairs for you to sleep in. Does that sound okay?"

"Where are you going to sleep?"

"Well, you're only here one night, so I can sleep downstairs on the couch."

"Are you sure? We can get a hotel room."

"I don't get to see you that often, and yes, I'm sure."

"Love you, Mom."

"Love you too. See you tonight."

"Okay, 'bye," Christine said on the other end, and then there was a click.

I hung up the phone, went to the kitchen, and poured myself another cup of coffee. I had every intention of prepping dinner, but decided to set the table in the dining room first. As I pulled out the tablecloth, I wondered if the phone call I'd missed had been Evan, and if it were, would he try back later?

The sideboard was full of my good dishes and centerpieces for me to pick from. I pulled out a few combinations to make the table look nice, because I wanted everything to be perfect for Christine and her guest. *She puts in long hours traveling for work and deserves to have a good home-cooked dinner.* My motherly need to feed was kicking in, and I couldn't wait to see Christine. I wished she could stay longer, but she'd never been one to sit still for very long and I'd be happy with what I got.

Before I know, she'll be gone and who knows when I'll see her again? I'd come to grips with letting go, because I'd had to and life went on. There were days, here and there, that I had this overwhelming sense of loss that filled my quiet times and I gave in to the relentless tears and had a good cry. Those are the days I questioned life, and asked why the days seemed so long, but the years short. My tears eventually gave in to the inevitable truth that time never stops for anything, not for me wanting to have more time with my husbands or my girls. It was hard getting older, but more than anything it was hard being alone.

Suddenly, I snapped back into the moment and remembered Evan hadn't called back, and I had no way of reaching him. All I could do was hope he would call sometime before he showed up. Now that the table was set, I needed to tidy up the house and then prep part of my meal. Neither one outweighed the other, so I picked up first. I got done by four, so I poured myself a glass of wine to take the edge off and went upstairs to soak in the tub.

48

I still hadn't come up with a good introduction for Evan, one that wouldn't create a hundred questions. My best option at that point was Evan could be the nephew of a friend at church who was out of town and he needed a place to stay. Neither one of my girls had been to my new church since I'd changed a few years back, so there wouldn't be any questions there. I leaned back, closing my eyes as the warm water hugged my shoulders. I reached up to get my wine when the phone rang, and almost dropped it as I scrabbled to stand up and grab a towel.

"Hello," I answered, as I pressed the towel over the front of my torso.

"Hi, Mom. Did I catch you at a bad time?" Claire asked.

"I'm taking a bath. Can I call you back in a bit?"

"Sure, sorry about that," Claire answered.

"Goodbye, honey," I said, as I pushed the end button and tossed the receiver on the bed.

The water was still warm and inviting as I nestled back down into the water, taking my glass of wine with me. I closed my eyes and drifted off to a time when my girls were small. I would put them in the tub together and they would play well after the water got cold. For the most part they got along well, thank goodness, because they roomed together and napped together, which gave me the time I needed to keep my own sanity.

My wine disappeared not long before the water got cold. I had to get out anyway, because I told Claire I would call her back. I toweled off again, used my rose-scented lotion, got dressed, and put on some lipstick. *Yep, Mom's ready to go*, I told myself as I looked in the mirror. I grabbed my empty glass and went downstairs to toss the salad and call Claire back.

The phone rang three times before Claire picked up, then there was a lag.

"Hello?" I questioned, wondering if she was on the other end or if my pointed chin had cut her off.

"Hi, Mom. How was your bath?"

"Relaxing, but I had to cut it short so I could toss a salad for dinner. Your sister and her friend should be here in the next hour or so."

"Who is she bringing?" Claire asked.

"A fellow she seems to like. They are going to be staying here, so I had to get both bedrooms cleaned up."

"Well, where are you going to sleep?"

"Downstairs on the couch; that is, unless Evan shows up," I said, in anticipation of what was to come.

"Who is Evan?"

"Oh, he's the nephew of a friend at church who needs a place to stay, because they're out of town. Actually, he stayed with me one other time and he's a nice young man."

"Why haven't you ever mentioned him before?"

"Oh, I don't know. I guess I didn't think it was any big deal. You'd like him, I'm sure of it. There's plenty of room here for all of us to find a place to sleep. It's just for one night anyway. I didn't want to mention Evan to your sister, because I wanted her to stay here instead of some hotel. To be quite honest, I'm not one hundred percent sure he's coming. He called a week or so ago, but things could've changed; plus, if he does show up it won't be until very late."

"I think it's great you're helping a friend, Mom, but don't get hooked into a being a hotel for your church," Claire said in a motherly tone.

"He's the only one I've helped, and like I said he is a nice young man. Whew, the salad is done. Listen, honey, I've got to get off here. Can we talk in a couple of days?"

"Sure. Give Christine a hug for me."

"I'll do it. Consider yourself hugged, and give little Jacob a big kiss from his grandma. Love you, honey."

"Love you, have fun. 'Bye," Claire said as she hung up.

I cradled the phone between my shoulder and ear as I rinsed off my hands and looked around for the kitchen towel.

I knew telling Claire about Evan was a good move; otherwise, Christine would be calling her when she left, and Claire wouldn't know anything about Evan. *Now, I can mention to Christine that Claire knows and hopefully that'll cut down on a bunch of questions.* I would rather keep things simple, and Evan posing as a nephew of a friend at church was perfect. *I'll just have to make sure Evan's okay with my story. I hate having to hide things from my daughters, but I'd be breaking the promise to Stephen about keeping our two lives separate.*

49

"Knock, knock, anyone home?" Christine hollered out as she came in the front door.

"Right here," I said, as I came through the kitchen door in her direction. "How was your trip?"

"We didn't have any trouble," she said, as she looked toward her boyfriend, Tom, and then introduced him as he set down their suitcases.

"It's very nice to meet you, Tom. Please, come in and make yourselves comfortable. Would you like a glass of wine?"

"Thanks, that would be great," Tom said.

"Let me help you, Mom, I can get the wine," Christine offered, as she followed me back toward the kitchen.

"Thanks. You'll find the glasses on the sideboard, and the wine is in the refrigerator," I told her, as I went to check on the meat.

"You look great," I told Christine, as she opened the wine, "and happy," I added. "Has my little girl fallen in love?"

"Maybe," she smiled, as she looked through the kitchen door toward where Tom had sat down in the living room. "This might be The One. He makes me happy, Mom. I do love him, but we haven't made any commitments yet. Tom is a lawyer, and between his job and mine, it's tough to think that far ahead."

Christine went into the dining room to retrieve the glasses.

When she came back, she asked me not to say anything.

"I won't say anything, Christine, but you know if you love him then you might have to make some changes to be together. Relationships are great, but they're also something you have to work at if you want them to last."

We had a wonderful dinner, and I could see why Christine was attracted to Tom. He reminded me of her father, with the dark hair and the same type of low-key personality. Christine smiled at him all through dinner, and I could tell by the way Tom looked at her that he cared deeply for her. After our dinner, we eventually moved to the living room and watched the news.

"I cleaned the rooms upstairs for the two of you when you get ready to retire," I told them.

"Great, I think I'll go up and get some reading done for my next case and let you two girls talk," Tom said, as he stood and walked toward the front door where he had placed their bags when they'd arrived.

As Tom started upstairs with the bags, Christine got up to help him. "Mom, I'll be back down in a minute."

"I'll be here. Would you like another glass of wine?"

"No. I think I'll pass, but I'd love a cup of coffee, if it's not too much to ask," she said as she headed upstairs.

"Sure," I told her.

I loaded the coffee pot, and then sat down in one of the kitchen chairs and listened to floorboards creak upstairs as they got situated. I could hear their muffled voices, and then things got quiet. My thoughts went to Evan, and how I was going to tell Christine about him. I must have been zoning out when she came back downstairs, because I didn't even notice when she came into the kitchen until I heard her voice.

"What are you doing in here, Mom?"

"Just thinking about what a nice dinner we had," I replied,

feeling ashamed of myself for fibbing. "Did you get settled upstairs okay?"

"We did, but where are you going to sleep if we take both bedrooms upstairs?"

"Don't worry about me. I'll do okay on the couch. Oh, by the way, I almost forgot, there's a young man who is supposed to stay here tonight. His name is Evan. He's the nephew of one of my friends at church who needed a place to stay while they're out of town. He's stayed here before for a night or two a couple months ago. Anyway, he's not supposed to get here until eleven-thirty or twelve tonight, so don't be alarmed if you hear something."

"Mom. Why didn't you tell me? We could've come another weekend."

"I didn't want to take that chance. You've got a busy schedule, and who knows when you could've come again?" I said as I stood up and got our cups.

"Well, Tom and I can share a room. It's okay, Mom, we're big people and we've shared before," Christine admitted. "You need to be in your own bed."

"That's very sweet, but sleeping on the couch is the right thing for me to do, especially with Evan coming in late," I said, as I poured our coffee. "Maybe I'll give him my room if you don't mind."

"Fine with me. That way no one's without a place to sleep."

We finished our coffee in no time flat and Christine headed up to bed. I pulled down the sheet and blanket I had stored earlier in the hall closet and started to make myself a bed on the couch when the phone rang. It was Evan.

"Hi, I hope I'm not calling too late."

"No, I was just getting ready to lie down. Are you still coming in tonight?"

"I should be there in an hour or so, if that's still all right with you?"

"Sure, what I'll do is leave the key under the front door mat. That way if I'm asleep you can let yourself on in. Oh, by the way, you'll be staying in my room tonight. My daughter, Christine, and her friend are in the other rooms. Before you say anything, I already told Christine that you are a nephew of someone at my church."

"I can stay at a hotel tonight."

"No, please don't. Besides, everything is fine here … really. Anyway, if I am asleep when you get here, please find your way in and we'll talk in the morning."

"I'm not too comfortable with this, Diane."

"I am, and plus I have some news for you."

"Really?" Evan's voice lifted.

"I can't wait to see you. Be careful now."

I hung up the phone, relieved that Evan had called. I could finally take a deep breath and relax, knowing that that day had turned out okay.

I hadn't quite fallen asleep when I heard Evan outside the front, fumbling with the key, so I got up and let him in. He looked tired, and quickly gave in to my insistent request that he sleep in my bedroom. As he went upstairs, I went back to the couch and laid in the darkness, rehearsing the introductions I would make in the morning.

50
Sunday in Blue Ash, Ohio

The next thing I knew, I'd made the SWITCH and was feeling disoriented, because I was still thinking about Evan meeting my girls, including Lauren. The house was quiet and I couldn't gauge what time it was, but knew it was after seven because it was light outside. I fumbled with the clock to see if I had overslept and perhaps missed Lauren, but then I realized it was Sunday. *Glorious Sunday,* I thought, *a day at home with Lauren and not too much to do.*

It was eight-thirty and I was shocked that I'd slept that late. As I brushed my hair in front of the bathroom mirror, I wondered why the house seemed so quiet. I couldn't remember what time it had been when we finally went to bed, but the pile of pictures lying all over the floor reminded me of my time with Lauren the night before and all the memories in that life.

In those couple of hours, I thought I had relived them all. All the laughs, touches, and special moments of my life there with Stephen were refreshed. I looked back at myself in the mirror and for the first time was thankful for the wrinkles I saw. The sweet memories of spending time with Stephen and having Lauren were both worth getting older.

The only way I knew Lauren was still asleep when I looked in on her, was by her blonde mop of a ponytail hanging out over the top of her covers. It wasn't too long after I went downstairs and got the paper before I heard the cuckoo clock strike nine, and couldn't believe I'd actually slept through the church bells and it was that late. Lauren must have heard the clock too, because she came down the stairs looking surprised. We sat for an hour drinking our coffee and watching the news three times before we noticed another hour had passed.

"What are you going to do with all those pictures?" Lauren asked.

"Oh, I don't know. I guess I haven't really thought about it."

"Maybe we can buy some albums."

"Would you like to do something like that?" I asked, with some hesitation and halfway surprised.

"It'd be nice to put them all in order. You know, get them organized. Would you be okay with that, Mom?"

"Sure." I paused, not quite knowing how to accept Lauren's willingness to look and talk about her dad. "I'm glad you want to do something with the pictures. It's a great idea."

"If you can't handle it, Mom, I'll understand," Lauren said, as she nodded at me with a motherly look.

It was like a role reversal right before my eyes. I tried to hold back my tears, but I couldn't, and the tears slid down my cheek. I wiped them away with the backside of my hand, as I reached over to grab Lauren's hand.

"I'm sorry, Mom."

"Don't be. It's a happy-sad I'm feeling. I'm happy you're ready to talk about your dad. I haven't been able to talk about him for all these years. I never thought about it before now, but I've never had anyone to talk to about him. That sounds profound, doesn't it? I guess I never knew if you'd ever be ready to talk about him, so I've tried to keep my thoughts and memories to myself. You're getting older, and that makes me sad, but you wanting to talk about the man we both still love makes me happy. I'm glad you want to talk about your dad. I'm really glad."

"I had fun last night, even if our pizza did get cold," Lauren said, as she laughed. "Maybe we can get some albums tomorrow and get started. I don't have much to do tomorrow."

"Sounds good to me," I responded, wanting to ask her *why not today?* but before I could ask, she told me her plans.

"I'm going to the gym this morning, and then I need to go to the library. Oh, and is it okay if Nicole comes over tonight?"

"Only if she's willing to stay over if it gets to be late. I don't think she lives in the greatest area and you're not used to driving downtown."

"Okay, I'm sure she won't mind," Lauren said, as she stood and stretched.

51

Lauren was dressed and out the door in an hour, and I was still sitting on the couch where I'd been parked all morning. I felt like I had a hangover or was coming down with a bug. It was almost noon when I got up, and that was only to fix myself a bowl of tomato soup. I wanted to go clean up, but all I could do was envision all the pictures of Stephen lying all over the floor in my bedroom. I blamed my procrastination on feeling sick, but the God-honest truth was I was physically drained and mentally exhausted from going through the pictures and couldn't yet bring myself to go upstairs.

I ate my soup and went back to the couch and found a good sleeping position. When I dozed off, I dreamed I was with Stephen.

We were at a restaurant in the Old Italy part of town. He had the blue sweater on that I had bought him for Christmas one year, and he looked so real. I reached out to touch him, but I couldn't feel him. He was there, though, because I could see him talking and hear him laughing. The sparkles in his eyes were dancing back and forth, and I could see my reflection in them. He told me I was beautiful, like he always did, and then he reached out and touched my face. I felt him touch me, but when I reached up to hold his hand it wasn't there. I started crying, and he wiped my tears away. He told me not to cry, and that he was glad everything was okay. I told him all about

Lauren and her school and cleaning out the garage. We both laughed. Then I started to tell him about Evan, and he got this concerned look on his face while he shook his head, but didn't say anything. That's all I remembered when I woke, and I chalked it up to a weird dream.

I looked at the clock and it was half past four. My hesitation to go upstairs to my bedroom and the box of pictures was gone, because I had a sudden urge to see Stephen's face. The pictures were still strewn across the floor as Lauren and I had left them the night before. They all seemed to be staring at me, so I sat down on the edge of the bed and looked at my life while I tried to shake how real Stephen appeared to me in my dream. I picked up one of his pictures, and thought to myself how young he looked. To me, Stephen would always be young, even when I was old.

Then my thoughts went back to my dream and I heard myself asking, "Why did you shake your head when I mentioned Evan? Is there some reason you don't think I should talk to him? I hope this isn't too much; it was really hard for me, too. I couldn't believe he figured it all out. I mean, who I was and … Stephen you'd be very proud of him. I know you would."

Of course, he didn't answer me, but I was sure he could hear me. All I could think was, *maybe there was more to Evan than I knew*.

"Mom. I'm home!" Lauren yelled, as she bounded up the stairs. "Who were you talking to?"

"I wasn't talking to anyone," I told her, in hopes that I hadn't been reliving my dream and talking to Stephen out loud.

Lauren smiled as she looked at her dad's picture in my hand and then gave me a couple of nods, like she was telling me it was okay to talk to the picture. Then she turned and started to leave.

"Oh, by the way, Mom, Nicole is coming over around six," Lauren said over her shoulder, and then grabbed her ponytail scrunchy with her right hand and pulled it down to release her hair.

"Okay by me. But I wasn't planning much for dinner."

"We'll go out somewhere, if that's okay with you," Lauren said, as she exited my bedroom and started down the hall.

"I wasn't planning on going anywhere, but you two can go. Although, you might have to put some gas in the car," I said loud enough so she could hear.

I heard the shower running, and for a moment I was relieved. I needed to gather my thoughts and get out of the pajamas I'd hung around in all day if Nicole was coming over. I chose a dressier set of sweats that were presentable, but still comfortable, and got dressed. I had stacked up some of the pictures when Lauren poked her head back in my room.

"Are you okay, Mom?"

"Yeah. I've just enjoyed my lazy day. I needed one."

"I'm glad, you deserve it. Hey, I'm going down, because Nicole should be here any minute. We're going to go out for Mexican, I think. You want me to bring you back anything?"

"I don't have much of an appetite, but thanks. I'm thinking about crawling into bed to read a good book."

"Sounds good," Lauren said, like she already knew my answer.

"Oh … can you lock up and turn off the lights when you leave?"

"Sure."

"Have fun," I said loud enough that she could hear as she headed downstairs.

"I will. Don't let the bed bugs bite," Lauren's voice trailed off.

I read for a couple of hours before I turned off the light. I was surprised I felt like I could sleep after my nap earlier and dreaming of Stephen. I didn't think I would be able to as I kept replaying the way he looked at me when I told him about Evan, but I had no trouble making the SWITCH.

52
Sunday in Ardmore, Pennsylvania

I woke with a stiff neck from sleeping on the couch, so I got up. Pulling on my robe, I walked to the kitchen and thought about how I was going to miss church that week.

My feathered friends on the back porch kept me company as I counted the scoops of coffee and waited for it to brew. The aroma filled the air and calmed my nerves because that was going to be the day that one of Stephen's boys was meeting one of my daughters. Stephen and I had been so cautious not to let our two lives blend, and now it seemed like they were colliding.

The first one downstairs was Tom, and he smelled like musk aftershave. He was dressed and looking for a cup of coffee.

"Good morning. I hope I didn't come down too early. That's what I get for retiring early. Please don't think rudely of me, but I could smell the coffee," Tom trailed off.

"I'm glad someone is up to drink the coffee with me. Did you sleep well?'

"Great, as a matter of fact. Thank you for sharing with us."

"Us? So, you like my girl, Christine?" I asked

"I love her," Tom confidently stated, as he leaned against the doorjamb. "I just wish I could get her to slow down and spend more time with me. I was hoping we'd have this conversation, so maybe you, being her mother, could talk to her."

"Well, she's a very strong-headed young woman, but I'll see what I can do," I told him, as I went to pour our coffee. "How do you like yours?"

"With cream, but let me help you."

"The half and half is on the counter, and here is a cup," I said, as I pulled a cup out of the dishwasher. "I usually get up early myself, along with my feathered friends," I added, as I looked out the back window.

"They're beautiful," Tom said, as he turned to look at the birds gathering around the feeders.

"Aren't they great? I think the nuthatches are my favorite. See them over there underneath the feeder? I like to watch them when they get all puffed up. Ah, the life of a bird."

"Yeah. I know what you mean."

We both sat in silence and watched the birds. There was something about Tom that was comforting and down to earth. I was just hoping Christine had noticed and could appreciate the quality of tenderness this young man had to offer. With that thought, she walked into the kitchen, not looking as dapper as Tom. She still had her pajamas on, and her father's dark hair pulled up into a ponytail on top of her head.

"Hey, what are you two doing?"

"Shush, we're watching the birds," Tom answered.

I could hear Christine over by the coffee pot. She was my loudest child, and just like now, I always knew what she was doing.

"What time is it?" Christine asked.

"Half past eight. I'm glad you got to sleep in," I answered.

She sat down on Tom's lap and seemed content to stare with us as we watched the birds. We sat there for five minutes before we ever said anything. It was a nice experience, and I wished that Claire could have been there to share the moment with us.

Finally, I heard some noise coming from upstairs, and I knew it had to be Evan getting up.

"Did your friend's nephew get in last night?" Christine inquired.

"Yes. In fact, I think I hear him upstairs. He should probably be down anytime."

"Where is he from?" Tom asked.

"Chicago, I think. He works in the advertising business," I said, as I anticipated the next question. "It's just too bad his aunt and uncle are out of town, but I didn't mind helping out. Like I said last night, he stayed here before a few months ago and he seemed really nice. On top of that, he's good company. Not to change the subject, but would you two like some breakfast?"

"After that big meal last night, I don't think I'll need anything else all day," Tom said.

"I'm okay," Christine chimed in.

I heard the sound of Evan's footsteps coming down the stairs, and my heart began to pound with just the thought of our two kids meeting each other.

"Good morning, Evan, did you sleep well?" I heard myself ask.

"Yes. Thank you."

"I'd like to introduce you to my daughter Christine and her friend Tom."

"Nice to meet you," Evan said, as he reached out to shake Tom's hand.

"So, my mom tells us you're from Chicago?" Christine asked.

"Yes. I was raised there."

"That's a great town. You'd have to like the blues to live

there."

"As a matter a fact, I do, and I brought your mom a new cd from one of our local blues bands that I thought she might enjoy."

"Evan, would you like a cup of coffee?" I interjected.

"I'd love one."

"Do you come to Philly often?" Christine asked Evan.

"My first time was just a couple of months ago. Your mom was nice enough to let me stay with her when my aunt and uncle were out of town. I never knew my aunt and uncle traveled so often, but your mom has been great to let me stay here with her."

I took a deep breath, relieved that Evan remembered what he was supposed to say. He looked over at me and I smiled to let him know his answer was good as he took his first sip of coffee, and then I turned back toward Christine.

"Where do you live?" Evan asked Christine, to return his interest.

Christine held up her hand motioning that her mouth was full of coffee and then answered, "I live in Boston, if you'd call it that, with the way I travel with my job."

"Do you get back to Philly often?"

"Not as much as I'd like to, and when I do it's not for very long."

"Christine and Tom have to leave this afternoon. They only came in for one night," I told Evan.

"Oh, that's too bad. I was going to see if I could take everyone out for dinner tonight," Evan offered, as he returned a smile my way.

"We'd take you up on it if we were staying," Christine said. "How about we take everyone out for lunch?"

"That would be fun," I replied.

"It does sound fun, but unfortunately I've promised a client

I'd take him golfing this afternoon," Evan said.

"Work perks, uh?" Tom asked.

"Yeah. Definitely a perk."

"Well, I guess I'll go and clean up if you guys are done upstairs?" Christine announced. Then she poured herself another cup of coffee and left the kitchen as loudly as she came in.

53

We all chose to skip breakfast. I straightened up the living room and put away the linens I had slept on, so we could all move out of the kitchen and find a more comfortable place to sit. By mid-morning, we had run out of things to talk about as Christine wore a path in the carpet, pacing back and forth like a trapped cat. None of us were taken by surprise when she announced she was going out for a jog. Tom decided to go with her, and they both went upstairs to change clothes.

In the meantime, I aimlessly browsed through a magazine that I had no interest in, as Evan made his afternoon plans on the phone and our two joggers left out the front door.

"Well, how did I do?" Evan asked me as he hung up the phone.

"You did wonderful."

"I'm sorry my being here made you have to make up some story."

"Evan, please don't feel like you have to apologize. Christine might be my daughter, and grown at that, but you are Stephen's son and your father meant the world to me. That makes both of you special. Unlike you, she doesn't know who you are and I'm not sure what good that would bring to the table. I've been through this a thousand times in my head, and my relationship with your father would only be hurtful to them. It's kind of like when you told me you never mentioned my name to your mother. Your father and I weren't unfaithful to our families, and neither were you to your mom. We just didn't want to hurt them."

"Sometimes I feel like I'm cursed. Ever since my dad died, things have never been the same, but I never thought I'd be chasing my dreams. Sometimes I feel like I should submit my stories to the *Unsolved Mysteries TV Series* or go see someone who can interpret them."

"I thought that's why you looked me up?" I asked in a joking manner to lighten up the moment.

"Maybe it was. Do you read palms, too?"

"There's the Evan I know. So, do you want to talk about the news I have for you?"

"Sure."

"I think I might have found the girl. Her name is Nicole. She's a sophomore in college and works at a café on campus. She has a mole on her neck right here," I said, as I reached up to touch the right side of my neck about two inches under my ear.

"It's a mole. No. Come to think of it, it might be a birthmark. I know you mentioned a mole one time. Does her name ring a bell?"

"Can you tell me any more?" Evan asked, as he scooted up on the edge of the couch.

"She lives with her brother in a downtown apartment. She takes the bus everywhere she goes. Her mother lives in Bowling Green, Kentucky. How am I doing?"

"How do you know all this?"

"It gets a little bit more complicated," I added.

"What do you mean?"

"Well, let me see, where do I start? Umm … I didn't tell you when you asked about my relationship with your dad if we had any children. Evan, your father and I married, and I took your dad's last name. We had a child together, and her name is Lauren. She's a freshman at the University of Cincinnati campus in Blue Ash. She still lives at home, because our house is in walking distance. Anyway, she has a job on campus at the Union Building Café′, and that's where she met Nicole and they became friends."

"I can't believe this. So, when I saw you in my dreams, you were in your dreams? I mean …" Evan paused. "I don't know what I mean. Does Lauren know about me?"

"I told her about you when she was eleven or twelve, only because she was so depressed when Stephen disappeared from our lives. She knows that your father and I had different families with children, and that we were with them when we fell asleep at night. I told her about you and your brother and my two girls. I'm not sure how much she remembered me telling her at that age, because she's never asked again. I don't know if she's afraid to rehash the old feelings and details or is in denial that I go somewhere else when I fall asleep. I think it makes her feel like she's not real, but she's as real as you are, and so is Nicole."

"I want to believe that, Diane."

"You should. Anyway, getting back to Nicole, I showed her the picture of you from your business card. She didn't act like she knew you, although later she told me she wanted to meet you."

"What?"

"Isn't that what you wanted, Evan?" I asked.

"Yes, how did you show her my picture?"

"I remembered your father told me one time he fell asleep with his cell phone in his hand when he made the SWITCH. His phone didn't work in Blue Ash, because it couldn't get reception, and he thought that was because it wasn't recognized. Anyway, I tried it with your picture and it worked," I told him.

Trying to take it all in, Evan sat there for a few minutes before responding. "Okay, that's weird. This whole thing is way too weird. I'm having a hard time grasping that this could be possible. What if it's not her? She should have known who I was, don't you think?"

"Maybe she didn't want to let on that she knew you, or maybe she's suppressed her dreams. I don't have all the answers, but she is all that I have come up with so far."

Evan got up and crossed the room. He stood at the window with his back to me. The way he stood there reminded me of his father, Stephen.

"I've only been with her once in the last week. I dream when I go to sleep, but she's not there. We used to see each other more often," he told me.

"Really? Well, maybe that's because she's busy with school or she's at my house," I said, as I got up to go to the kitchen, remembering that I wanted to pull out the pork chops to thaw. When I came back into the living room, Evan was still standing by the window.

"I think the first thing I should do is take a picture of her. That would narrow things down, don't you think?"

We both turned to look at the front door when we heard Christine's voice. She was saying something to Tom that wasn't quite audible. Evan got busy leafing through an atlas that happened to be lying on the top of some magazines. I headed toward the front door in case it was locked.

When I opened the door, Christine was stretching her calves and Tom was sitting on one of the steps. Both looked flushed from their run, but that didn't keep them from teasing each other. Evan and I watched them deposit their shoes inside the front door as they headed upstairs to take their second shower of the day, and it wasn't even noon.

54

By the time they came down, Evan had left to meet his client for lunch and golf. I had retreated back to my comfort zone in the kitchen, tidying up, when Christine swung open the service door, looking around.

"Where'd Evan go?"

"Oh, well, he had to leave to meet his client. I guess they decided to meet early and get something to eat before their golf game. He did ask me to tell you that he had a nice time talking with you and Tom this morning and that he hoped you had a safe trip home. I think he's as much on the run as you are, honey," I replied as I dried off the coffee pot.

"Well, why don't the three of us go out to lunch?"

"Sounds like a great idea to me," Tom chimed in, as he appeared out of nowhere. "The least we can do after that beautiful dinner last night is treat you to lunch."

"Well …"

"Oh, come on, Mom, let's get out of the house for a while."

"Sure, why not," I said in agreement.

We ended up at a neighborhood diner within walking distance. The kind of place where you seat yourself, and wipe off the table with a paper napkin before you dare think of resting your arms on it. The place smelled of French fries, and two-day-old cobbler.

"Remember when we were kids and used to eat at places

like this? What was the name of that place? I didn't know these places still existed," Christine said, as she picked up the saltshaker to inspect its cleanliness.

"I think I know which one you're talking about, but I can't remember either. You and Claire used to get thick strawberry milkshakes that were a godsend to me because you couldn't possibly spill them."

"So, are you telling me Christine was a little piggy?" Tom asked, as he laughed.

"My girls took turns winning the piggy award," I told him.

"A strawberry shake sounds pretty good," Christine said, as she pointed to the menu. "See, they have them right here, and I'm going to have one for old time's sake."

"Go all out," Tom said, as he winked at her.

By the time we got through eating, I felt fat as a pig and greasy all over, and all I wanted to do was go home, take a shower, and lie down for a nap. The heavy food didn't seem to bother Christine or Tom. In fact, they acted like it gave them a second wind. I tried to dismiss the way I was feeling to keep up with the conversation Christine and Tom were having about making it to the airport on time, but all I was thinking about was taking a nap.

I loved my children to death, but the great divide was starting to happen; and sometimes I wondered if they saw me lagging behind as much as I realized I did. Maybe the whole Evan and Christine meeting wore on me more than I thought. I was just glad it was over.

"Hey, Mom. Are you still with us?" Christine asked, as she looked over her shoulder and interrupted my thoughts.

"Of course, sweetie. Maybe it was the food. I think I ate too much."

"Well, why don't you take a nap after we leave?"

"I just might do that," I replied, as I wondered if my being tired was that apparent.

Before I knew it, they were waving goodbye to me from the back of a cab as it pulled away. Christine looked happy. I hoped for her what every mother wants for her daughter: a companion who is loving and loyal. I knew I should be more worried for Tom, because it seemed he really cared for Christine, and she still hadn't slowed down any. She never once tried to talk to me about Tom while she was there, and that was not a good sign. It had always been all about her, and maybe that was my fault for spoiling her because she was my first. It was funny how different all three of my girls were.

I changed all the linens, and started a load of laundry. Then I took a bath and went straight to bed. It didn't take me long to fall asleep. I slept hard, and had sleep lines on the side of my face to prove it when I finally climbed out of bed at five o'clock. I couldn't believe I'd slept that long.

Evan came back around six-thirty and told me he was still full from lunch and thought he'd pass on dinner, which was fine with me after all the greasy food I'd eaten. I did open a bottle of wine to take the edge off the last twenty-four hours and Evan was game to have a glass with me.

"Hope you like Merlot, because that's all I have around here that doesn't need to be chilled," I told him, as I walked back toward the living room.

"Sounds great to me. So how did I do, I mean with your daughter and all?"

I handed Evan his glass of wine and sat down on the couch. "You did great while they were here. I'm just sorry that I put you in that position."

"What do you mean?" Evan asked.

"I never wanted to make you feel like you had to lie, and that's exactly what I did. I'm sorry," I apologized, and took a sip of my wine.

"Don't be sorry. If I hadn't showed up on your front step asking questions and looking for my dream girl, then you'd never have been in this position. Anyway, I could've stayed at a hotel, so don't give it another thought."

"Well, then, let's talk about this girl I found."

"Nicole?"

"Yeah," I said, as I set down my wine glass. "I've been thinking about it and at first I thought maybe you could find me in your dream, and I could take you to her. Then I thought, *what if it's not her and she sees you?*"

"Is that bad?"

"It could be, if she likes what she sees and she's not who you're looking for."

"Oh … I get it," Evan agreed.

"So, I thought if I could get a picture of her and Lauren together on my cell phone, then maybe I could transport the phone with me when I make the SWITCH like your father once did. I'm thinking we wouldn't need a signal on my phone to look at my stored pictures, right? This might just work. Anyway, it's worth a try, and it'd be great if you could see a picture of Nicole."

"All right. So, how soon are you thinking?"

"Maybe by tomorrow, if I'm lucky. Nicole might have stayed all night at the house last night, depending on how late they stayed out after I went to bed. I'll see what I can do."

We turned on the Sunday night news, and settled into our bottle of wine. I think we were both happy it was just the two of us. There was a comfort level Evan and I had with each other because of his father, and the possibility of him being able to SWITCH. It was ironic, but I thought he knew me better than anyone else in the world. We were both ready to turn in early, maybe because we both wanted to make the SWITCH.

55
Monday in Blue Ash, Ohio

I woke up early, and for the first time in days I felt recharged. I could breathe easier knowing I'd survived the overlap of my two worlds, even though I knew it wasn't quite over yet.

I freshened up and tiptoed down the hall to see if Lauren was still asleep, but when I got to her room it looked untouched. My heart started racing, and I went downstairs to see if the car was in the garage, but it wasn't. I ran to the telephone to see if the message light was blinking, but it wasn't. I picked up the phone and dialed Lauren's cell phone, but the recording told me to leave a message. I hung up the phone and stood there, frozen with worry.

My mind was racing. *Where was she? Why hadn't she called?* I didn't have Nicole's cell number or my car to go looking for them, and that wasn't like Lauren. *I should have stayed up and waited for her to come home,* I thought, as I pried myself from the kitchen and went back up to Lauren's room. I thought, *maybe I could find a phone number or something that would tell me where she was*. Then I turned around and realized it was only six a.m. I told myself to relax. *Maybe Lauren had stayed with Nicole and was still asleep, but why didn't she call last night and tell me?* I laid down on her bed, motionless, and waited for her to call.

It was seven-twenty when the phone rang, and I jumped up

so fast that I had to catch myself from falling forward.

"Lauren?"

"Mom?"

"Where are you?"

"I stayed at Nicole's because we ended up eating at some Italian restaurant closer to her apartment, and then going back to her place. It got late and I thought you wouldn't want me driving home. I'm sorry, and I hope you're not mad."

"Half mad, but I've been more worried. You've never done anything like this before, and I was scared something had happened," I told her.

"I'm sorry, Mom."

"Well, I'm just glad you're okay. Are you coming home soon?"

"Yeah, I've got to get ready for school."

"Good. Be careful," I added, before saying goodbye.

I was relieved as I hung up the phone, but still wired, so I went downstairs and drank almost a whole pot of coffee before Lauren got home. I was pretty cranked up by the time she walked in and ready to throttle her — that is until I saw Nicole walk in behind her.

I was glad to see Nicole, but not naïve, and knew Lauren probably brought her home as a buffer. It was probably a good thing she had brought Nicole, because otherwise she might have been grounded from using the car or given an indefinite curfew. I kept wondering what Stephen would've done, and reminded myself that "Old Mom" just might have to lay down some new rules; however, I was just glad to see she was okay.

They didn't stay in the kitchen long, maybe because they knew Lauren was in trouble. They traipsed upstairs as I continued to tidy up around the kitchen, which was long overdue. Other than the low rumble of their voices and a radio playing in the background, the house was quiet except for my screaming headache. I found some aspirin to take and then went upstairs to take a shower. As I turned on the water, my thoughts went to Evan and I wondered if Nicole was his girl.

The steam was starting to cling to the inside of the shower door as I stepped in and let the hot water massage my back and run down the back of my legs. I could've stood there all day or until the water turned cold, but my conversation with Evan about getting a picture of Nicole kept me moving. As I washed my hair, I contemplated how I was going to get a picture of the girls after the shenanigans of the night before. All I knew was if I didn't seize the moment, there might not be one.

So, after getting dressed, I tapped on Lauren's door and asked the girls if they wanted to go out for breakfast. They seemed surprised, and took me up on my offer.

We ended up going to a mom and pop bagel shop the girls suggested. The place specialized in healthy cardboard-like bagels. I'd never thought about eating sweet potato or pesto bagels, but the selection of bagels and cream cheese was fabulous. We all left full and happy with the choices we made. The girls were either slap-happy from staying up too late, or relieved that I wasn't mad at them for the night before and let me take a few pictures of them with my cell phone.

When we got back to the house, Lauren raced upstairs to take a shower while I chatted with Nicole about her day and looked at their pictures. I was surprised how good the pictures turned out. The girls were both smiling ear-to-ear, and very photogenic, but then again that could have something to do with their age.

Little did Nicole know that Evan might be looking at her picture in a few scant hours. I showed the pictures on my cell phone to the girls as they were walking out the door, and then carefully tucked my phone back into my purse.

Somewhere between straightening up and laundry, the

hours passed quickly. Lauren came home later and ate some dinner, then said something about Nicole coming over to study and spend the night as she headed up to her room.

I wasn't far behind her, and retreated to my bedroom. I changed into my pajamas and got into bed. Holding on to my cell phone, I closed my eyes as I thought *about Lauren, and her staying at Nicole's the night before. I needed to know where she was at night, and that she was safe. I didn't want to leave her, but knew I had to make the SWITCH for Evan.*

56
Monday in Ardmore, Pennsylvania

I made the SWITCH with the cell phone in my hand. When I woke up, it was there. I opened it up to see if I could bring up the pictures, and I could. With one quick yank on the bedspread, I made the bed and went downstairs with my phone still in hand.

The kitchen was void of any smells of food or coffee, and the early light of dawn barely lit the space around me. I turned to flip the under-counter light switch on, when I caught the silhouette of someone sitting at the table out of the corner of my eye, and I jumped.

"It's me," I heard Evan say. "I'm sorry if I scared you. I couldn't sleep."

"Is something wrong?" I said, as I went toward the coffee pot and slipped my hand into the pocket of my robe and felt for my phone.

"Not really … well, it wasn't one of our best days together, if you'd call it that; for some reason, I couldn't do anything right. I know I shouldn't have left, but I came back early."

"Well, you know Evan, relationships are like anything else in life. They're a lot of work."

Evan stood up and walked toward the cupboard for a cup. "Yeah, I know that. It's just, I don't understand girls sometimes," Evan said, as he waited for the coffee to brew. "I don't know," he added in a monotonous voice.

"Things will work out, honey," I said, reaching over to pat his arm.

"Thanks."

"Hey, I've got something for you," I said, with some hesitation because of the mood Evan seemed to be in. "A picture of Nicole. But maybe we should wait until later?"

"You're joking, right?"

"What, that I have a picture or that this isn't a good time?"

"I'm fine, really," Evan said, with a pleading look.

I poured our coffees and we sat down at the table. Then I pulled the cell phone out of my pocket and said, "It worked. I don't have any signal, but I can pull up my pictures," I told Evan.

Bringing up Nicole's picture, I handed Evan the phone. The moment seemed endless as I watched him look at it. My adrenaline was pumping, and I knew it wasn't from drinking too much coffee. I didn't have to wait long, though, before Evan shifted in his chair and looked up at me.

"Where is she?" he asked.

"In that picture, she's in my kitchen in Blue Ash, with my daughter, Lauren." I paused. "Is it her?"

My question didn't echo or bounce off the walls, but came to an abrupt halt as I watched Evan study the picture. I could see him smiling and knew at that moment Nicole was his girl.

57

Evan didn't say anything as he clicked back and forth between the pictures of Nicole on my phone. I watched him in his silence and wondered what he was thinking. What would he say to Nicole? Would she remember Evan from when she fell asleep or believe that some people can SWITCH to another life when they go to sleep?

The questions took me back to the morning Stephen and I were alone in the breakroom at work, and how I prayed he would step forward and say something about meeting me every night. I wanted him to tell me that he dreamed about me every night, because I wanted to tell him I loved holding him. I loved him, and wanted to be with him every chance I could.

Fortunately, Stephen did acknowledge he knew me, and our nights together turned into a lovely romance and we had a great life together for as long as it lasted. *I just hope for Evan, that Nicole recognizes him and is open to what he has to tell her. I don't know what Evan will do if she doesn't.*

"I can't believe she's sitting in your kitchen. I mean, just right there, and with your daughter, or my stepsister. It's all too unbelievable," Evan said.

"Are you happy?" I asked, as I mentally brought myself back to the here and now.

"Am I happy? Ecstatic. Yeah, but scared, too," he added. "I'm not sure what I'll say. Do you think she'll know who I am?"

"I don't know, Evan. Your father recognized me, and I'm still not sure how the whole thing works. I wish I could tell you that she'll know you, but I'm not sure," I said, as I went to retrieve the coffee pot.

"After seeing your picture, she told me she'd like to meet you. Which makes me think she can't remember her dreams or is in denial if she does. All we can do is get you with her, and then figure out things from there."

"But our situation is different. I can't talk to her during the day, like you could with my father." Evan paused. "I don't understand; how can she want to meet me if she possibly already knows me? Do you think she recognized me in the picture you showed her, and she's just pretending not to know me?"

Not intentionally ignoring Evan's questions, I had already mentally moved on. "Well, let me think now. Today is Monday, which means Nicole might have spent the night."

Evan chimed in, "Spent the night? I think I just figured why lately there have been nights we didn't hook up. It's because Nicole's been crashing at your house with Lauren after work or school, and staying up half the night. No wonder she had more time to be with me in the summer. She had more time to sleep."

"What do you do on those nights?" I asked Evan.

"Nothing. Roam around, look at music, and look for Nicole."

"Well, that's a new thought for me. I never thought about you two not being together every night when you SWITCH over."

"I wish we were, but our relationship isn't quite there yet. If she's at your house, then I probably won't see her," Evan concluded.

"Not unless you come over to my house tomorrow. Tell

you what, I'll give you my address and you can stop by, but no later than seven in the morning, because I don't know if I can keep her around long. That is, if she stayed the night."

"I can make it happen."

Then it was like we never had the conversation. I was back to watching my birds, and Evan was staring at the pictures. The coffee disappeared long before the quietness of our morning thoughts, and when the kitchen phone rang it about knocked both of us out of our chairs. I thought it was probably Claire, but it was some man for Evan.

I handed him the phone and moseyed into the dining room to put away the placemats that were still on the table from Saturday night. As I picked them all up, I thought about the dinner with Christine and Tom, and what a lovely time we had. *Seems like Saturday night was weeks ago, with all that has happened in the last twenty-four hours.*

The service door from the kitchen swung open and Evan appeared, not looking very happy. "I have to meet a client for lunch."

"Must be something important," I said.

"Just a deadline on a project we're trying to meet."

"Well, you go ahead and try to make the most of it. I'm going to go for a walk and get some fresh air. We'll talk about things later. Okay?"

"Okay. I guess I better get cleaned up," Evan said, as he looked at the wall clock.

"You and me, both." I motioned for him to go. "We'll talk later today."

58

I walked by a church and felt guilty for not going the day before. So, I found a bench close by and sat down to give my thanks to God and pray for some normalcy in my life. There was no choir singing or preacher with a consoling smile standing behind a podium, but I could still feel God everywhere.

As I walked home, the sun beat down on the side of my face and I knew He was with me. Somehow, the whole devotional experience renewed my outlook, and lowered the stress that had settled in my neck and back muscles.

When I got back, the house was empty, and I felt lonely even before I made it upstairs to take off my walking shoes. I had to laugh at my mood swing. What happened to feeling renewed? I sat on the bed wishing I had a good book, but my stomach growling reminded me it was past lunch time.

So, I went downstairs, fixed a sandwich and tried to call Christine. After five rings I hung up and ate in silence, wondering what Evan was doing. I could feel my anxiety building because I knew it was going to be a long day.

How was I going to pass the time before my SWITCH over to see Lauren? Would Nicole be there? What would Nicole do when she saw Evan? Would she know him, and if she did, would she let on? Would Lauren have a zillion question? How would I answer them?

No wonder my heart is racing, I thought, as I carried my

dish to the sink; and if that wasn't enough, I wondered if Lauren would have a normal life. I wanted that more than anything for her. I wouldn't have Lauren if it wasn't for Stephen and I being able to SWITCH, and make a life together. I wouldn't trade it for anything. But watching what Evan was going through scared me, because I wasn't sure I wanted Lauren to be able to SWITCH between two lives.

I couldn't sit still, so I put my coat back on, and walked to the corner grocer to get some stuff for a soup pot. The cool autumn breeze pushed all my questions aside and passed through me as if cleansing my soul and making me realize that it was a good day and I should be enjoying it. On the way back, I stopped in a coffee shop and splurged on a large hot chocolate to take the chill off as I walked.

By the time I got home, I was tired, so I put the produce away and went to lie down. When I woke, it was a little after five, and already dark outside. I got up, half expecting to see Evan when I went downstairs, but he wasn't back yet. I went ahead and got started making soup, and poured myself a glass of wine. By seven o'clock, I was two glasses into the bottle and getting hungry, so I went ahead and fixed myself a bowl. I finally put the rest in the refrigerator, and headed upstairs for the night.

As I got ready for bed, I hoped that Evan remembered to show up by seven in Blue Ash the next day, but then I remembered he didn't have my address. I found an old envelope and wrote it down on the back with a short note, then slipped it under the door to his bedroom.

Evan, I got tired and went to bed. If you're hungry there's soup in the fridge. See you on the other side at seven a.m. Hopefully, Nicole will be there.
My address is on the back.

I got into bed and turned out the lights. My last thought was a worry, as I made the SWITCH. I didn't know about what, but I could feel the tension building in my body.

59
Tuesday in Blue Ash, Ohio

When I woke I was thirsty, and I had this funny metallic taste in my mouth. My stomach was a mess, and I spent the first few minutes in the bathroom feeling sick and jittery. I decided to check in on Lauren, to make sure she was in her room. Through the crack in the door, I was happy to see both Lauren and Nicole sleeping.

I made my way downstairs and put on a pot of coffee, not for me but for the girls when they got up. I was hoping by then I'd feel like having a cup myself. The kitchen's clock ticked loudly and ricocheted off the back of my head as I stood in front of the kitchen sink. I felt edgy and annoyed at the clock, although I knew it was my nerves getting the best of me.

My two worlds were once again going to collide and it felt like a two-ton weight on my chest. It was crushing, and then a sharp pain shot through my arm and shoulder blade. Was I having an anxiety attack? I fell to my knees in the kitchen as my peripheral vision went black. I could hear what was going on around me, but I couldn't get up.

I must have made a thud when I fell or else the glass I was holding broke, because I could hear Lauren and Nicole coming down the stairs.

"Mom!" Lauren called out. "Oh, God. Mom, please talk to me."

I could hear the girls talking about calling 911, but I couldn't respond. Lauren was sitting by me and brushing my hair back when I heard the doorbell ring.

"That must be the paramedics," Lauren told Nicole.

"I'll get it," Nicole said, as she rushed towards the front door.

"Nicole? Tell them to come in here. Nicole? Nicole, what is going on?"

"It's not the paramedics," Nicole answered.

"Hi, I'm Evan. I'm a friend of Mrs. Winthrop's."

"Who is it?" Lauren yelled.

"It's a friend of your mom's," Nicole said, as she stared at Evan. "Huh, we have a problem. Can you help us?"

"Sure, what is it?" Evan said, as he perked up.

"Mrs. Winthrop has collapsed in the kitchen. We called 911. We thought you were them," Nicole rambled.

"Nicole!" Lauren yelled.

"We're coming," she said, as they ran toward the kitchen.

I could hear sirens in the background, and then it was a blur. The next thing I knew, I was in the ambulance and Lauren was sitting by me crying. I smiled at her, but I didn't know if she saw it. Then my mind flashed back to the kitchen. Evan was there with Nicole and Lauren. *Why did I have to get sick now? Wonder if....*

"Mom, we're at the hospital. They're going to move you now, and I'll be close by."

I squeezed her hand, and she squeezed back, so I knew she felt it. I was weak, but had come-to a little, and noticed an IV in my arm. The nurses had been in to ask a bunch of questions, and others had strolled in and out to take my blood pressure and make sure I was comfortable. There were two doctors talking with Lauren outside the glass sliding door as she looked at me. She had that five-year-old scared look on her face as she nodded to the doctors and then they all came in.

"Hi, Mrs. Winthrop. I am Dr. Buckingham, the ER doctor, and this is Dr. Penske, he's a cardiologist. We've got your labs back and ran an EKG, and apparently you had a heart attack this morning."

"You're stable now," Dr. Penske added. "I would like to perform a cardiac catheterization to get a better look at what happened and see if there is any vessel damage that needs to be repaired. I will need your approval to do this."

"Mom, I think you should let them check you out. I'll be right here waiting, and they said I could see you in a few hours," Lauren said.

"Mrs. Winthrop, we strongly advise you have this procedure and then we'd like you to stay one night so we can keep an eye on you. You can go home tomorrow if everything works out like we hope."

I nodded and reached for Lauren's hand.

"Mom, you'll need to sign a consent form, okay?"

"Okay," I said, as I reached for the clipboard Dr. Penske was holding."

I signed the bottom of the consent form as he talked about what he was going to do, and told me about all the risks associated with the procedure, and then he left.

"I'm sorry, honey," I told Lauren. "This isn't what I had planned for the day."

"It's okay, Mom. Don't worry about anything. I'll be right here waiting for you. We've been through tough times before, and we're not going to let this one kick us in the butt. You're who taught me to be tough," Lauren said, as she patted my arm.

"You're going to be just fine," she added, as two people dressed in scrubs arrived and told us they were taking me down the hall to see Dr. Penske.

60

When I was taken to my room, Lauren was already sitting in the chair beside the bed they transferred me to. I wanted to hug her, but I felt groggy. She sat and watched the nurses come and go for a while, before she made her way over to the bed.

"Hey, Mom. The doctor said you were going to be just fine. He said your heart is as strong as a horse," Lauren told me, as she pulled up my hospital gown on one shoulder.

"The doctor said he'd be in later to go over what they found. He thought you'd probably be able to go home tomorrow."

I closed my eyes, because I was feeling unusually tired.

"I rode with you in the ambulance, do you remember?" Lauren asked.

"Yes," I heard myself say, as I was still trying to process what had happened. The idea of having a heart attack seemed impossible and surreal.

"Anyway, we left in such a rush that I'm not sure we locked the front door or turned off the coffee pot. I need to catch a ride and get back home, and while I'm there put a bag together for you and get the car. Okay?"

Before I could muster up another yes, Lauren bent over and gave me a kiss.

"I'll be back in a couple of hours."

Lauren didn't say anything about Nicole or Evan. *Did*

Evan tell her who he was? The question echoed in my brain as I continued to think. *We never planned his introduction or how I knew him, because of his uncanny resemblance to his father, Stephen. Did Lauren know who he was without having to ask me? Maybe Nicole told Lauren that Evan was her boyfriend, or maybe Evan made his own introduction. If he did, who did he say he was? Had Nicole recognized him?*

I had a thousand questions and until I saw Evan, I wouldn't know what happened.

My eyes were heavy, so I gave in to sleep. It must have been the medication they gave me. I was sleeping hard when I heard Evan's voice.

"Diane? Can you hear me?" he asked.

I tried to wake up, but I was floating in between that moment and the next.

"That's okay, close your eyes. I saw Lauren leave, so I thought it would be a good time to visit. Nicole didn't recognize me, or if she did, she didn't show it. We didn't get to spend much time together. The ambulance came right after I did, and Nicole ran off during all the commotion. Lauren was so worried about you, that we never got the chance to say hello. I'm not making much sense I know, plus I'm not even sure you can hear me."

When I finally woke up, Lauren was moving around the room. She had picked up some fresh flowers and had set them in the window. She had also brought a pillow and afghan and piled them on the chair. She seemed restless, and much older.

"Hey," I said, in a voice I didn't recognize.

"Mom, you're awake. How do you feel?" Lauren asked

"Hungry. Maybe if I'm lucky I'll get some yellow Jell-O."

"You're funny. I can ring the nurse."

"What time is it?" I asked, as I looked at my arm. "Do you have my watch?"

"It's shortly after five, and yes, I have your watch and your purse, if you need it."

"All I remember is feeling sick to my stomach when I got up this morning and not feeling like I wanted to have my usual cup of coffee. I had looked in on you and Nicole, and then went downstairs. I don't remember too much after that."

"We heard a loud noise and came downstairs, and you were lying on the floor. I was so scared. Thank God, Nicole was there to help me, she called 911. Then … there was this guy…" Lauren's voice trailed off at the sound of a knock at the door.

"Hi, Mrs. Winthrop. I'm Dr. Penske, your cardiologist. How are you feeling?"

"So-so, I guess."

"I'm going to adjust your bed into a sitting position for you, because I'd like to listen to your heart. Can you take some deep breaths for me? Good. Good."

"Let me tell you what I found during your procedure. You had some blockage in an artery on the front part of your heart. So, I cleaned the artery out, and placed a stent into it to help keep it open. Other than that, all the other arteries look pretty good. You have good collateral arteries that helped to make the damage to your heart less severe. You're a lucky lady."

Lauren politely interrupted, "So, did my mom have a heart attack?"

"Yes, she did. Fortunately, you got her here quickly, though, and the damage was minimal," Dr. Penske answered, as he turned back around to me.

"Tell me, Mrs. Winthrop, did your mother or father ever have a heart attack?"

"Neither one of my parents ever had a heart attack."

"How about your brothers or sisters?"

"No. I only had one brother but he died as a child."

"Well, at least there isn't a family history," he remarked, and then continued, "You don't smoke, you're not overweight, you don't have high blood pressure, and all your blood tests came back within normal range. You've been fortunate this far in life and not had to take any medications, but this heart attack changes things. You'll have to take a couple of medications for at least a year or so. I'll leave my instructions with the nurse and I want you to follow up with your family doctor in the next two weeks. I'll review your chart in the morning and, if all is good, you'll be able to go home. This is earlier than I would normally discharge someone, but you're quite a trooper."

Before Lauren and I could blink an eye, he was gone, almost like he had never been there. Within a minute, the nurse was standing at my bedside sharing the wonderful menu items I could pick from, and yellow Jell-O was one of them.

61

"Well, this is fine dining," Lauren said, as she took a second bite of the sandwich she'd picked up in the hospital caféteria.

My food looked good, but I'd lost my appetite after hearing that I definitely had a heart attack.

"Mom, are you okay? You look like you're going to get sick."

"I don't have much of an appetite. Can you take this and set it somewhere?"

"Sure."

Lauren turned on the evening news for us, but I couldn't concentrate on what they were saying because I was lost in my own woes. For the first time, I felt awake enough to think about what had happened, and it scared me. Being there in the hospital forced me to think about not being there with my children.

I closed my eyes and started praying to God. *I thanked Him for watching over me, and for giving me more time with my children. I asked Him to heal my damaged heart, and to watch over my kids and give them the strength to carry on throughout this life.*

Lauren didn't say anything while I laid there with my eyes shut, maybe because she thought I went back to sleep or didn't want to bother me. It wasn't long before someone came in to take my blood pressure, and that's when I opened my eyes.

Lauren was asleep in the chair with the afghan spread over her. She looked exhausted, even though she was sleeping. I felt bad for putting her through that, and hated the fact that my stressing had probably put me there. I watched a rerun of an older-than-dirt sitcom, before I closed my eyes again. Sleep didn't come easily because I was worried about Lauren. Lauren had been through a lot in her short life, and the thought of putting more on her broke my heart.

What would she do if something happened to me? I've always wanted her to have a normal life, but maybe I'd rather her have the ability to SWITCH over so she could be with Christine and Claire. God, am I going crazy? Why am I thinking this way? Is it because Evan has crossed over?

Then my thoughts shifted to Evan. *I wondered about where he was, and why Lauren hadn't mentioned him to me today.* I couldn't sleep, and the more I tried, the harder it got. The nurses coming on the hour didn't help matters. The only good thing was that Lauren slept through it all. One of the nurses even made some comment about how soundly Lauren was sleeping.

After the sitcom, there wasn't much on television but the news, but it did make for good background noise, and seemed to tone down all the weird hospital sounds and noise from the hallway.

My bottom was getting tired from lying in one position, and all I wanted to do was go home. I buzzed the nurse to see if she could bring me another pillow so I could change positions, and then asked her for a newspaper to read. The paper would be better than watching the newscasters deliver all the bad news in the world. At least with the paper, I had the choice to read something good.

The hospital wasn't exactly a spa, but the service was good. The nurse must have been waiting outside my door. She even talked me into trying to eat, by telling me why I needed to, after what I'd been through. I'm not sure she talked me into eating or if I just conceded after getting tired of listening to her.

After eating a little and thumbing through the paper, I turned the volume down on the television and closed my eyes to pray again.

Dear Lord, thank you for another day here with my families. Please watch over my children, and give them the strength they will need to get through life. Open their eyes to life's mysterious blessings, and the meaning of true love. Teach us all to be understanding of each other's needs, and help us to get through the days ahead. Keep our eyes on the goodness of life and our hearts true to the life in the hereafter. Amen. Oh, and Stephen, I hope you can hear me. Your daughter is about to find out who Evan is and I'm scared. I wish you were here. I really need you right now, and so do Lauren and Evan. If you can hear me, please stay close to us. I'm going to need your words of wisdom.

My prayer turned to tears, and then the tears to sleep and I made the SWITCH.

62
Tuesday in Ardmore, Pennsylvania

When I woke, I wasn't in the hospital but in my bed at home with a bad case of terrible heartburn. I had this awful taste in my mouth, like a vitamin had been stuck in my throat all night.

I got up to get an antacid and a glass of water from my bathroom, with the idea of staying up, but ended up sitting back down on the bed in a daze. It must have been an exhausting night, because I didn't feel like I'd slept a wink. I got back into bed and tried to remember what had happened the night before, but I couldn't. I didn't think anything of it, because there had been times I hadn't remembered.

It was eleven in the morning before I got up and felt like going down to make some coffee. The house was quiet. I figured Evan came in after I went to bed, and he was probably still sleeping.

After feeding the birds, having a bowl of cereal and two cups of coffee, I wandered back upstairs to get dressed. I stopped outside Evan's bedroom door to see if I heard anything, but I didn't. I started to knock, but decided to let him sleep.

I got dressed, went downstairs and put on my coat, then went outside to sweep off the back deck. I only lasted about two minutes before I became winded, so I decided to go back inside and put my feet up.

The hours had passed like minutes while I slept, and it was nearly four-thirty when I woke. I got up and went upstairs to see if Evan had come and gone, but his door was still shut. I put my ear to the door, but heard nothing. My knuckles made a soft knock, but there was no reply.

The door opened as I turned the knob, and his bed looked untouched, like he hadn't been there at all. Where was he? Had something happened where he couldn't cross back over? It was Tuesday morning, and he was usually returning work calls by that time. Where could he be? I needed to talk to him before my day and night formally met again. How was I going to do that if he didn't show up? Then I started to worry that something bad had happened.

The rest of the day and evening I spent snoozing off and on across the hall in my bedroom, half hoping that Evan would show. The last thing I remembered before my SWITCH was feeling hungry, and wondering why I still felt so tired, and feeling like I could sleep forever.

63
Wednesday in Blue Ash, Ohio

Lauren was standing by my bed when I woke.

"What day is it?" I asked, and then tried to swallow, but my tongue felt like a dry sock.

"It's Wednesday, and you're still here at the hospital, Mom," Lauren answered in a motherly voice.

"Rise and shine," she continued, as she waltzed across the room to pull the curtains open.

"Can you get me a drink of water? Oh, that's bright," I said, as I wondered what time it was when I finally had gotten to sleep.

"Sure, I'll get you some water. It's a pretty day outside. I thought you might be getting cooped up and could use some sunshine. I have my sunglasses if you want to borrow them," she said in a joking voice, as she handed me a glass of water she'd found on my bedside table.

I took a long swig of water and then tugged at the neckline of my gown to loosen the grip it had on my neck from squirming around in bed all night.

"Wouldn't I be a fashion plate? A pair of sunglasses and a hospital gown that looks like the material came off the same bolt as my grandpa's boxers."

"Well, at least you sound like you're back to normal. How do you feel?" Lauren asked, as she pulled the curtains together a little.

"Like I could eat something more than Jell-O. A cup of coffee would be great."

"Let me go down to the nurses' station and see what I can find out."

I clicked through the television channels, and had just settled on some crazy talk show when the phone started to ring. After three rings, I managed to answer it, hoping all along it was Evan, but it was the minister at my church. He asked how I was doing, and then asked if he could stop over to the house in the next couple of days. I was hanging up the phone when Lauren came back in.

"Who was that?"

"That was the pastor from church."

"Mom, you haven't gone to church for a long time. Wonder how they knew you were here?"

"Okay now, be nice. What did the nurse say about having some coffee?"

Lauren pulled a brush out of her purse and sat down on her makeshift chair-bed.

"They said a nurse would be by soon to put in your breakfast order."

The room got quiet, and I knew what she was thinking. She wanted to know who Evan was, and if she asked, I'd have to tell her.

64

The morning flew between breakfast, discharge papers, and Lauren pulling around the car. A nurse helped me get into the passenger side of our car that Lauren had warmed up. One the way home, we chatted about having soup for lunch, the weather, and a new guy at the café, but never Evan. I knew she was deliberately avoiding the question, maybe because she thought it would upset me, but why?

When we arrived home, Lauren got me settled on the couch and then brought me the afghan that was draped over the back of the leather recliner.

"I'll fix lunch for us. You just sit there and relax," she said, as she scanned the room, looking for the clicker.

"Would you like something to drink?"

"Honey, please don't go overboard. I'm going to be fine."

"Mom, you were collapsed on the kitchen floor yesterday morning."

I half-heartedly laughed, because I knew she was right. Even though it seemed like yesterday was a long time ago.

"What are you laughing about?"

"Life … just life. I love you. You are the best part of being here, you know that?"

"Mom, now you look like you're going to cry. You're worrying me," Lauren said, walking toward me.

"Don't worry. I'm going to be fine. Remember the doctor said I was a real trooper."

"You might be, but I still think you need to lie low for a few days. It'll be fun. We can watch TV, lie around, do nothing, and lie around some more."

"That does sound like fun, but," I said, as I got up, "does that include sitting at the kitchen table?"

"Only when you want to read the newspaper and have a cup of coffee."

"Who's the mom around here anyway?"

"You're the only mom I have, and I want to keep you."

"Honey."

"Mom, I was so scared," Lauren started to cry. "I'm not ready to be in this world by myself. I still need you."

I got up and put my arms around my little big girl. I wanted the moment to last forever. The thought of her being scared and lonely frightened me as much as it did her. I led her to the couch, and we sat for the longest time holding on to each other until eventually we lounged back and fell asleep.

Lauren woke up first and announced that dinner was a must. I agreed, along with my stomach, so we moved to the kitchen for a change in scenery and to stretch our legs.

We ate a sandwich and talked about everything but Evan. Lauren finally told me she had a paper she needed to be working on, but I could tell that she wasn't going up to her room until I went up. So, I made it easy for her by telling her I was ready for bed, even though I wasn't because we'd napped all afternoon. The truth was, I did have a good book to read, and I could stand to lie back down.

My own bed felt like an old friend who was there to comfort a restless soul. I tried reading, but I couldn't seem to concentrate. *My mind kept replaying the look on Lauren's face as she told me how scared she had been.* The thought of her being alone scared me, too, and the next thing I knew I was crying. I wondered if my emotions were off balance from the medicine or if what had just happened to me was finally sinking in. My pillow was soaking wet by the time I got around to turning it over.

If Stephen were there, I wouldn't have anything to worry about. But all I had was Evan to count on. It was a godsend that he could cross over. He was my only hope of not leaving Lauren totally by herself. I decided right then and there that Evan needed to know my wishes if anything were to happen to me. Where was Evan? Why hadn't he stopped by or tried to call? Why didn't Lauren ask who he was? I knew I needed to calm down or I'd end up back in the hospital, but I couldn't help but wonder if I'd survive the merging of my two worlds.

65
Wednesday in Ardmore, Pennsylvania

I woke bright and early, feeling much better after my SWITCH. As I got up and left my bedroom, I paused at Evan's door to see if I could hear anything, but there wasn't a sound. I don't know what I was expecting, because I'd never heard him snore. I didn't dare knock for fear of waking him, but I was hoping he would hear me going down the stairs and get up — that is, if he was even there.

A cup of hot coffee was calling my name, so I headed toward the kitchen. As I got ready to turn the light on, out of my peripheral vision I saw someone moving around on the back deck. I crept to the back door with every intention of turning on the outside light, when I realized it was Evan.

He had his back to me, but by the way he was standing I could tell there was something wrong. I decided not to turn the light on, because I didn't want to startle him, so I gently opened the back door.

"Evan, are you okay?" I asked through the screen door.

"Yeah. I guess."

"Where have you been? I've been worried about you."

Evan turned around and I could tell by his bloodshot eyes that he hadn't gotten much sleep.

"I'm sorry, Diane. I am so sorry." Evan's head drooped down in between his hunched shoulders.

"About what?" I asked, as I stepped out on the deck.

"If it wasn't for me, you might not have had a heart attack. This is too much for you, isn't it? I mean, trying to help me and then me coming to your other house?"

"Evan, no one is to blame," I interrupted him in a motherly way. "You can't blame yourself for what happened to me. I don't blame you. You're just trying to find yourself, like I once did. Please, come on back inside, and let me make you a cup of coffee."

Evan followed me in like a lost pup. He sat down hard at the kitchen table, planted his elbows on the table, and cradled his bowed head in his hands. I listened to the quietness as I scurried around to make coffee, with only the morning light creeping through the windows to light my way. I thought about turning on some lights, but by the looks of Evan I knew lights were out of the question.

"Evan, I remember you in the kitchen with Lauren and Nicole, but that's it," I said, as I put his cup of coffee in front of him on the table.

He didn't say anything, so I turned around and went to get my cup.

"Lauren never asked me about you all day. Here. Try some coffee; maybe it'll make you feel better," I said, scooting his cup closer to him, and sat down across from him. "You don't look like you got any sleep last night."

"I didn't," Evan mumbled.

"Evan, why don't you go lie down for a while and catch up on your sleep?" I consoled him, as I reached across the table and laid my hand on his arm.

"I'm not thinking very clearly; maybe I should," he said, as he stood. "Please don't think that I'm rude or let me sleep too long because I do need to talk to you about some decisions I've made."

"Well, go get some sleep and we'll talk later when you get

up."

Evan slowly walked out of the kitchen and made his way upstairs without making a sound. I didn't hear the floor creaking upstairs as he closed his door and walked across the room.

Two cups later, I was still sitting at the table and wondering what decisions Evan had made. I finally ate some breakfast and wandered outside to sweep off the back deck, but sweeping the steps got me winded, so I stopped short.

"Good morning," I heard Jackie say from her patio.

"Jackie, how are you? It's good to see someone else is up enjoying this beautiful morning."

"These dogs keep me on a schedule," Jackie replied.

"They're good company for you, aren't they?"

"They're all I've got. You should think about a pet, Diane."

"I'm not ready to stay put yet, and that's what I'd have to do if I had a dog."

"Well, we're going in to have breakfast," Jackie said, as she cut the slack in the leashes she was holding.

"It was good talking to you, Jackie. Have a good day," I told her, as I made my way back up the three steps I'd just swept.

With the kitchen door shut behind me, I went to empty the dishwasher but opted not to in fear of waking up Evan; so I headed upstairs to see if I could muster up enough energy to think about going by the church for my call list. The God-honest truth was I physically couldn't and knew better than to push myself, so I opted to lie down in bed and read a new magazine that had just come in the mail.

I must have fallen asleep, because I woke to Evan's bedroom door shutting. I slowly pulled myself up and went downstairs to find Evan using the phone.

"What are you doing?"

"I've got to go back to Chicago," Evan said, as he looked away.

"Right now? You just found Nicole."

"She acted like she didn't know me, Diane," Evan pointedly said.

"What do you mean?"

"The morning you went to the hospital. After the ambulance left, I turned to Nicole and asked her if she knew who I was. She just stared at me and shook her head. Then she took off, and I ended up looking for her all day and night, but never found her."

"So, that's why you weren't here on Tuesday?"

"Yeah. I just couldn't stop looking. I don't understand how she couldn't know me."

"Evan, maybe she knows who you are and can't understand how it could happen, or else the incident with me upset her. I don't know."

"I've thought and thought about it, but what if she doesn't want to hook up anymore?"

"I don't know the answer to that question, but we do know where we can find her. Let me ask you, Evan: You met Lauren that morning; why do you suppose she hasn't asked me who you were?"

"I don't know. Nicole answered the door Sunday morning. I told her I was a friend of yours. I don't think she had time to tell Lauren that, because Lauren was busy taking care of you. Maybe Lauren thought I was a friend of Nicole's. I don't know, but I do know I need to disappear."

"Disappear, why?"

"Maybe Nicole will come back to you and Lauren if I'm not around."

"I hope she does, but what then?"

"Can you talk with her, please?" Evan asked. "I can't do any more if she doesn't want to admit she knows me."

"Let's hope she comes back."

"Diane, I think this is the best decision for now, plus I need to get back to the office. Show my face. You know, stir up some dust and make some money."

"I understand. You do what you think is best. I'll hold the fort down and see what I can find out. Thanks for helping me understand what happened that morning."

"Diane," Evan said, as he reached out for my hand. "I'm sorry for all this."

"Evan, don't be sorry. What time are you flying out?" I asked, as I squeezed his hand.

"This afternoon at three; that way I can be in the office tomorrow morning."

"Well, let me fix you a bite. You go pack."

66

After Evan went upstairs, I must have stood there for fifteen minutes in a daze. My mind blanked out both worlds until the phone rang and made me jump.

"Hi, Mom," Claire said.

"How are you, angel?

"Fine."

"How's Jacob?"

"He's busy painting you a picture for your refrigerator. I'll mail it to you later this week."

"That would be lovely. I sure would like to see him."

"Well, come on over," Claire joked.

"Wish it were that easy, sweetie," I said.

"Why shouldn't it be, unless you've got company or something?" Then there was a long pause.

"So, what do you say? How about coming to visit for a couple of days?" Claire asked.

"Well, let me think about it."

"Mom, are you okay? You sound a little out of breath; are you sick? Nothing's wrong or anything, is there?"

"No. Nothing's wrong, honey. I'm fine," I fibbed.

"Good. Why don't you let Jacob and me pick you up? I'll arrange a return bus ticket for you on Saturday morning. I'd like to see you, and Jacob would love it. Say yes, please, Mom? Jacob and I could make the drive in and pick you up tomorrow."

"Okay, then, yeah … I'd love to spend a couple of days with you."

"I'll call you this afternoon. Mom, you don't sound like yourself, you're worrying me."

"Your mother is just fine, not to worry."

"Good. Talk later. I've got to run. Love you."

I hung up and wondered if I was truly up for the trip. I didn't want her to know I hadn't been feeling well. Maybe, then again, a break was just what I needed. My mind and heart could use a few less stressful moments, and I had a feeling I was going to need all the strength I could get to help Evan and be there for Lauren.

Before I knew it, I was sitting at the dining room table making a mental list of all the things that I needed to get done before I left the next day. I wondered to myself if other people my age had to sit down to make a mental list. Was it my age? I seemed foggy sometimes, like my brain was full of sludge. I could blame the episodes on hormonal changes, but in my heart, I knew it was stress.

The sound of the shower upstairs forced me to get up and stop feeling sorry for myself. I went to the kitchen to see what was in the refrigerator, but all I found was wilted lettuce and some sliced ham that had gotten slimy. There was a chunk of cheddar that was still edible and a small bottle of pimentos. So, I grated up the cheese and added the pimentos and the mayo, hoping that Evan liked pimento cheese sandwiches. His father loved them. We used to have them along with a bowl of soup on the weekends.

"Do you need some help?" Evan inquired, as he leaned up against the frame of the door.

"No. I got it taken care of," I said, as I stirred the iced tea. "I didn't have much to work with for lunch, so I'm hoping you like pimento sandwiches?"

"Love them. Boy, that sure does bring back some memories. My grandmother used to fix pimento sandwiches for us when we were kids."

"Well, that explains why your father loved them."

The sound the dishes made as I put them on the table was like a pin dropping. We both smiled at each other as we sat down.

"You miss your father, don't you?"

"Wish he were here …" his voice trailed off.

"Eating a sandwich with us." I tried to finish his thought, but then I realized for him that was probably not what he wished.

"Sorry."

"Don't be."

We finished our sandwiches in silence. Evan jotted down his cell number, we gave each other hugs, and I promised to let him know when I saw Nicole. He seemed reluctant to leave, but at the same time excited about starting a new project at work. We said our goodbyes three times before the taxi pulled up, and then he was gone.

I went to bed early, hoping to fall asleep right away, but the harder I tried the longer it took. I wanted to see Lauren, I felt like so much had happened. I needed to be with her. I needed to know she felt safe, and then I thought of how I forgot to talk with Evan about my wishes for him to take care of her if something were to happen to me. I was worried all over again and my chest felt like it was going to explode. I wanted the feeling to go away. I wanted to know I would see Lauren married someday, and know she was secure and happy.

67
Thursday in Blue Ash, Ohio

When I made the SWITCH, I woke to the darkness of my bedroom with a sliver of light coming through a crack of my bedroom door that had been left ajar. After my eyes adjusted, I could see Lauren's silhouette. She was sitting on the floor at the foot of my bed with her back to me. When I reached across to turn my lamp on, she turned around with that smile that reminded me of nine years ago.

After Stephen disappeared, she slept with me for months. On those mornings, she would wake with a worried smile on her face that belonged to someone else way past her years. Time helped to ease Lauren's sadness and fears, and she gradually bounced back to her happy-go-lucky self.

So then, when I saw that worried smile on her face, I knew something was wrong. I knew she wouldn't be sitting in the dark, at the foot of my bed if there wasn't.

"Good morning, honey," I said. "What are you doing here? What time is it?"

"It's six. I was waiting for you to wake up."

When she talked, I smelled alcohol. So, I got out of bed to get a better look at her, and when I did Lauren turned away.

"Lauren, look at me. Have you been drinking?"

"No."

"Honey, please don't lie to me. I know alcohol when I smell it."

Lauren got up and walked toward the door, but stumbled and hit her head on the doorframe. I ran to help her. Blood was trickling down her forehead, and she began to cry.

"Sorry, I'm sorry. I've been …"

"You're bleeding, honey. Sit down here on the floor and let me get you a cold washcloth," I said, as I headed for the restroom. "What would make you want to drink and how did you get home?"

There was no answer as the warm water soaked the washcloth. I looked in the mirror at myself and wondered what had brought this on. Were there signs and I didn't see them, or was this just a college blunder? I turned the water off and wrang out the washcloth.

Lauren was still propped up against the wall, looking a little out of it, as I pushed her hair back and held the cloth to her forehead. She was lucky the cut wasn't a gash that needed stitches. I cleaned her up, and then walked her down the hall to her own bedroom, where I left her in bed.

I didn't know whether to be angry or sad. The morning seemed to drag on as Lauren slept. I picked up around the kitchen and den, but wasn't too motivated to pay bills, or start the laundry. My life was in shambles: Lauren drinking, my heart attack, and Nicole not knowing Evan, were making my heart palpitate.

I wasn't sure I could handle the chaos my two lives were throwing at me. I wished my two older girls knew my secret, and that I didn't have to pretend anymore. Stephen and I never wanted things to be this way. We never wanted our children to be involved or ever know, and now I knew why. I wanted to cry, but I didn't know what I would be crying about.

Would the tears be for me wanting Stephen back, or worrying about how much stress my heart could take and if Lauren would be okay without me? Or would they be tears for

Lauren's drinking, or Evan leaving because Nicole ran off, or possibly for my older girls who didn't know this side of their mother?

Lord, no wonder I'm a basket case. I slumped over from where I was sitting on the couch until my head passed over my knees and my knuckles touched the carpet. I was alone with my thoughts and I felt lost.

The doorbell rang, and I jumped. *Who in the world would be here at seven in the morning?* I wondered, as I walked through the kitchen. When I got to the front foyer, I saw Nicole standing on the front steps with her back to me. When I opened the door, she turned with her tear-streaked face, looked up at me, and then started to cry.

"Nicole, here honey," I said, as I opened the storm door. "Come on in. Let me have your coat."

"I didn't know where else to come," she said, between gasping for air as she cried.

I started to take her coat off of her, but she pulled back and blurted out, "It's my brother. He's in trouble."

"What do you mean?"

"These guys shot him last night."

"Where is he?"

"I stayed with him all night. He's bleeding. He wouldn't wake up," she gasped.

"Nicole, calm down. Let me get you a box of Kleenex. Sit down here on the bench."

"I didn't know where else to go. Can you help him?"

"Did you call the police?" I asked, as I came back with the tissues.

"No, he told me not to call anyone, that he'd be okay. He kept telling me it was nothing."

She was in shock, and kept rambling on. I couldn't make sense of why she hadn't called the police or an ambulance for her brother. In the commotion, Lauren had come downstairs and was standing in the front hall behind me. She hadn't said anything, and I was too busy with Nicole to ask her how she was feeling.

68

I asked Lauren to stay with Nicole, so I could get her a glass of water to help calm her down. As I turned the faucet on, I heard both the girls run into the front restroom. When I got there, Lauren was holding Nicole's hair back as she vomited into the commode.

That's when I noticed that Lauren's hands and the edge of her sleeves had blood on them. I went into panic mode with a hundred questions on the tip of my tongue, but knew I had to wait until Nicole calmed down.

Twenty minutes later, we were in the kitchen and I had the girls sitting at the table. While I made some coffee, they sat there and stared into space without a word. I wasn't sure where to start with my questions, and it didn't look like they were going to share any information. As I waited for the coffee to brew, I tried to collect my thoughts.

I took the girls their coffee and sat down. The Lazy Susan in the center of the table squeaked, as the girls turned it to reach the sugar bowl. After two or three swallows of coffee, Nicole began to cry again.

"Don't cry now, honey. Where'd the tissue box go?" I asked, because I could have sworn I brought it with us, as I rose to go back to the restroom to grab it.

"I'm worried about your brother. Why didn't he want you to call the police?" I asked, as calmly as I could as I came back into the kitchen.

"Mom, I'm sorry," Lauren broke in with a half sob between words. "You went to bed and fell asleep so early last night. I know I shouldn't have left you, but the last couple of days have been so scary with you in the hospital. I've been so scared of losing you that I felt crazy inside.

"I tried to sleep but couldn't, so I caught the bus and went down to Nicole's and her brother's apartment. We hung out for a while with him and his friends who made us a couple of drinks.

"Then we went out and got some pizza. We weren't drunk, just hanging out, and nothing bad happened. Well, not until Jake got shot. We were walking back to the apartment after we ate when it happened." She paused as she squirmed in her chair.

I told myself to take a deep breath and stay calm. "Lauren, you've never drunk alcohol before, that I know of. Was it worth it?"

"Mom, I wasn't drunk. I didn't think two or three drinks would hurt, and I didn't fall this morning because of the drinks. I tripped on the carpet."

"Nicole, where is your brother now?"

"He's at our apartment. I put him in his bed."

"You said your brother was shot. Where was he shot?" I asked.

"I think it was in his side. I couldn't tell. A car drove by, and the next thing I know is …" Nicole started to cry again.

"What is your brother's name?"

"Jake," Nicole said, as she wiped the tears away with the back of her hand. "He wouldn't let me look. He just wanted to go and lie in his bed. I shouldn't have left him. He was so … so … uh …"

"Why don't you try to call him?"

"I need to go back to my apartment to see him. Will you

come with me? I'm scared."

"I'll come with you, but you need to call the cops first. Why don't you go do that and then we'll go over there?"

"He told me not to."

"I know he did, but you know shootings have to be reported. The police need to catch who did this to your brother. Why don't you go wash your hands and face, and then maybe you can clear your head enough to call them? Lauren, go upstairs and find something Nicole can change into that's clean. She's got blood all over her shirt and jeans, and while you're up there wash your own hands and change your top."

I picked up our cups and set them in the sink, as I leaned up against the kitchen counter to steady my emotions, and then took some deep breaths so I could think more clearly. My heart was racing, and I knew I really didn't need that kind of stress right then, but what could I do?

The girls came back after changing and looked much cleaner.

"What do I do with these?" Nicole asked, as she held out her bloody clothes.

"Why don't you put them on top of the washer? The police might want them for evidence."

Nicole looked at me, puzzled.

"I helped him up the steps, and into the apartment. He was all bloody."

"I know, honey, but better safe than sorry. Okay?"

Nicole walked toward the den in slow motion. It could have been because she was so drained, but my hunch was she didn't want to call the police because she promised Jake she wouldn't. She wasn't my daughter, so I didn't feel I could push her too hard.

Lauren sat quietly at the table, looking pale and drained from the horror of her night. I walked over behind Lauren and placed my hands on her shoulders.

"How are you?" I asked, as I rubbed her upper back. "Lean back and let me take a look at your forehead here in the light."

"I'm okay, Mom. I just feel so bad for Nicole. Her brother didn't look so good. I hope he is okay."

"Did you see him get shot?"

"Yeah. I was on the sidewalk closest to the building when it happened. It all happened so fast. We didn't even realize it at first. We just thought Jake was acting silly. He was all bent over. At first, I thought he was picking up something or bent over laughing. I didn't know."

"Honey, I'm just glad you're okay. I don't know what I would do if …."

"Mom. I know I shouldn't have gone. Maybe none of this would've happened if I would have just stayed home."

Nicole came out of the den and walked right by us on her way to the bathroom. I gave her a few minutes and then went and tapped on the door.

"Nicole, what did the police say?"

She didn't answer.

"Do you still want me to take you to your apartment?"

"Yes, I need to go back," she said through the door. "I'll be out in a minute."

"Have you called your parents?"

There was a pause, and I thought I heard a sob as she turned the faucet off. "No, I haven't called them yet. I just want to go see Jake first."

"Okay. Well, Lauren and I will be in the car."

The car ride was quiet, and no one was in the mood to listen to the radio. The tires hummed as we rode in silence.

69

There were two police cars parked outside of the old brownstone when we pulled up. Nicole jumped out of the car and ran toward the entrance, as one of the policemen stopped her. Lauren and I sat in the car as we watched them talking. It didn't take but a moment to understand the look on Nicole's face. Her brother Jake was dead.

"Mom, I've got to go over there with her," Lauren said, as she pushed open her car door; and I was quick to follow on my side.

I introduced myself to the officer, and told him what I knew, and how the girls had ended up back at our house this morning. He wanted us to come down to the precinct with him to answer a few more questions. He explained to me that the coroner was on the way, and he thought it would be best if I followed him down to the station before the coroner arrived, for the girls' sake.

It was another quiet car ride. I looked in the rearview mirror as we pulled into the parking lot behind the police car. Nicole's curly shoulder-length hair was hanging limp around her face that was all blotchy from crying. Her lips were parted and chapped, and her eyes dull. You hear people say that being in shock can suck the life right out of you, and that's what Nicole looked like as she stared out the window.

Lauren and I both got out first, and then Lauren opened

Nicole's car door and helped her out. Once we got situated in one of the interrogation rooms, I went and got all of us a bottle of water from the vending machine.

An officer, maybe in his early forties I guessed, due to his hairline and midsection paunch, walked in with a notepad and shut the door behind him.

"Hi, I'm Detective Matthews, and I need to go over a few questions with you," he said, as he looked at Nicole and scratched the top of his head.

"Your name is Nicole Scheider, is that correct?"

Nicole took a drink from her bottle before answering. I looked at her and nodded, signaling that everything would be okay, hoping that would get her through the next couple of hours.

"Yes, that's my name."

"Your brother had a different last name."

Nicole squirmed in her chair before looking up to meet his gaze.

"We found his wallet in his jeans pocket."

"Oh, well, I called him my brother," she said, with some hesitation as she looked back down to pick at the cuticle on her thumb.

Lauren looked at me. By the look on her face, I could tell she was caught off guard by this new revelation. She'd thought Jake was Nicole's brother, because that's what Nicole had told her. Why would Nicole lie about something like that? I was the typical mom, worrying about how twisted this was going to get, and how I could protect Lauren.

"So, he's not your brother?"

"No, he's just a friend. I called him that because it made me feel safe. He was okay with it, my calling him my big brother. I met him on campus when I first moved here. We had a class together and became friends. I was renting a room by the month, in a house near the university. I really wanted my own apartment but couldn't afford one by myself. That's how we became roommates. We've lived together for almost a year. You can check our lease."

"Where are you from, Nicole?"

"Bowling Green, Kentucky."

"That's where your parents live?"

"Yes. My mother. My dad died when I was in grade school."

"Have you called your mother, yet?"

"No. Not yet. I didn't want to worry her."

"Maybe you can call her in a few minutes."

"Nicole, do you know who would want to shoot your, uh ... roommate?"

"No. He quit school last semester, so I didn't see him very much. I think he was having money problems; anyway, that's why he quit school and went to work at some bottling company."

"Do you know which one?"

"No, but I do know Jake filed everything in a cabinet in the dining room."

"We'll need to search your apartment. Is that okay with you?"

"Sure."

"Where were you when Jake was shot last night?"

"I was with him."

"Detective, both girls were with him." I motioned with my hand, waving between Lauren and Nicole.

"I'm Lauren's' mother, Diane Winthrop."

"Both girls? How do these girls know each other?"

"They're both students at the University of Cincinnati campus in Blue Ash, and met this year working together at the Union Building Café'," I answered.

"I see. I'll tell you what; I'm going to need to question the girls separately. So, why don't I start with, uh, Lauren, and that'll give Nicole the opportunity to call her mom?" the officer said, as he looked up from some notes he was making.

"There's a lounge at the end of the hall with some vending machines and a phone. When Lauren is done, I'll come down to the lounge and get Nicole. You'll probably be here most of the morning."

I gathered up my purse and stood, while Nicole aimlessly walked towards the door. The two of us walked down the hall in silence until we made it to a generic-looking breakroom. It reminded me a of a school classroom with the painted concrete block walls, standard-issue clock, and bulletin boards with postings and regulatory information tacked in place.

The air smelled stale, but there was coffee, so I automatically poured two cups — one for Nicole and one for myself. Nicole looked like she needed a boost, and I'm sure that's part of the reason the officer was questioning Lauren first.

70

Back in the interrogation room, Lauren was being questioned.

"Lauren, can you tell me what happened last night?" Detective Matthews asked.

"I wasn't tired, and Mom had gone to bed early. I decided to take the bus and go to Nicole's. Her brother," Lauren stopped. "Well, who I thought was her brother, Jake, was there. We all hung out until about nine, and then decided to go out and get something to eat. We ate at a pizza place, but I'm not sure where because I'm not real familiar with where they live. I do know it took us about twenty minutes to walk there."

"Lauren, you said we all hung out. Was it just you, Nicole, and Jake?"

"No. A couple of his friends came over for a couple of hours, but then they left when the three of us walked out to get something to eat."

"What were their names?" The officer tapped his pen on the table as if playing a drum.

"John and, uh … I don't honestly remember. I think Jake works with them, because they talked about one of the machines breaking down and some supervisor guy they didn't like."

Lauren added, "They brought some bourbon and Coke with them and we all had a couple of drinks."

"What time did you go out to eat and where?"

"Around eleven, it was some pizza place."

"What time did Jake's friends leave?"

"The same time we did."

"When did Jake get shot?"

"When we were walking back to the apartment."

"Do you remember what time it was?"

"Maybe around twelve-thirty. Anyway, we were right outside the apartment when this car drove past."

"What kind of car?"

"It was silver, but I'm not sure what make, because the car was quiet and just came out of nowhere. Anyway, we thought Jake was joking around because we were all laughing and he was bent over. Then, that's when Nicole saw the blood on the side of his shirt.

"Next thing I know, she's yelling at me to open the door to the apartment building. I went up the stairs ahead of them because the stairs are kind of narrow, and Nicole was helping Jake. Then I remember Nicole handing me the keys, and her leading him into his bedroom.

"I just stood there and waited. She told me he didn't want us to call anyone for help. So, we didn't. Most of the night I sat on the couch, while Nicole stayed with Jake in his room. Then when it started to get light outside, I took a bus back home. I never planned on staying all night, but I didn't want to leave Nicole."

"So, you didn't see who was in the car?"

"No. I didn't think anything of the car. I didn't think what I heard was a gun shot, because we were all laughing and I wasn't paying much attention."

"Were there any drugs involved?"

"No," Lauren adamantly replied.

"Okay, I think that's about it. Let's go find your mother and Nicole." The officer stood and motioned to the door.

Lauren walked in the room toward me and reached for my hand at about the same time the officer started talking to Nicole.

"Nicole, you can bring your tea with you if you like. We're going back to the same room we were in before, okay?"

Nicole nodded as she pushed in her chair, and started walking towards the officer with her cup of tea in hand. Lauren and I watched her step in front of the officer, whose pants were two sizes too small around the waist and needed a couple of inches taken off the length. He reached to help open the door for them, as Lauren sat down beside me to wait.

71

"Take a seat, Nicole," Officer Matthews said, as he shut the door behind them.

"You're not in trouble, we just need as much information as you can give us, so we can figure out who shot Jake," the officer said, as he sat down and looked at his notes.

"Where and when did you meet Jake?"

"Jake was in one of my classes my freshman year. We became friends."

"How did you become roommates?"

"I was renting a room and wanted someplace bigger, and so did Jake. He was in a dorm, and said he didn't like his roommate. We decided to share an apartment. It saved me $40.00 a month. The only downside was, I didn't really like the commute to school on the bus, but it still saved me a little money."

"So, you moved in together when?"

"Last March."

"So, not even a year?"

"Yeah."

Officer Matthews shuffled through his notes. "Now, let's see, you said earlier that Jake quit school?"

"At the end of his freshman year. He told me he needed to take a break to earn some money. He planned on going back."

"Where did he work?'

"At a bottling company. I think it's called Wright

Brothers. I think, something like that. We really didn't spend much time together. Our schedules were different."

The officer was writing as he talked. "Do you know many of his friends?"

"Not really, just their first names."

He looked up at her without asking, and Nicole knew he wanted their names.

"John, Dave, and Sean. No, wait; maybe it's Dan instead of Dave. I'm not much help, am I?"

"You're doing fine. Who were his friends that came over last night?"

"Dan and Sean."

"Did you see who shot Jake?"

"No."

"Where were you when he got shot?"

"We were walking home from getting some pizza. We were just outside our apartment, on the sidewalk. I was walking in the middle, yeah, Jake was closest to the street."

"Did you hear the gunshot?"

"Yes, but it took a couple of seconds for me to figure it out. Jake was doubled over, and I thought he was picking up something on the sidewalk or acting silly or something. I don't know. The gunshot didn't make a loud sound."

"Did you see where it came from?"

"It had to come from the car that drove by."

"Could you identify the car?"

"No. Not really. I think it was red. It was dark. I'm not even sure it had four doors or two."

"Do you think it was an older car?"

"No. Not really. It looked like any other car. I don't have a car, so I guess I don't pay too much attention to cars."

"If I brought in a chart with some cars on it, do you think that would help you remember anything else about the car?"

Nicole shrugged because she didn't know, and then picked at the tea bag string that was draped over her cup. She started thinking about Evan's picture that Mrs. Winthrop had shown her. *Maybe she shouldn't have lied about not knowing him*, she thought to herself. *Lauren and her mom are going to think I lie all the time. Why did I have to tell them Jake was my brother? They must think I'm crazy. If they find out I know Evan, they'll really think I'm nuts. Especially, if they find out I only know him from my dreams. Evan's not going to be happy. He's told me several times I need to move closer to the campus. He doesn't think where I live is safe. Lord, am I going crazy? Hello, Nicole, it's just a dream!*

"Nicole? I know you didn't get much sleep, but I just have a few more questions."

"Okay," she said in a fogged state.

"Will you look at some pictures of cars for me?"

"Sure."

"I'll be right back."

Nicole folded her arms on the table and lowered her head to rest on top of them. She didn't know how long the officer was gone, because she dozed off.

"Nicole?" the officer said, as he cleared his throat.

"I'm here," she said, as she stood up and ran her hands over her hair.

"Take a look at the pictures. If anything looks familiar, let me know."

She looked through all the pages, but cars all looked the same to her. *He's going to think I'm such a buffoon. Colors, yeah, I can do that, but taillights, forget it. I already told him I didn't know. God, I am so tired.*

"Like I said, they all look the same to me. It was dark, and I wasn't paying much attention to the car."

"Okay," the officer said, with no emotion as he scooted the

chart down the table.

"Well, how about the people in the car?"

"I didn't get a good look. We were all laughing about something, and I really didn't realize anything was wrong until Jake didn't stand back up right away. That's when I saw the blood and ran over to him. Lauren helped me get him inside. He wanted to go and lay down in his bed."

"Why do you think he didn't want you to call for an ambulance or the police?"

"I don't think he thought it was that bad."

"Do you think Jake was in trouble?'

"I don't know."

"Do you know where his next of kin live?"

"Gosh, I think his parents are divorced. I only met his dad once, right after we moved in. He came to visit and took Jake out to eat and to buy him some clothes. He drove a black SUV. I don't think Jake saw him that often. Maybe Indianapolis, but I couldn't swear on it."

"We're going to search your apartment this afternoon. Is that okay with you?"

"Sure. Where is Jake?'

"He's at the city morgue."

Nicole heard herself choke and sob at the same time as she grabbed the side of her chair. She couldn't think straight, and her stomach was queasy. *If I sit here too much longer, I might pass out*, she thought.

"Nicole, I think that about does it. I'll need the clothes you're wearing, just for evidence," Detective Matthews told her.

Nicole looked up at him. "I changed clothes at Lauren's house this morning."

"It's procedure, they're just for evidence," he said as he stood and walked over to the door.

"I think I need some food in my stomach. I'm not feeling very good," Nicole told him, as he opened the door to the lounge.

"I'll have someone bring you a sandwich in a few minutes," he told Nicole. "Lauren? Mrs. Winthrop? Would you like something to eat?" the officer asked as he leaned against the doorjamb.

"I'll have a sandwich," Lauren said, as she looked at her mom who was shaking her head no.

"All right, two sandwiches. I'll be right back."

72

The girls were unwrapping their sandwiches, when the officer and I left to go down the hall. It was my turn for questioning.

I felt jittery, probably from the stale and strong coffee in the breakroom. The metal chair was cold, and even though the room had a sterile feeling, it looked like it needed a good scrubbing down. The concrete block walls had a yellow tint to them that I knew could be due to old paint, but more likely they were probably never cleaned after the no-smoking law went into effect.

"So, Mrs. Winthrop, right?" the officer asked to draw my attention.

"Yes," I didn't offer Diane to him since he'd been so formal all morning.

"Did you know Jake had been shot last night?"

"No, I was awakened by my daughter, Lauren, this morning and learned myself that she had left last night after I fell asleep and had gone to Nicole's apartment," I answered, as I looked at a pen mark on the officer's cheek.

"That's when you learned of Jake being shot?"

"Yes, who at the time I thought was Nicole's brother. Nicole arrived at the house about seven this morning and was a mess. I told her she needed to call the police. Apparently, her brother, or Jake, had asked her not to call anyone. Maybe he thought it was something he could take care of on his own. I don't know."

"Nicole and Lauren said they changed clothes at your house?"

"Yes, Lauren took a shower this morning, and Nicole changed clothes and washed up before she called the police station, and we went back to the apartment to check on her brother. I mean, her friend."

"We'll need to pick up those clothes at your house."

"That's fine. I thought you might want them. They had some blood on them, from her apparently helping him up the stairs last night."

"Is there anything you'd like to add, Mrs. Winthrop, before we call it a morning?"

"No, I don't think so," I heard myself say.

"My partner and I will follow you back to your house, to pick up the clothes."

"That's fine."

The girls were as ready as I was to go back to the house. On the way back in the car, I told Nicole she was welcome to stay in the extra bedroom for as long as she needed. I could tell she was still in shock and desperately needing a long nap to catch up on the sleep she didn't get the night before.

She didn't say much. I didn't know if it was because she had lied about Jake being her brother, or she was tired, or because Jake was dead. A combination of all three probably, and we couldn't get back to the house soon enough. I looked in the rearview mirror to check on the cruiser following us, and tried to shake the feeling that this was never going to be over.

As we pulled into the driveway, I told Lauren to get Nicole an extra blanket out of the hall closet and take her to the extra bedroom. Also, that I thought it might be a good idea if we all closed our eyes for a bit.

There was no argument as they both got out of the car and

walked in through the man door on the garage. I wasn't far behind them, as I scooped Nicole's soiled clothes and the top Lauren had been wearing and put them in a large kitchen trash bag, and then returned outside to meet Officer Matthews walking toward me.

"I hope you find out who killed this young man," I told the officer.

"I hope we do, too. We've got four men working on it. Maybe some of Jake's friends can help or we'll find something at the apartment."

"Well, let me know if we can help any further. Nicole will be staying with us until she's feeling better," I said, as I turned to walk back into the house.

We all slept most of the afternoon. The girls were both quiet and sluggish when they finally came down, so I ordered some pizza. I didn't think they would mind eating it two nights in a row, and on top of that I was too drained to fix dinner. We ate with our own thoughts and soon all turned right around and went back to bed for the night.

73
Thursday in Ardmore, Pennsylvania

My SWITCH came easily, and the hot shower water felt refreshing as it hit my chest and sprayed up into my face. I finally felt like I was getting back some strength since my heart attack. Today I was actually looking forward to packing a small bag and getting out of town for a couple of days.

After I cleaned up, I pulled my bobbed hair back in a clip, and went downstairs to make some coffee. While I waited for it to brew, I wandered around the living room thinking how nice it would have been to have all three of my daughters there at one time. The beeper from the coffee pot reminded me that would never happen, and that I needed to get packing if I was going to be ready by ten when Claire and Jacob arrived.

I decided to dial Evan at work after I got my bag together, because I knew he'd want to know why Nicole didn't show up in his dream last night, and try to explain what happened with her pseudo-brother, Jake.

"Hello, is Evan Winthrop in, please?" I asked, and then was put on hold.

"Hello."

"Hi, Evan, it's Diane. I'm sorry to call you at work. I tried your cell phone, but there was no answer, and I needed to talk with you. Do you have a minute?"

"Is everything okay?"

"Well, Nicole and Lauren had a rough night last night. Nicole's roommate, Jake, was shot and killed, and they were with him when it happened."

"What? You mean her brother, Jake?"

"I thought it was her brother too, so did Lauren, but we found out at the police station that Jake was just a friend she made when she first moved here. Lauren and I were both shocked as well. I don't think she wanted anyone to know he was just a friend. Who knows? Maybe for safety purposes she liked telling everyone he was her brother, especially living near downtown. Anyway, they're both fine but extremely drained from the ordeal."

"Well, that explains why I couldn't find her last night."

"Evan, don't give up on her, she's a good girl."

"I've got to do something, Diane. I can't concentrate at work or even get through my normal workout at the gym, and my appetite is shot," Evan said, as he paused to take a drink of his lukewarm coffee.

"We'll figure out something. In fact, Nicole has an open invitation to stay at the house until she figures out what she wants to do, and I thought maybe you could stop over. She's going to need a shoulder to lean on after this ordeal, and it might as well be yours. I think she's confused and scared. Who knows? Maybe that's one of the reasons she ran from the house."

"Scared of what?"

"I don't know, Evan. Maybe she recognized you, or else me lying on the kitchen floor might have frightened her off. I've thought about it over and over and I'm sure there's a good reason. All I know is, she told me she wanted to meet you.

"Hey, not to change the subject, but Claire is going to be here anytime to pick me up. I plan to stay with her a couple of days and then take the bus home on Saturday. So, I thought I'd better call you before I left."

"I'm glad you did."

"So, do you want to stop by my house and meet up with Nicole?"

"Yeah, I'll stop by," Evan answered, with a nervous laugh.

"Well, you're welcome to stop by anytime. Do you still have my address?"

"I do. What about Lauren? Have you told her about me?"

"No, but I will. Let me worry about that," I said bravely.

"All right," Evan conceded.

"Then I'll see you tonight."

"Or tomorrow, however you want to look at it," Evan replied.

It wasn't but about five minutes after I hung up with Evan, that Claire and Jacob were ringing the doorbell. We had a few quick hugs, and then were on our way to the Children's Museum before going to their house to make spaghetti for dinner.

Jacob did a good job entertaining us during dinner, by sucking down each lone noodle one at a time. I had forgotten all the funny things little kids do, or how excited they get picking out a couple of books before bedtime. The day had flown by and before I knew it, I was lying in bed patiently waiting to fall asleep, but my SWITCH wasn't coming easily.

74
Friday in Blue Ash, Ohio

When I woke up, the house was quiet, so I did my usual and went downstairs to make coffee, and then went outside to get the paper and wait for the girls to get up.

There was a small article in the paper about the shooting. I guess I didn't know what I expected, but it was a big deal in our lives. That boy's tragic death didn't make sense, unless he'd gotten mixed up in something. Maybe Nicole or the police would come up with some answers.

Aimlessly, I got up and went out into the garage with my first cup of coffee to look at all the boxes I had stacked in my efforts to start cleaning before my heart attack. My desire to think about this project was fleeting.

Instead, I found myself sitting on a cold concrete step with my hands wrapped around my coffee mug in a daze wondering how I was going to explain Evan to Lauren. I thought of several scenarios as I watched the residual cream swirl around the edges of my cup. A noise in the kitchen startled me, so I got up and went in.

Lauren, who was now a couple inches taller than I, was standing at the kitchen counter with her back to me. I walked over and put my arms around her and laid my head on her back and melted into the moment.

"How are you, honey? Did you sleep well?"

"Yeah. I slept hard," she said, as she turned around. "Mom, you still look tired. Are you sure you're feeling okay?"

"I'm fine, honey, and getting stronger every day. I've got a heart as strong as a horse," I said, to lighten her concerns.

"Here, come over here to the table and sit down with me. We can enjoy our coffee together."

Lauren sat down like a sack of potatoes, and then reached for a napkin to clean up the coffee that had sloshed over the brim. Her hair looked like she had tossed and turned all night, and her lips were chapped to the point of cracking.

"Lauren, sweetie, I know you have yesterday on your mind, but you need to call work to find out if either you or Nicole have to work and talk to your boss about what's going on. Also, you might want to get a hold of your professors, if you don't feel like going to your classes …" I heard myself trail off.

"Yeah. I think I have to work this afternoon. I'll call my boss. I want to see what Nicole is going to do today, before I decide what to do."

"I think that's a good idea, but we need to let her sleep. She's been through a lot, and she was pretty worn out."

"I'll wait as long as I can," Lauren said, as she set down her cup.

"Lauren, I have been meaning to talk with you about something," I hesitated. "I'm not sure this is the best time, because of what happened yesterday, and I probably should have told you earlier."

"What is it, Mom?"

"Well, remember when you were younger, and I told you how your father and I met? You asked me if there were other kids, you know, when we fall asleep. Do you remember that conversation?"

"Yes," Lauren pensively replied.

"Well, your father had two boys. Evan and Johnny. Evan is in his early twenties now, and Johnny, his younger brother, is a senior in college."

"Why are you telling me this?"

I swallowed hard. "Let me finish. I have two other daughters, Claire and Christine. They're both older than you. Claire is married and has a little boy named Jacob, and Christine is my career girl. Anyway, until recently, I had never met either of your father's boys."

"So, I have stepbrothers and sisters?"

"I guess you could think of it that way. The reason I'm telling you this is because recently I met the older boy, Evan."

I stopped to take a sip of coffee and steady my quivering voice. "I'd like you to meet him."

"What do you mean?"

"He's kind of like me, in that when he falls asleep, he comes here."

Lauren stood up and walked toward the coffee pot. "You mean to Blue Ash?" she asked, with her back to me.

Then she turned around, leaning against the kitchen counter, and directly aimed her sarcasm towards me, "Do you think that everyone like you comes to Blue Ash?"

"No, I don't think they all come here. I've never thought of that before now, but no, I don't think so. I only thought your father and I did, until I met Evan."

"I don't understand."

"Lauren, I'm not sure I've figured it out either, but I told Evan he could stop over sometime, and I wanted you to know who he was before he came over."

"Does he know who I am?" Lauren asked, walking back to the table.

"Yes. He was here once. I don't know if you remember, but he told me he stopped by the morning I collapsed in the kitchen."

"That was Evan?" Lauren's question sounded more like a statement as she sat back down.

"Yes, and I've wondered why you never asked me who he was."

"I don't know. I guess I thought he was a friend of Nicole's. I was more concerned about you." Lauren's answer confirmed what I had thought all along.

"So, this is awkward. Why did you tell him he could stop by?"

"I thought it would be nice if you two could meet," I heard myself say, because I couldn't bring myself to tell her the real reason he was coming was to meet Nicole.

"You're going to like him, he's a great guy," I heard myself say.

Lauren rolled her eyes, as if to say she was put out by the idea, and took a sip of her coffee.

"I think I'll go upstairs and take a shower," she said, as she got up and walked toward the stairs.

I took a deep breath and counted to ten as our conversation began to play over in my head. What did I expect? I knew she wouldn't jump up and down with joy, or welcome what I had to tell her, but what choice did I have? My two worlds were colliding, and it felt like a storm was rolling in. To take cover, I retreated to my bedroom to change the linens and try to get a new perspective.

75

It wasn't long before I heard the two girls talking in Lauren's bedroom. Then Lauren eventually poked her head in my room to tell me she'd decided to go on in to work, and that Nicole had off. She said she was scheduled at eleven and she'd be home around five-thirty.

I reclined on my bed and listened to the shower running in the hallway bathroom until I fell back to sleep.

I woke when the doorbell rang and couldn't believe I'd slept until twelve o'clock.

Evan was standing on the front steps looking nervous as I opened the door. He relaxed a bit as we sat at the kitchen table and caught up, until Nicole came down the stairs. Then the air felt thick and uncomfortable as she sat down to join us. She did look better. Her eyes weren't swollen, and she'd regained her coloring. Passing on the sandwich I offered, she sat on the edge of her chair and barely made eye contact with me, maybe because she was embarrassed she'd lied about Jake being her brother.

"Nicole, you remember Evan from the picture I showed you?" I asked her, to break the ice as I made Evan and myself a sandwich.

"Yes, I remember."

"Well, Evan was in the area, so I invited him over," I heard myself say, as I looked over my shoulder to catch a glimpse of her expression.

"I hope I'm not too much trouble," Evan chimed in to ease the awkwardness of the moment.

"Not at all," I said, carrying the sandwiches over. "Would you two like some raspberry lemonade?" I offered.

"That sounds good. Can I help?" Nicole offered, finally looking at me.

"No. You just sit there and relax. How about you, Evan?"

"Sure, I'd love some."

I mixed up the lemonade, poured it over ice in two glasses, and carried them to the table.

"Evan, I hope you don't think I'm being rude, but I really need to go upstairs and clean up. I fell asleep earlier and never got it done," I said, and then paused to gather my thoughts.

"You know, it's such a beautiful day. Why don't you two go out on the back deck and get some fresh air? There are some cushions already on the chairs." I motioned toward the sliding glass door. "I shouldn't be long."

Turning on my heel, I left the room without looking back.

"Well, do you want to go outside?" Evan asked Nicole.

"Sure, why not?" Nicole shrugged.

They sat in the two chairs, as a slight breeze kicked up and blew a tapestry of colorful leaves across the deck. The sun's rays ricocheted off the branches and found their way down to the deck, but couldn't compete with the fall chill. Evan took off his jacket and handed it to Nicole, hoping she would accept the gesture, which she did.

"So, you're friends with Diane's daughter?"

"Yeah, Lauren and I met this year on campus. We both work at the same place."

"You didn't have to work today?'

"No. Thank goodness. I had a rough day yesterday," Nicole said, as she swirled the ice in her glass.

"Diane told me something happened to your roommate?"

Evan thought the question sounded stupid, when he really wanted to ask her why she'd led everyone to believe Jake was her brother.

"Yeah. He got shot," Nicole said, as she set her glass on the table in between them and then looked out across the yard.

"He died."

"That's horrible. I'm sorry, Nicole. If there's anything I can help with, I will."

"No thanks, but thanks for offering. I still can't believe he's dead, and maybe he wouldn't be if I had called 911, but he didn't want me to."

"You were there?"

"Lauren and I were there. We had gone out to eat and were walking back when it happened."

"Was he mixed up in something?'

"I don't know. We had different schedules and I didn't see him that often, but I don't think so. He was a good guy, and his friends seemed normal."

"Did you call his family?"

"No, I never met them. He was from some town near Indianapolis, I think. The police said they would get in touch with them," Nicole said in a monotonous voice.

"Diana said you might stay here until you feel better."

"Yeah. I don't know what I'm going to do. I can't afford the apartment on my own, and I need some place closer to campus, so I've got to move."

I opened the door as I stepped out on the deck with my hand stretched above my eyes to avoid the sun.

"How are you two getting along? Would you like another glass of lemonade?" I asked.

"No thanks, Diane. I was thinking about going on a walk to stretch my legs, and take in the lay of the land," Evan said.

"Sounds nice. I've got some housework to catch up on,

and dinner to prep. Lauren said she'd be home around five-thirty. Nicole, are you doing okay?"

"Yes. Thank you."

"Did you ever call your mom?

"No. Not yet. Thanks for reminding me," Nicole added.

"Not to change the subject," Evan said as he stood up. "Would you like to go with me, Nicole? I don't plan on walking all that far."

"Yeah. I think I will."

76

Nicole handed Evan back his jacket as they got up and went back into the house to get her sweatshirt. They took off out the front door, and walked a few blocks before finding a park bench next to a small pond in a neighborhood park.

"It's chillier than it looks. The sun is deceiving, isn't it?" Evan asked Nicole.

"Yeah. It's cold today."

Evan shoved his hands down into the pockets of his jacket to keep himself from going crazy. He had so many questions and didn't know where to start. The last thing he wanted to do was to upset Nicole or scare her off again.

"I'm sorry, I'm not being very gentleman like."

"What do you mean?"

"I was just thinking back on some things. Zoning out, I guess, but I'm back now," he said with a chuckle, trying to lighten the moment, but feeling pretty awkward

"Do you remember the day Diane collapsed, and I was at the house?"

"Yeah."

"Well, you left in a hurry, before the ambulance came. I just wondered if seeing Diane on the floor, or something I said at the door was what upset you?"

"No. Not really," Nicole answered, as she bent over to pick up a red oak leaf.

"Not really?"

Nicole looked at Evan and then rolled her eyes. "I just thought I'd met you before, and it spooked me. You know, like deja vu?"

"Wow. I must have made a bad impression on you, for you to leave like that."

"No, actually you weren't bad at all," Nicole said, as she smiled at Evan.

"So, now I'm not that bad? How about the deja vu part?"

"Where are you from, Evan?" Nicole asked, making him think she was trying to change the subject.

"Chicago. Where are you from?" he asked her back.

"Bowling Green, Kentucky. Well, that's where my mom lives. My dad died when I was eight."

"Sorry."

"Thanks. Anyway, I was trying to figure where I might have met you," Nicole said, running her fingers under the ribbing of her sweatshirt sleeve. "It doesn't matter."

"Yes," he said in a hoarse whisper. "It does."

"Why's that?"

"Because I want you to remember me."

Nicole laughed, and then realized he was serious. She looked anywhere but at Evan, and he wondered if he'd moved too fast.

"Nicole?"

"Yeah."

"Let me explain, okay?" he asked, as he reached over and touched her forearm.

Nicole turned to look at him, and he knew the only way he knew to explain, was to kiss her. So, he did. It was probably the most intense moment of his life, but he had to take the chance. He was hopeful their kiss would shock her into remembering him or that she would relax and enjoy it. Evan couldn't gauge her reaction when he pulled back, and she looked down; so he plunged into talking again.

"I dream about you and me. I've dreamt about us more than once. You and I, we a ... well, you know, we were together in my dreams. God, I can't believe I'm telling you this," he looked up and then back over at her. "Why are you, uh ... smiling?"

"That's the deja vu."

They both laughed.

Then Nicole said, "I've been with you before in my dreams, too."

"You remember? Why didn't you just say so?" he asked her.

"Who goes around telling someone you barely know that you dream those kinds of things about them?"

"Me, I guess." Then there was a long pause, and Evan knew he had to continue.

"You know, Nicole, there are people who can dream together. I mean they both have the same dream. Well, not the same dream every night, but when they go to sleep, they dream together and it continues every night. Like another life exists between them."

Nicole started to laugh, then stood up and walked down to the pond. Evan got up and followed her to the water's edge. He picked up a couple of rocks at his feet and skipped them across the top of the water.

"Evan, I don't know who told you that, but there's no way. It's just not possible. Why would you believe that?"

"I just do. Let me ask you a question."

"Okay."

"Are you sleeping right now?"

"What do you mean?"

"Well, I believe there are two sides to every day. You

know, day and night, twenty-four hours in a day, but eight or twelve hours of each day is night. However you want to look at it," he paused, as he assessed the look on her face.

"I can tell by the way you're looking at me, you think I'm crazy. At first, I thought I was, too, but I'm not. Just hear me out," he told her, as they stood face to face, and then asked her again. "So, are you?"

"Am I what?"

"Asleep?"

"No, I'm awake. Evan, it's not nighttime here, in case you haven't noticed." Nicole looked up at the sky.

"Nicole, have you called your mom since your roommate got shot?"

"What does that have to do with dreaming?" Nicole asked.

"You can't, can you? Does she know you are a college student, and live in Blue Ash?"

"What do you mean?"

"You know what I mean. Does she know you're here?"

"I can call my mom, anytime I want," Nicole pulled her cell phone out of her sweatshirt pocket. She started dialing a number, but stopped.

"You're right, I can't call my mom." Then she reached out and laid her hand on my shoulder, leaned in to me and pressed her lips to mine.

"What was that for?"

"You feel real to me."

"I'm real. I'm just as real as you are. Nicole, I'm not here by chance. I've been searching for you for weeks. I had to find you, because there were days when I couldn't find you anywhere, when I wanted to be with you."

"How did you know where to find me?"

"Diane found you and told me you were going to be staying with her and Lauren for a few days."

"When did she tell you that, because I didn't decide to stay with them until last night?"

"Uh, well, while you were in Bowling Green with your mom. You know, on the other side of day. Those other eight or twelve hours."

"I am so confused."

"It's very confusing, I know, but when you go to sleep tonight, you'll go to Bowling Green, I'll go to Chicago, and Diane will go to Philadelphia," he said.

"Lauren's mom goes to Philadelphia?" Nicole asked.

"That's only part of it," Evan told her.

"Well, how do we know which part of day is day and which is night?"

"I guess where I grew up with my family is day. I don't totally understand it myself, and sometimes when I overthink things, it gets more confusing. I do know one thing though: I'm glad I found you."

77

Nicole was deep in her thoughts as they walked out of the park. Evan wasn't quite ready to go back to Diane's house yet, so when they got back up to the street he noticed a shopping area a couple of blocks up.

"Is there any place up there we can get something warm to drink?" He pointed toward the buildings.

"There's a donut shop."

"Do you want something?"

"Warm sounds good."

They walked the two blocks in silence. Even though he knew Nicole had questions and he needed to answer them, all he wanted to do was hold her. They sat down at a table by the front window and stirred their hot chocolates to avoid the awkwardness of the moment.

Evan was wondering how this was going to play out. Would she choose to avoid him, out of denial? What if she stopped coming over to Diane's house? Evan had so many questions, and the thought of losing her again scared him.

"So, this donut shop doesn't exist?" Nicole broke the silence.

"It's real in our world. Nicole, this is all new to me, too. I just found out myself that this other side of day existed," he told her, and then took a sip of his hot chocolate.

"Let me try to explain." He paused to collect his thoughts.

"When I was a teenager, my dad and I were in a car wreck.

My dad didn't make it, but right before he died he yelled out Diane's name. I didn't know who Diane was, because my mom's name is Kathy.

Anyway, it always bothered me and I was determined to find out why he called out another woman's name. I found out dad and Diane met at work in Philadelphia where there was a branch office he visited. When I found out where Diane lived in Philadelphia, I went and confronted her. She told me how they met and discovered they were sharing the same dream. They ended up getting married, had Lauren and lived here in Blue Ash."

Nicole started to say something, but Evan held up his hand to stop her.

"I was having a hard time believing Diane's story myself, but I was having these dreams with you and me, and I thought she could help me. Why? Because when I saw Diane for the first time, I recognized her. She was also in my dreams, like in the background sometimes. So, at first, I thought you lived near Philadelphia, and Diane was helping me look for you, but then she found you here."

"So, Lauren is the daughter of your dad and Diane in this other life?"

"Yeah. Crazy, huh? Lauren knows who I am, but we've never talked face to face."

"Is Diane married in her other, uh ... what should I call it?"

"Her husband died a few years ago, but she has two grown daughters and a grandchild."

"No way. This is crazy."

"I know."

"I wonder if all the people here in Blue Ash are dreaming or living on the other side of day? Can everyone do this? I mean, how does this happen?"

Nicole stopped talking and looked down at the hot

chocolate that she'd hardly touched, and then asked Evan without looking up, "Does Diane know you're telling me about this?"

"Nicole, I honestly don't know about all the other people here in Blue Ash. Just like I don't know why I'm never tired, or if everyone can cross over. I've stopped trying to figure it out, because all I wanted was to find you. Although Diane did tell me she drove to Blue Ash one time to see it during the day, and it was different."

"How do you mean?" Nicole asked.

"Diane said the buildings, streets, people were all different. She thinks Blue Ash is some kind of portal, and that at night it falls into some kind of black hole or void. She compared it to the Bermuda Triangle. Crazy, huh? The Blue Ash Triangle."

"I feel like I'm having a bad dream."

"Please don't say that, because I'm happy I found you."

Nicole started to reach across the table, but then withdrew her hand, "I'm sorry."

"It's okay, I know this is a lot, and like I said I'm still trying to absorb it all myself." Evan stopped to take a drink of his hot chocolate. "On top of trying to figure things out now that I've found you, I'm still worried how Lauren will take all this."

"Why?"

"Well, we've never officially met and my being here might bring back too many memories about our dad. The other thing I'm worried about is that she was born here, unlike us or Diane, so I'm worried that will make her feel alienated or not real?" he said trying his hardest to voice his concerns.

Nicole took the lid off her hot chocolate. "The whole thing is awkward. Diane knowing our secret relationship, Lauren feeling left out, and me with my roommate fiasco. I don't know if I can handle all this," she said as a tear rolled down her cheek and fell into a curl of her dark brown hair just below her chin line.

"Hey, I'm here," Evan consoled her, as he reached over and took her hand. "I won't leave you. We'll get through this."

78

Lauren walked in from work as the three of us were sitting at the kitchen table. She didn't say anything, and her uneasiness with the situation made me feel as if I'd caused all her discomfort.

"How was work?" Nicole asked, breaking the silence. God love her.

"Fine," Lauren said, as she walked past us to get a glass out of the cabinet.

"There's raspberry lemonade in the refrigerator," I offered.

She poured herself a glass before walking back over to the table to sit down in the only chair left.

"You look like you swallowed a cat," Lauren said to me.

"That bad, huh?" I asked with a stutter.

"Let me make my own introduction, Mom," Lauren announced as she sat down and put her glass on the table. "I'm Lauren, and you must be Evan," she said sarcastically.

"Lauren, he's your half brother. So be nice," I said sternly.

Lauren was staring at the table and didn't respond, and I knew that if I didn't start talking between my heart's erratic palpitations that she might get up and leave.

"Lauren."

Lauren held up her hand as if telling me she'd had enough.

"You need to hear this," I told her, and then continued. "Evan found me a couple of weeks ago at my condo in Ardmore. He told me that your father died in a car wreck.

That's why he never came home. He didn't leave you or us, Lauren," I reached over and took Lauren's hand to ease the tension in the room. "I told Evan where we lived and all about you, and asked him to come over, honey. We've been waiting for you to get off work."

"To come on over. Just how does that work, Mom?" Lauren blurted out.

"I've been wanting to tell you, but I didn't know how," I tried to explain, as I reactively reached up to a sudden sharp pain in my chest.

Lauren jumped up. "Mom, are you okay?"

"I'm fine, honey. I don't know who's having a more difficult time with this, you or me? Maybe I just need something to eat. Why don't we get out of here and find something for dinner?" I asked everyone, as I got up.

"Maybe it'll do us all some good to get some food in our stomachs and talk," I said, as I moved toward the coat rack.

Awkwardly, they all got up and went through the motions of following my lead to find their coats.

"Oh, Lauren, you don't mind driving, do you?" I asked her, because of the jabbing chest pain I'd just had.

"Sure, Mom," Lauren answered in a motherly tone, with a concerned look on her face, which told me she knew my heart was still weak.

At the restaurant, we slid into a booth and they promptly ordered the nightly special, which were humongous hamburgers with steak fries and shakes. I was the exception and ordered a salad.

"You look like my father," Lauren told Evan, after the waitress had left our waters.

"He does, doesn't he?" I added.

"Are you from Philadelphia?" Lauren asked.

"Chicago," Evan answered.

"So, how did you find out about my mom?"

"My dad, or I mean, our dad," Evan stammered. "Well, we were in a car wreck and before he died, he yelled out your mom's name. I didn't know who she was, but I wanted to find out, so I went to all our dad's offices and asked if anyone knew a Diane who used to work there," Evan explained.

Things got very quiet, and I could tell by the way Lauren's eyes were traveling from one item to next around the restaurant that she was thinking. *She's trying to digest this other world she's never seen,* I thought, as I tucked both my hands under the sides of my legs.

"You were here the day my mom collapsed," Lauren said, changing the subject.

"Yeah. I was."

"Why?"

"To be honest, I was trying to find Nicole, so I could talk with her."

"I don't understand," Lauren said, in a shaky voice, as she moved her water glass and napkin to make room for the hamburger platter that the waitress had brought.

"Lauren, Evan's from Chicago, but when he goes to sleep, he comes to Blue Ash, like I do. While he was here, he met Nicole. Do you understand?" I tentatively asked, not wanting to upset her or make her feel any more alienated then she had for years.

"I think so," she said, without looking up, as she picked at her fries.

"Anyway, Evan got here earlier this afternoon, and Nicole and he took a walk, and then we all waited for you to get home," I explained, trying to make her more comfortable with the wide array of feelings she was experiencing.

We let our own situations sink in as we ate in silence, and tried to digest how all of our lives had changed in the last few hours. I knew we'd crossed the bridge, but still had a long way to go. At least I hadn't had any more chest pain, and everyone's food seem to be hitting the spot.

We finished within thirty minutes, and were walking back to the car, when Nicole noticed a parked car that looked like the car she'd seen the night Jake was shot.

Nicole pulled Lauren back and whispered, "Look, Lauren. Does that car look familiar?"

"Maybe. Why?"

"Hey, girls, what are you doing back there?"

"We're coming," Lauren answered, as she looked at the car, and then the two guys sitting in it.

When we got back to the house, I fixed up the couch for Evan to sleep on, and told him I probably wouldn't be able to call him the next day because I was staying with Claire, so I would see him when I woke up here. He understood.

I then went and found the girls upstairs and told them I was going to bed. *I survived*, I thought, as I closed the bedroom door behind me and went to get changed.

"Mom," Lauren said, as she knocked on the door and came into my room. "Are you feeling okay?"

"Yes, honey."

"You promise?"

"Yes, I promise."

Lauren walked over close enough that I could hug her. "I love you, Mom."

"I love you more," I told her.

"No. I do."

"No. It's my turn today," I said, and then kissed her good night.

79
Friday in Ardmore, Pennsylvania

Jacob's little hands were softly touching my arm, as I made the SWITCH. He was smiling ear-to-ear, and raring to go. He led me downstairs to his train set, where Claire quickly redirected his attention to breakfast and offered me a cup of coffee. We watched The Weather Channel and decided to take Jacob to the zoo.

Everything in Jacob's world was magical, and I had forgotten how exciting it was to see a monkey or giraffe. Although, I'd have to say the choo-choo train was Jacob's favorite, and a lifesaver for me because I'd gotten short of breath. Out of my peripheral vision I'd seen Claire looking at me quizzically, so I tried to cover it up by focusing on Jacob. I didn't want another daughter worrying about my health, or pushing me to go see the doctor.

We watched Jacob squirm in his seat as the conductor yelled, "All aboard" and blew the whistle. It was the grand finale to a wonderful afternoon.

Jacob fell asleep in the car, and Claire carried him into his bed when we got back to her house. He'd worn himself out, and slept the rest of the afternoon.

This gave Claire and me some quality time together prepping dinner, while I listened to her plans for the holidays, and how she was going to paint Jacob's bedroom.

Her husband, Mike, came home and we had a wonderful

dinner together as a family. I wished for Claire that her father could've been there to see how grownup she was and to play with his grandson. He would have been delighted to have a boy in the family.

When Jacob's bedtime came around, I got to read Jacob a couple of his favorite books. Then, when we got up to his room, we turned off the lights and played with his flashlight, making different shapes with our hands on the ceiling.

Eventually we all said our goodnights, and I sank into bed and felt myself drift as I made the SWITCH.

80
Saturday in Blue Ash, Ohio

I awoke to the phone ringing, but by the time I answered it no one was on the other end. Looking at the clock, I couldn't believe I'd slept until eight0, and someone had the nerve to call so early.

I got up wanting to get some laundry started, but when I got downstairs Evan was still asleep, so I retreated back to my bedroom.

Lying down on the bed, I glanced across the room at the box of pictures that I had planned on carrying up to the attic but never got around to it. My memories went to the night Lauren and I'd sat on the floor and gone through them, and then to Stephen. I closed my eyes, and willed Stephen to hear my thoughts. *Have I done the right thing, by inviting Evan to the house to meet Lauren? Would you have approved? You'd be so proud of the both of them.*

The bathroom door in the hallway shut, so I ventured back downstairs to see if I could at least get the front steps swept off. Evan was still asleep, so I quietly got the broom and went outside.

When I came back in, I heard Evan's voice, and was happy to see Nicole sitting in front of the couch on the floor. Leaving them alone, I went to start the laundry.

"You both want some coffee?" I asked, as I came back into the kitchen.

"Sure, if you're making some," Nicole replied, as she helped Evan fold up his bedding.

"Did someone say coffee?" Lauren asked, as she came lumbering down the stairs in her sock feet, pulling her hair back in a ponytail.

"It's brewing," I answered.

"Who called so early this morning?"

"I don't know. Why?"

"I thought maybe it was work. I'm not sure if I have to work or not. Anyway, they said they'd call if they needed me."

Lauren redirected her conversation to Nicole, who was now sitting at the kitchen table with Evan. "Are you working today?"

"Yeah, just to cover the lunch crowd from eleven to two," Nicole said, as she rolled her eyes and then added, "I'm hoping it's busier than last Saturday, because I could really use the extra tips for the apartment now that I'm by myself."

"Nicole, under the circumstances, you could probably break the lease. Have you thought about that? You know, find something closer to school, and get out of the city proper," I suggested, as I poured our coffees.

"You know, you can always stay here until you figure it out," I told her.

"You've been awful kind, but I don't want to be a burden or overstay my welcome."

"You're not a burden. I would feel better about you staying with us until you find a new place, and I'm sure your mother would agree with me."

Lauren chimed in as she put sugar in her coffee, "Did you get ahold of your mom?"

"Yeah, I told her what happened." Nicole nudged Evan's leg under the table to alert him that she wasn't telling the truth. Not because she wanted to lie, but because she didn't want to explain that her mom didn't know she was even here attending college in Blue Ash. Evan glanced across the table at me, maybe to see if I was going to respond, but I didn't.

"Well, that's good. Does she know you're staying here?"

"Yeah, I told her I was staying here for a couple of days until I could figure things out. Anyway, I'm supposed to talk to her later today." Nicole stopped to take a sip of her coffee.

"I think I'll go call in to work to see if they need me, so I can plan my day," Lauren said, as she reached up towards the ceiling to stretch.

"Is anyone hungry?" I offered.

They all said no in one form or another, and I knew how they felt. I was still full from dinner myself. One by one, we got up from the table and got cleaned up for the day. The girls ended up working, Evan left to find some gym clothes and toiletries, and I finished the laundry and then took off around noon to run errands.

81

Evan was back at the house waiting for Nicole when she got off work.

"Hey, I didn't expect to see you until after 2:00," Evan said as Nicole walked through the kitchen door.

"It was slow, so I opted to leave. Lauren said she was going to stay, so here I am," Nicole said as she took off her coat. "I was hoping you were going to be here."

"And, why is that?" Evan asked.

"Because being with you, helps me to figure things out. Hey, I'm going up to change out of these clothes, okay? I'll be right back," Nicole said as she spun around on her heel and headed towards the stairs.

She didn't know it, but he was two seconds behind her and pushed on the door as she was trying to close it.

"Can I help you with those clothes?"

"What?"

"You heard me."

"That's probably not a good idea. What if someone comes home and you're in my room?" Nicole said with a smirk.

"Everyone is gone. It's just you and me. Don't tell me you don't want my help," Evan said, as he reached over to help her take off her shirt.

"Evan," she said, as she looked towards the door.

"I locked it."

"Evan."

Their time together flew by in ecstasy.

Ten minutes after they got downstairs Lauren came home and joined them, where they were sitting in the living room.

"You got off early?" Nicole asked.

"Yeah. I left at two-thirty because the place was dead," Lauren answered. "Where's Mom?"

"Your mom went shopping a couple of hours ago. She told me she had several places to go," Evan told her. "Which reminds me, I didn't get to a drugstore this morning. Is there one close by?"

"There's one a few blocks from here," Nicole told him. "I'll walk down there with you."

"I'm starving," Lauren said, as she started toward the kitchen. "I think I'll fix myself something and then get some studying done."

They hadn't walked a couple of blocks when Nicole slowed down and was looking at a car that had pulled to the side of the road ahead of them.

"What are you looking at?"

"That car, with those two guys in it. I thought I saw it last night, too, when we left the restaurant."

"Really?"

"Yeah, it kind of spooks me."

"Why?"

"It looks like the car I saw the night Jake was shot."

"Are you sure?"

"Not positive, but pretty sure. Maybe it's just a coincidence."

82

Lauren was upstairs when Evan and Nicole got back from their walk. I was unloading a few groceries, when I heard them talking about asking Lauren something.

"Hey, you two, if you're looking for Lauren, she's upstairs studying," I chimed in, trying not to sound like I was eavesdropping.

"Thanks," Nicole said as she trotted upstairs.

"How are you two doing, Evan?" I asked.

"Good. Real good in fact," Evan smiled, as he shifted his weight.

"Great. I'm glad. Hey, just so you know, when we SWITCH I should be back home from my visit with Claire. Maybe we can catch up then, if you'd like?"

"Okay," Evan agreed, not knowing what he would share with me.

"Hey. Not to change the subject, but I bought pork chops for dinner. Will you grill them up for us while I toss a salad?"

"Sure. Do you want me to start up the grill?"

"Well, it's almost five, so why not? We'll have an early dinner. I'm not sure about everyone else, but I'm starving. I should've eaten something before I left earlier today. How about you? Did you get some lunch?"

"No, I didn't eat either. So, a pork chop sounds good," Evan, said with a broad smile.

Evan zipped up his jacket, and took the lighter outside to

start the grill. I got busy cutting up a salad and was setting the table when the girls came down, looking as if they could eat a horse.

"Where's Evan?" Nicole asked.

"On the deck, grilling us some pork chops. Here, take him this platter to put them on," I said, handing the platter to Nicole, knowing she wanted to be with him.

As Nicole closed the door behind her, I turned to give Lauren a hug. She looked upset, and I thought maybe she'd had a bad day at work, or having Evan here was too much for her to handle.

"Honey, you look like you've lost your best friend. What's wrong?"

"Nothing, Mom."

"I know you better than that. What is it? Does Evan being here upset you?

"No. Even though him being here is weird. Not just him, but the idea that he goes somewhere else when he falls asleep, like you do. Sometimes I wonder if I'm dreaming ..."

"What?"

"Like, my life is a dream, or worse, I'm just part of someone else's dream. You know, like a figment of someone's imagination."

"You're real, honey." I reached over and took her hand. "I know, because I made you, and I'm real, and so is Evan. I'm not sure why some people can fall asleep and go somewhere else, and I've often wondered myself which part of my life is day and which is night. There's just a fine line between the two. Please, don't let it cloud your thoughts or it'll drive you crazy."

"I love you, Mom."

"I love you, Lauren."

"They really like each other, don't they?" Lauren said, as

she looked out towards the grill.

"Seems so."

Evan had done a great job grilling, and the pork chops were perfect. There wasn't much talking going on, and my sixth sense told me the silence was more than just being hungry. I wondered if Lauren and Nicole were getting along, or if I was just imagining there was tension in the air.

After dinner, the girls helped me clean up, and Evan disappeared outside. Darkness was creeping into the days earlier, which made it seem later than it was, but that didn't keep me from putting on my PJs. I was ready to get off my feet, and leave the downstairs for the big kids to hang out in. I wanted to watch TV to take my mind off worrying about Lauren, because I wasn't feeling good about making my SWITCH and leaving her alone.

83
Saturday in Ardmore, Pennsylvania

I woke up at Claire's, feeling anxious. I couldn't shake being worried about Lauren as I got dressed and packed my overnight bag. Pulling the linens off the bed, I made my way downstairs to the laundry room and then into the kitchen. I was trying to figure out how to make her coffee pot work when she came in and took over.

"I didn't wake you up fumbling around down here, did I?"

"No. I needed to get up anyway," she said, as she came over to help me. "I like to have a few minutes in the morning to myself, before Jacob gets up and our day gets started."

"Yes. I remember those days. They can be long and tiring."

"Yeah, they are sometimes. Are you hungry, Mom?"

"I'm still full from dinner last night, but a cup of coffee sounds good."

Claire had just poured us both a cup, when Jacob came barreling down the stairs and running into the kitchen carrying his favorite stuffed toy; a white, dingy bear that looked like it needed a bath in the washing machine.

"I think you left. You not in your room," he told me in two-year-old talk.

"I wouldn't leave without giving you hugs and kisses," I consoled him, trying to bring a smile to his pouty face.

"Hey, Jacob, we're having some coffee. Would you like some juice?" Claire asked him, as she scooped him up. "You know, we've got to leave soon to take your grandma to the bus station."

Jacob and I played for the next hour, while Claire cleaned up so we could leave. They walked me into the bus station where we said our goodbyes, and before I knew it, I was back in Ardmore.

I ran some quick errands and then ended up sleeping most of the afternoon. Evan arrived around four-thirty. He said he'd stopped by earlier but didn't think I was home, so he went to the gym.

"Sorry, I didn't hear you come in. I must've really been tapped out."

"Are you feeling okay?" Evan asked.

"Yes, why?"

"It really hasn't been that long ago since you were in the hospital. You probably need as much rest as you can get." Evan raked his fingers through his hair.

"Seems like every time I turn around, I'm going to sleep."

Evan chuckled, "But do you ever sleep?"

"When I take naps, but you're probably right, I do need to slow down. I could use something to drink. I'm feeling kind of sluggish after sleeping all afternoon," I explained, as I wondered how long it would take me to recoup from my hospital stay. "How about you? Would you like something to drink?"

"I think I'll just have a glass of water. Thanks."

Evan joined me in the kitchen, and we sat down at the table with our glasses of ice water. He was quieter than usual, and I wondered if it was because he was thinking about Nicole or his work.

"You look worried. Are you and Nicole doing okay?"

I didn't want to pry, but I was curious to know if Nicole was part of Lauren's world or if she was making the SWITCH when she fell asleep, like us.

"We're doing good." Evan looked up briefly from his water. "I'm happy. It's just that I wish we could be together all the time."

"I know. I think about Lauren everyday when I'm here, but I have to keep telling myself she's asleep and I'll be with her in a few hours."

"But, Diane, Nicole is not asleep."

I paused to gather my thoughts, "Where does she go, Evan?"

"Bowling Green, Kentucky. She lives with her mom, her dad is deceased," he told me, before stopping to take a drink of water. "It wasn't easy the other day, when we went for a walk. At first it was awkward, and then she had a ton of questions and some of them I couldn't answer."

"Like what?"

Evan stood up and walked to the window. "Oh, let me see, like why some people can make the SWITCH while others can't? Or, how do we know which part of our life is day and which is night? They were all good questions, but I didn't know how to answer them. She wanted to know if Lauren came here with you when she fell asleep."

Thinking about that made me sad, because I'd always wished I could bring Lauren with me. I don't know how I would've introduced her to Claire and Christine, but I know they would've accepted her.

"Hey, why don't I get cleaned up, and we can walk out to get some dinner? Does that sound good?" I asked as I stood up, because we both needed a breath of fresh air to lift our moods and clear our thoughts.

84

We ended up at the corner café', where we had first eaten together. We beat the Saturday night rush by just a few minutes, and found a table in the back corner. We both ordered off the specials list, and sipped on our wine while watching people filter in and fill the tables.

I was always amazed at how many people ate out. I looked at the couples, and wondered if they were going to see a movie or take in a play after dinner. I missed that type of companionship. I looked at Evan, and he reminded me of Stephen. I missed his father. I missed both my husbands for different reasons, but having Evan there made me think of Stephen.

"You're awfully quiet tonight," I said, but it sounded more like a question.

"Sorry, I don't mean to be. I was just thinking about Nicole and Lauren's conversation last night."

Evan pushed his napkin and silverware over, so he could rest his forearms on the table.

"Nicole has seen this car a couple of times in the last few days that reminds her of the car that drove past them the night that her roommate was shot."

"Where did she see it?"

"Well, Nicole and Lauren both saw it the night we all went out for dinner, and then yesterday Nicole thought she saw it again when we walked to the drugstore."

"Did you see the car?" I asked Evan.

"Yeah. I saw it."

"Tomorrow morning, we need to get hold of that detective, and let him know the girls have seen this car," I told Evan, as I tried to steady my voice and stay calm. My worst fear was staring me in the face; that I couldn't SWITCH anytime I wanted to help Lauren if she needed me. I felt my heart racing as I took a sip of my wine, and watched Evan look towards our waitress who was carrying our dinner.

"Tomorrow's Sunday. Do you think he'll be around?" he asked, as he scooted his glass out of the way.

"I hope so. If not, though, I'm sure someone will call us back."

There was a lull in the conversation as we began to eat. I was trying to convince myself that the girls were being paranoid after witnessing what they did, but my gut was telling me they could be in danger.

Evan broke my train of thought. "Can I ask you something?"

I nodded, as I swallowed a bite of food.

"Do you think everyone can dream with someone else or live another life?"

"No. I don't believe everyone can."

"How do you know for sure?"

I paused to use my napkin. "Well, I know Lauren can't, and one time I tried to broach the subject with Claire, but she didn't even get close to understanding." I twirled some pasta with my fork to take another bite.

"Why some and not others, I wonder? Do you think it's a gift, or that you have an extra sense that can be tapped into?"

"I've tried to figure it out for years, and then you came along and threw all my theories out the window," I joked. "Although, there is one common thread. We've all lost at least one parent; I mean, you, Nicole, your father and I. Maybe I'm reaching, but what if that deceased parent could dream or cross over, and once they're gone it can be passed on to a child?"

"So, what are you saying?"

I didn't care if my pasta was getting cold, because I thought I was finally on to something that I'd questioned for years. "Maybe when they die, their child inherits the ability to SWITCH. I don't know."

"I also think a person's ability to make the SWITCH is a subconscious decision," Diane said. "I mean, you subconsciously made the decision not to SWITCH when you went back to Chicago for a few days.

"That's true," Evan agreed.

"What if there's more than one child?"

I gestured for him to give me a moment as I swallowed. "You were the only one with your father when he passed away, right? So was I. Or maybe, if you're an only child, it's automatic."

"Wonder if Nicole was with her dad?"

"Good question."

We finished up our dinner, walked home, and put our day to bed so we could SWITCH, and be with our girls in Blue Ash.

85
Sunday in Blue Ash, Ohio

I found Evan sitting on the front steps when I went out to get the morning paper. He said that the girls were still asleep and that he was going for a run, and would be back shortly.

I retied my robe, thinking how mild it was for a fall day. I sat down where Evan had been sitting, opened up the paper, and skimmed the headlines. There wasn't much worth reading, which was probably good because I was more interested in every car that drove by.

I finally decided to go back inside and boot up the computer in the kitchen, so I could look up Jake's obituary. I didn't know why, but I was curious to find out where he was from. I was on edge knowing about this suspicious car the girls had seen a couple of times and was determined to alert the police, voicing my concerns.

The coffee had finished brewing by the time I got off the computer, and I heard shuffling around upstairs, so I quickly sliced up fruit and pulled some bread out to make toast. Both the girls came down at the same time, with their hair tied up in ponytails and wearing sweats.

"Good morning, did you sleep well?"

They said their good mornings, then poured themselves some coffee and sat down. I put breakfast on the table and the girls didn't waste any time eating.

They were both reading the comics when Evan came back from his run. He said his hellos, and then made a quick exit to clean up. We'd all just poured our second cups of coffee when he came back downstairs, looking refreshed.

I wanted to give him a couple of minutes to sit and eat before I asked the girls about the mysterious car. I didn't want to make them think Evan and I were talking behind their backs, but I couldn't take any chances.

"Evan mentioned to me that you girls have noticed a car hanging around in the area. Do you think it could be an unmarked police car?" I asked, trying to ease the situation, and then added, "Maybe it's just police policy to hang around for a bit, until they find out who shot Jake."

Nicole was rubbing the edge of her coffee mug with her index finger as she listened to me, and Lauren was staring at Nicole.

"I was concerned after I heard you talking last night," Evan confessed. "I want you to be safe, that's all."

"I know." Nicole smiled at him and then looked in my direction. "It doesn't look like an unmarked police car. I wish it were, but we both think it's the car we saw that night. I haven't been able to get a good look at the two guys, though. Do you think they think we can identify them?"

I reached over and took Nicole's hand. "Listen, I'll call Detective Matthews this morning and tell him. In the meantime, I don't think you girls need to be walking anywhere. If you need to go anywhere, let me take you and pick you up. That would make me feel better, until the police can put our minds at ease. But, if you see the car again, please point it out to me and Evan so we can be on the lookout for it, too, okay?"

"I've got to be at work at eleven," said Nicole.

"Well, when you're ready, I'll take you."

Lauren didn't say much except she had the day off, and she

was going back to bed. She looked tired as she got up. I just hoped she wasn't in one of those shutdown moods where she slept all day, because I was looking forward to spending some time with her. I wasn't far behind her when I decided to go upstairs to clean up for the day, and leave Nicole and Evan to themselves.

After a quick shower, I sat down by the side of the bed and called Detective Matthews' cell phone. I was surprised, but relieved, he picked up. I told him about the car the girls had seen a of couple times, and he said he would stop by the house mid-afternoon.

As I drove Nicole to work, I mentioned to her that Detective Matthews was stopping by the house. She told me she didn't know much about makes of cars, but maybe Evan could tell the detective what kind of car it was since he was with her yesterday when she saw it. I asked her if she recognized the two guys, but she didn't know them and told me they looked like they were in their twenties.

Lauren didn't come down for lunch, so Evan and I ate a sandwich and decided to hang around the house and wait for Detective Matthews, who showed up around two-thirty.

I told him the girls had seen the car twice. The first time was Friday night when we came out of the restaurant, and then yesterday when Nicole and Evan were walking to the drugstore. I told him I had taken Nicole to work, because I didn't want her walking alone and that, from my conversation with her, she didn't know the make of car, and didn't know the two guys.

Evan told him that it was a silver Honda Prelude with four doors. It was an older model, and it had a dent on the back quarter-panel of the driver's side. The detective wanted to talk with Lauren, so I got her up.

I offered everyone something to drink, but had no takers.

Lauren came down long enough to tell him that the car was silver, older and had two guys in it that she didn't know. She thought it could've been the same car, and that Nicole was the one who saw it first and pointed it out to her.

Detective Matthews said they had a couple of patrol cars assigned to the neighborhood, and thought it might be a good idea for the girls not to go out alone. He also asked to be called if any of us saw the car again. At first, I couldn't tell if he thought the girls were being paranoid or if the two guys in the Honda were really following them. The look in his eyes when he was leaving told me he was downplaying his concerns to ease our minds.

I picked up Nicole from work, and on the way home we spotted the patrol car, but neither hide nor hair of the mysterious silver Honda. I didn't know what I was expecting, but when we got home, I was relieved we were all in for the evening.

86
Sunday in Ardmore, Pennsylvania

I'd made the SWITCH, and was laying out my church clothes, when I heard the front door shut. So, I went downstairs and found Evan in the kitchen drinking a glass of water. He told me he'd been out for a run, and that he was planning on flying back to Chicago late morning.

I guessed I'd always known he'd go back to Chicago, and now that he'd found Nicole there wasn't any reason for him to miss any more work than he already had. He reassured me that I'd see him in Blue Ash the next day, and asked if he could stay a couple more nights there until he found a place to rent. I was relieved that our goodbye would be short-lived, and told him he was welcome to sleep on the couch.

My motherly instincts kicked in, and I gave Evan a quick hug before excusing myself to go get ready for church.

Even though I didn't feel like going, I knew I had to retain some normalcy in my life as I left the condo. The cool air hit my face and bit at my cheeks as I made my way to the bus stop. All the while, I thought of Evan leaving and Lauren back in Blue Ash by herself and asleep.

When church was over, I returned home to find Evan gone, and myself alone. I tried to call Claire, to thank her for having me come visit, but she wasn't home. I tried to call Christine, but there was no answer, so I left her a message.

I wanted to call Lauren, but I knew I couldn't. Then I

began to panic, because I wondered if she was safe. She was the only one at the house; Nicole was in Bowling Green; Evan was on his way to Chicago; and I was here. I was going to have to figure out a way to keep her safe without scaring her. I tried taking a nap, but all I did was stare at the ceiling.

Finally, the phone rang, and it was Claire calling me back. We talked while she fixed dinner, and she filled me in on Jacob and what their week looked like.

After we hung up, I meandered to the kitchen to eat a bite myself, but instead poured a glass of wine to calm my nerves. After two glasses, I went upstairs to climb into bed and read my book, hoping to pass the time until I could make my SWITCH and be with Lauren. I needed to know that she was safe. I needed to go to sleep and be with her.

87
Monday in Blue Ash, Ohio

When I woke up, I went to check on Lauren, and I found her still asleep, so I padded back down the hall to my own bed. It was nine o'clock when I woke again to the sound of someone shuffling around downstairs, so I got up. It was Evan making coffee, and, at first, I thought he was the only one up; but then, when I went out the front door to pick up the paper, I found that Lauren had beaten me to the punch.

She was just about to come in when a gust of wind rippled through the pages and sent a couple of inserts tumbling across the front lawn. Lauren had started chasing one of them, when I noticed a silver car approaching. My stomach lurched and I started running toward Lauren, and screaming for her to come back. I watched Lauren look back at me, confused as to why I was running. I could feel myself running as the moments slowed between us, and the car moved closer. Then I was lying on the ground with Lauren under me, and I couldn't move. I couldn't feel a thing.

"Mom!" I could hear Lauren's voice.

"Somebody help!" she screamed, and then whispered. "Mom, you're bleeding."

Evan came rushing out the front door, running toward us. He lifted me so that Lauren could get up, and then he knelt down beside me.

"She's bleeding," Lauren said, in between her sobs, as she knelt down beside Evan.

"How?"

"She was screaming at me. Then that car drove by." She sobbed. "It was them."

"Get inside the house, Lauren," Evan told her, as she wiped her nose with the back of her hand.

"Go, now!" he screamed at her to get her attention. "Go! Call 911! Hurry!" Evan screamed again.

I could hear the kids talking, but they seemed far away.

"Stay with me, Diane. You're going to be okay."

"Lauren," I said, but wasn't sure my mouth was moving.

"She's fine. She's in the house. We're going to get you help, so hold on," Evan said, as he looked back toward the front door and saw Nicole coming out.

"Go back inside, Nicole!" he yelled, as she kept walking toward him.

"Go back inside with Lauren. It's not safe out here for you. Please, just go!" he yelled again, as he turned back to me. "Stay with me, Diane."

I could hear sirens but couldn't tell which direction they were coming from.

"Do me a favor?" I said, but I wasn't sure if Evan understood me because my tongue felt thick and dry.

I thought I was dreaming, and that Lauren was trying to wake me up, until she reached for my hand and a pain shot through my arm.

"Mom. Don't move. You've got an IV in your arm," Lauren said. "I'm right here. Go back to sleep."

"Don't go," was all I could say, and I wasn't sure if she heard me.

I heard voices, and then Lauren crying. Evan's voice came in and out, but the words were mumbled. I tried to open my eyes, but I couldn't focus.

"She's awake," Lauren said, as the doctor came to my side.

"Diane, I'm Dr. Cowen. You're in the Critical Care Unit at a hospital here in Cincinnati. You've been shot, and the bullet is lodged next to your heart. We're trying to keep you comfortable. Try not to move around too much. There is a team of thoracic surgeons looking at your chart right now, and we'll soon know what we can do to help you."

Evan stepped up beside the bed, when the doctor left.

"The police are looking for the guys in the car, Diane. The girls are safe, they're here with me, and Detective Matthews has a policeman outside your hospital room."

"Talk to you," I said.

"What?" Evan asked.

"Take Lauren with you."

I must have been whispering, because Evan's face got close to mine and I thought I could feel his breath.

"I won't let her out of my sight. Not until they catch these guys."

"No, take her."

"Where?"

"Promise me."

"Okay, I promise. But ... where do you want me to take her?"

"Tonight."

Evan stepped away from me, and looked at Lauren and then at Nicole. He wasn't sure they understood what I was asking him to do, but he did.

88

My hospital room got smaller all of a sudden, as Dr. Cowen walked in with an entourage of nurses.

"We've decided to take your mother to surgery," Dr. Cowen said, looking at Lauren, as he motioned to one nurse to call the OR and then the other two nurses to wheel me out of the room.

"You're her daughter, right?" Dr. Cowen asked Lauren, as she stood up.

"Yes."

"We're going to do the best we can."

Nicole put her arm around Lauren's shoulders and urged her to sit back down, while Evan followed Dr. Cowen out into the hall.

"What are her chances?" Evan asked the doctor.

"Not good. The risk of bleeding is great and her heart's not strong, which is probably due to her recent heart attack. We'll do the best we can."

"How long will she be in surgery?"

"Hard to tell, maybe a couple of hours. Then she'll be in recovery for a while, so probably late afternoon. I'll stop by to check on her when I make my evening rounds. We'll have a better idea by then about her recovery." Then he turned and walked away.

Evan went back into the room and told the girls that I would be in surgery for most of the morning, and then recovery. He suggested they find the caféteria and get a bite for lunch. He didn't know about them, but the last thing he wanted to do was stay in a hospital room waiting all day.

"I need to get out of here," Lauren whispered.

"Let's go outside then; we'll take a walk until we find a place. How does that sound?" Evan asked, as he grabbed his jacket.

"Give me just a minute," Nicole said, as she went into the restroom.

Lauren walked to the window with her back to Evan as she waited for Nicole. She didn't have the energy to talk, because her heart was breaking, and she was scared she'd never speak to her mom again.

Nicole reappeared and grabbed her purse, and then went to Lauren's side in hopes of finding the right thing to say.

"Come on, Lauren, the time will pass faster if we get out of here. The fresh air will probably do us all some good. Are you ready?" She looped her arm through Lauren's and guided her towards the hall.

"Where are you going?" the undercover officer outside the door asked.

"For a walk, and to get something to eat."

"There's a caféteria downstairs," he suggested, as he motioned towards the elevators.

"We're looking for some fresh air," Evan told him.

"Well, my assignment is to stay close to you. I'll need to radio it in."

Evan shrugged and started walking behind the girls who were already headed for the elevator. They made their way outside under a canopy of clouds and a threatening sky, and walked in silence. Weaving in and out of people, they were oblivious to being followed by an undercover officer, and when the clouds opened up to rain they quickly ducked into the closest restaurant. It was an old-looking diner-type place, with red vinyl booths and middle-aged waitresses wearing aprons; but under the circumstances, they didn't care where they ate as long as it wasn't in the hospital.

89

Lauren slid into the booth first, and pulled two napkins from the silver napkin holder on their table to wipe at the tears she couldn't seem to control. Nicole sat down beside her and wondered if they'd be able to talk at all without upsetting Lauren more than she already was.

"Would you like some menus?" the waitress asked, as she glanced over at Lauren's blotchy red face.

"Sure," Evan said. "Oh, we might be here for a while. We're waiting for someone to get out of surgery at the hospital. Is that okay? We'll give you a good tip."

"No problem," she said, as Evan watched her turn and walk towards the counter. He then noticed the undercover cop, by the shoes he was wearing, sitting a few booths down from them.

Nicole leaned close to Lauren and whispered, "Do you need to go to the restroom?"

Lauren shook her head no.

"Let's get something to eat. It'll pass the time," she told Lauren.

Lauren nodded yes.

"I'll order us something," Nicole said, as she looked at Evan.

The waitress came back with their menus and took drink orders.

"Lauren, I know this is hard and you're scared, but your

mom is a strong woman," Evan said, as he reached across the table toward her.

"I can't lose my mom. She's all I have," Lauren gasped, and reached up to cover her face with both hands.

"Look at how well she did after her heart attack. If anyone can pull through this, she can," he told her, even though he wasn't so sure she would.

"They were trying to shoot **me**," Lauren said, as she reached up and tapped on her chest.

"Your mom wasn't going to let that happen," Evan told her.

"She loves you too much," Nicole added, as she put her arm around Lauren's shoulders and then got lost in her own fears of losing her mom someday.

"But what if …?" Lauren trailed off.

Evan's gut told him that he needed to prepare Lauren just in case, but he didn't know if she could handle it. He knew he had to tell Lauren what her mom had asked him to do, even if he himself was questioning whether it would work or not.

Could he take her with him tonight when he made the SWITCH? Would it work? What if she didn't want to go? Could he keep his promise to Diane, and make sure Lauren was safe? What if the guys who shot Diane were also able to make the SWITCH? Would they be able to track them? What about Nicole? Would she be willing to come with them?

Evan wondered if he could ever keep Nicole and Lauren totally safe, because the real question was, could they subconsciously stop themselves from making the SWITCH back to Blue Ash when they fell asleep each night?

The waitress came back by, saving all of them from their own fears by taking their orders. When she left, Evan knew it was now or never.

Lauren made it easier for him when she asked, "What was

my mom talking to you about, Evan?"

"She wanted to know if ... um ... well, if I'd take you with me," Evan answered. He knew it sounded crazy and he was questioning it himself.

"What do you mean? Why would she say that?"

Lauren had as many questions as he did, and now Nicole was looking at Evan across the table as if she couldn't believe what she was hearing.

"Your mom is covering all her bases, Lauren. She wanted to know you'd be taken care of … if …" he stopped. "Look, she's just as scared as you are, but more scared that something's going to happen to you. She probably thinks that these guys in the Honda are after you and Nicole, because they think you can identify them.

"She's not the only one that thinks that either, otherwise there wouldn't be an undercover cop camped outside your mom's hospital room or an undercover cop sitting a few tables down from us now," Evan said, as he nodded across the way.

Lauren and Nicole turned at the same time to look, and then Lauren asked Evan, "What did my mother mean by take me with you?"

"She meant if something were to happen to her, she wants you to come with me back to Chicago."

"But, how?" Lauren asked, as she stopped playing with her wadded-up napkin.

"I don't even know if it'll work, but your mom thinks it's possible. You see, before I came here, I gave your mom my business card with a picture of me on it. Then she held onto it one night as she fell asleep, hoping she could transport it with her to Blue Ash, and it worked. Your mom wanted to show my picture to Nicole to see if she knew me."

Evan stopped talking and looked at Nicole. "Do you remember looking at that picture of me, Nicole?"

"Yeah, I remember," Nicole, said as Lauren turned to look at her in disbelief. "I saw Evan's picture. Your mom showed it to me. It was after we first became friends, and I came back to your house to get something I'd forgotten. A book or something."

"I wouldn't have come here to Blue Ash if Nicole hadn't been here. Remember when your mom took some pictures of you and Nicole on her cell phone?"

"Yeah," Lauren replied.

"Your mom fell asleep holding that cell phone, so she could show me Nicole's picture. We were in Ardmore, Pennsylvania, when she showed me those pictures. She transported that cell phone when she made the SWITCH."

Evan stopped to take a drink of his water.

"Let me finish explaining. Lauren, your mom also believes that I can SWITCH when I fall asleep, because my dad could. She thinks that maybe it's passed on to a child, like when our father died it was passed on to me. Then I could make the SWITCH, even though I didn't even know that was what I was doing.

"I mean, I thought Nicole was a girl in my dreams and your mom was a lady in the background of my dreams, until I found your mom and figured out she wasn't just a figment of my imagination and neither was Nicole.

"Anyway, back to your mom; she thinks a person's ability to SWITCH is passed on from a deceased parent."

Lauren's head was nodding back and forth, like she thought Evan was crazy. He kept waiting for her to say something — anything — but she didn't.

"Lauren, my dad died," Nicole said.

"What are you saying?" Lauren said, as she physically turned around to face Nicole.

"I'm saying my mom lives in Bowling Green, Kentucky,

and that she couldn't afford for me to go to college and it's all I ever dreamed of."

"Wait. No, no, I don't believe it. No." Lauren's voice was trembling and had dropped an octave. "This can't be happening."

"Lauren," Nicole reached over to touch her arm.

"Don't touch me," Lauren said, and pulled away.

"Lauren, I would want to go with you and Evan."

"If we have to leave here, I'd want both of you to come with me. We could all be together. Lauren, for Christ's sake, you're my half sister," Evan said, trying to pull Lauren back into the conversation.

Lauren sat frozen, as Nicole and Evan stared at each other while waiting for the waitress to leave as she put their plates of food in front of them.

90

When they got back to the hospital, the room was still empty. Evan rang for the nurse and asked her to find out how Diane was doing, while Lauren paced back and forth in front of the window.

Evan stepped outside the door to talk with the police officer, but it was a new guy. He introduced himself and Evan asked if they'd caught who shot Diane. He told Evan as far as he knew they were still looking for them. Just as Evan stepped back into the room, a nurse came in right behind him.

"My name is Melinda, and I'm the nurse who will be taking care of your mom," she said, as she looked at Nicole.

Nicole pointed to Lauren, so the nurse would know that she was the daughter.

"Your mom is in recovery," Melinda said, redirecting her attention to Lauren. "She'll probably be there for a few hours until the doctors feel she is stable enough to be moved into the ICU. As soon as I know something more, I will let you know."

"Did they get the bullet out?" Lauren asked.

"I don't have details from the surgery, but I do know she is still in critical condition."

Lauren gasped and her eyes started to tear up. Nicole stood up from where she'd sat down on the edge of the chair and walked over to Lauren.

As the nurse turned to walk out, Evan thanked her, and then returned his attention to Lauren.

"Why don't you sit down, and I'll go and get you something to drink?" Evan looked at Nicole, wishing like hell that they didn't have to be here and that Diane was okay.

"Okay. Be back in a couple of minutes."

He told the cop he was going downstairs to the caféteria to get some drinks, and asked him to stay close to the girls. When he got back, they were still in the same place he'd left them. They drank their drinks like zombies and watched the clock, but the more they watched, the slower the afternoon went. Then, finally, Melinda opened the door and told them to follow her to the ICU, and that only two of them could visit Diane at one time. So, Nicole let Lauren and Evan go in.

Diane looked peaceful, in a motionless type of way. She was sleeping or else still so drugged up that she couldn't open her eyes. Lauren stood close, willing her mom to wake up as she held her hand. She wanted to see her mom open her eyes, wanted to talk to her, and wanted her to be okay.

The doctor came by and told them they got the bullet out, but there was more damage than they thought, and it'd be touch and go for the next few hours. There was nothing comforting about his manner or words of encouragement, and then having the hospital chaplain stop in right afterwards left Lauren rattled, and all of them feeling depleted.

It was after nine o'clock when Lauren thought she felt her mom's hand move.

"Mom, can you hear me? I'm right here. Mom," Lauren's voice waivered, as it cut through the stifling stiffness of her anticipation. "Can you squeeze my hand, Mom?"

"I felt her," Lauren looked up at Nicole and Evan with tears in her eyes. "She moved her hand. She can hear me."

Diane's pulse must have changed, or something, on one of the monitors, because her nurse, Melinda, came in and began to check her IVs, and then made some notes on her chart as she read the monitors.

"I think she's trying to wake up," Lauren told the nurse.

The nurse smiled and patted her on the arm. "I hope so. She's been through two traumas today."

Lauren gave her a puzzled looked.

"The trauma of being shot, and the trauma of surgery," she said, as she straightened the sheets at the end of the bed. "I'll be right down the hall at the nurses' station if you need me. The buzzer is right here," she said, pointing to the cord attached to the side of the bed.

Two hours later, Diane opened her eyes. They could tell she was trying to focus. "Lauren?"

"I'm right here, Mom," she paused. "I love you."

"Love you," Diane said. Then she opened her mouth to say something, but nothing came out.

"Mom?"

"I need you to go with Evan."

"Evan's right here, Mom."

"Evan?" Diane said, as she shut her eyes. "Take Lauren with you. To her sisters," she whispered.

Lauren began to cry. Then the monitors began to beep, and within seconds there were nurses running through the door toward Diane. Nicole pulled Lauren back to make room for the nurses.

"There's no pulse."

"Call for the doctor."

"Signal for Code Blue, we need the crash cart."

They stayed as long as they could with Diane. Even after the doctor told them she was gone, they stayed. The next couple of hours were surreal, and it wasn't until the police officer stepped into the room and asked if he could take them home that they realized they had to leave.

They were both exhausted, but Evan still needed to

persuade Lauren to leave her mom. The police officer finally told Lauren that her mother would be moved soon, and that he needed to take them home so they could get some rest.

Evan looked at Lauren and Nicole as they rode home in the police car. By the hollow and blank look on their faces, he hoped they'd collapse and eventually fall asleep when they got back to the house. He had made a promise to Diane to take them with him when he made the SWITCH, so he desperately needed them to fall asleep. Lauren wanted to be in her mom's bed, which was probably a good idea. At least there they could all be touching when and if they fell asleep.

91
Monday in Harrisburg, Pennsylvania

"So how was your visit with Mom?" Christine asked.

"It was good," Claire told Christine. "She looked tired, though. I asked her if she felt okay and she claimed everything was fine. I don't know, I worry about her sometimes."

"Yeah. I know. She called me yesterday and left me a message," Christine added. "I tried to call her back this morning, but she wasn't home. I'll try her again this afternoon."

"She tried calling me yesterday, too, but we had a busy day and I never got the chance to call her back. I'll probably try her later today. Hey, are you coming to Mom's for the Thanksgiving holiday?"

"Probably. I'd like to bring Tom with me again, but I think this time we'll get a hotel room. It'd be practical for you guys to stay there with Jacob, and all. Plus, I think Tom would feel more comfortable with his own space."

"Is this getting serious?" Claire asked. "Give it up, tell me. Is my little sister finally falling?"

"No, well, maybe. It takes some longer than others."

"Hey, hold on a minute. I've got someone calling in on the other line." Claire pushed the button. "Hello."

"Hi, um … my name is Lauren."

"Yes. Who are you looking for?" Claire asked, but didn't

hear anything. “Hello? Hello?”

Claire clicked on the button. “Christine, you still there?”

“Yeah. I’m here.”

“That was strange, some girl named Lauren. Uh-oh, there’s my phone again. My caller ID says Chicago. Sorry, hold on.”

“I’ll call you back later. If you talk to Mom though, tell her I love her,” Christine said.

“Okay,” Claire told her, and then clicked over to the other line.

“Hello,” she said, as she got up to refill her coffee cup.

The End

About the Author

Rachel Ruth was born and raised in the Midwest. She graduated from the University of Evansville, Indiana, earning a MA in Marketing Management. Rachel worked as a marketing professional in Evansville, Indiana, Nashville, Tennessee and Erie, Pennsylvania for more than twenty-five years, and now resides in Fairhope, Alabama with her family, focusing on writing.

www.ingramcontent.com/pod-product-compliance
Lightning Source LLC
Chambersburg PA
CBHW030537310726
48979CB00010B/1937/J
9781945190865